PRAISE FOR THE IN-BETWEEN GIRL

"Alison Hart brilliantly weaves family background, history, and lyrical imaginings into the story of a Black mixed-race family whose journey from the underground railroad to the US Civil War through the horrors of racism sheds a uniquely compelling light on the nuanced evolution of mixed-race people and their identities, past and present. This bold, seductive drama winds its way into your heart and soul, lingering long after you reluctantly finish the final page."

— TaRessa Stovall, blogger at Mixed Auntie Confidential and author of the Mixed-race memoir, *Swirl Girl: Coming of Race in the USA*

"Traveling over great time and distance, this poignant chain of one family's story reveals the long threads that both connect and confine us. A deeply American tale of history and heartache."

— Alix Christie, author of *Gutenberg's Apprentice* and *The Shining Mountains*

"Weaving Native and African American spiritual thought into an immediately immersive multi-generational family saga, Alison Hart ushers us into a world of complicated betweens. Here, the past—and the passed—remain ever present in an interlocking continuum of societal injustice, unresolved trauma, and recurring dreams. In some cases this chain is bondage, in others it is an opportunity to strengthen bonds of love. Often, it is both, tying together the generations of this family, and society at large, in intimacies that span the human capacity for beauty and cruelty, while candidly reflecting on the space between fragility and resilience that houses so much of human existence."

— NANA EKUA BREW-HAMMOND AUTHOR OF *BLUE: A HISTORY OF THE COLOR AS DEEP AS THE SEA AND AS WIDE AS THE SKY* AND *MY PARENTS' MARRIAGE: A NOVEL*

"In *The In-between Sky* we are confronted with the unacknowledged American epic, a multi-vocal testament of survival within slavery and the harrowing escape routes north and south. Alison Hart's deft sense of scene and dialogue pulls us deeply into how power is exerted in the details of daily actions in a novel that spans from 1852 in Richmond, Virginia, to the 1990s in the San Francisco Bay Area. Even as the forms of racism change, the daily anxieties echo across time and place. Once you open the covers of this book, you won't put it down."

— SHARON D. COLEMAN, POET & EDUCATOR

"With *The In-between Sky*, Alison Hart once again demonstrates her extraordinary gift for bringing characters, time, and place vividly to life. A captivating story from the first page, Hart's prose seamlessly weaves together scenes of rich historical detail and emotional depth."

— LUISA SMITH, BUYING DIRECTOR AT BOOK PASSAGE

"Equal parts heartbreakingly beautiful and beautifully heartbreaking, The In-Between Sky is an unforgettable, sweeping deep dive into the cruelty that has haunted our nation since its inception. From the Slavery Trail of Tears and the descendants of those bound in coffles still shackled by prejudice today, to Native Americans exiled and erased, Alison Hart lays bare how trauma and resilience echo across time. In raw, unflinching prose, she reminds us that what was endured is not past but still present—yet within that presence are voices of strength, memory, and love that refuse to be silenced."

— SHARON BIALLY, AUTHOR OF *VERONICA'S NAP* AND FOUNDER OF BOOKSAVVY PUBLIC RELATIONS

FROM THE LIBRARY OF Elisa Clowes

THE IN-BETWEEN SKY

THE IN-BETWEEN SKY

Alison Hart

For Elisa —
♥ Alison Hart

Front cover design by Gladys Kathman

Rear cover design by Michael Karpa

Author photo © Elaine Dennis

Cover photo © Alison Hart

Published by Mumblers Press LLC, San Francisco CA USA

ISBN 978-1-963221-06-0 (paperback) | 978-1-963221-05-3 (e-book)

LCCN 2025919110

For my brother Scot

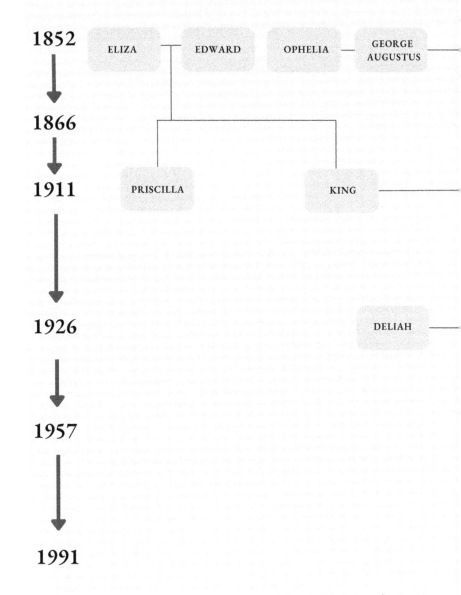

1852

ELIZA — EDWARD   OPHELIA — GEORGE AUGUSTUS —

1866

1911

PRISCILLA   KING —

1926

DELIAH —

1957

1991

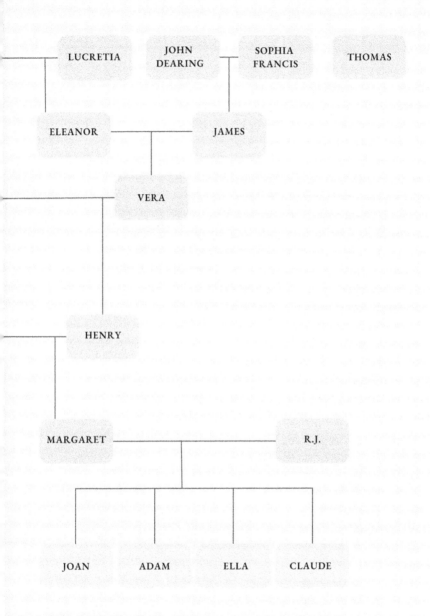

PART ONE
RIVERS

After the trans-Atlantic slave trade ended in 1808, the domestic slave trade flourished in the United States. Virginia was the main hub where close to a million enslaved people, coffles of women, children, and men, were forcibly marched through the countryside to be sold further south down the Mississippi River to the sugar and cotton plantations. Historian Edward Ball coined the phrase "The Slavery Trail of Tears" to describe this massive deportation.

ELLA

DREAM

A dark blue bonnet with white lace trim frames the young woman's ebony face and high cheekbones. She sits on the edge of a bed with shiny brass bedposts. Across the room, the wind gently blows white curtains through a half-open window.

She says nothing except with her eyes. Tears stream down her face like tiny rivulets. A man stands nearby, wearing a brown, worn leather hat and tan work boots, holding a fiddle. He turns his head away from me. She reaches her thin hand across the bed; I take it and know I must tell their story.

ELIZA

COFFLE

RICHMOND, VIRGINIA, 1852
He sent hounds on her this time. They won't catch her: she's hiding with the Indians. The last time Ma refused him, she ran. She didn't want no more babies born light—not like me, black as coal. Not like Ma neither, dark as night. So many babies born and sold, born and sold. Ma gone into some kind a madness. That's why she's in the woods, don't want no more children.

My pa's from another plantation. He come here one time without his pass and paddy rollers got to him. Strung him up and hung him from a tree like they do. I don't remember him.

Why He don't sell me, I don't know. I tend to little ones with Nana and bring water to the field workers. I sing and pray into the wash bucket at night like Ma showed me, so they don't hear nothing.

Ma kneels on the dirt floor, her arms rise across the bucket. It is the quiet time when we are supposed to be sleeping so we

can wake up at crack of dawn. I kneel, stretch my arms out—
they are thin as sticks next to hers.

Her prayer is a song. Ma says the sea is mother of all. She is
not like the white Jesus the white folk pray to; she's black like
us. You pray to her; she comes to you. She is our mother.

Crickets chirp, mosquitoes buzz, the cabin is dark. I can make
out Cato and Sissy's stubby legs sticking out under the patch-
work quilt, molasses-colored legs twine together like roots—
that them breathing? My eyes and ears play tricks on me, they
sold, they gone. A white man came on a brown horse with a
whip coiled like a snake at his side. The first thing I seen was
his whip— and his crooked yellow teeth.

Under the big oak tree, the cooks walk weary-like, carrying
pails full of corn mush. They pour it in the big wooden trough—
same kind they use for the pigs—children so hungry, we rush over
with oyster shells, scraping up the mush before the flies get to it.

A white man watches us high on that horse, wipes sweat
from his head with a kerchief, his hair stringy and brown like
wet hay. He spits, it lands on dry dirt, leaves a dull wet mark.
He got two pigs in a cart behind his horse. They sniff around,
snouts push against the edge of the cart like they trying to get
out. I suspect they hungry, too.

Here He comes, out the big house, down the porch steps
with his long beard, long beak nose, tall black hat and dressed
in the suit coat he wears on special occasions. He wears it on
Christmas. No one dare look at him. Too hot for such a heavy
coat, must be important company to wear that on this
scorching day. The white man gets off his horse and points to
Cato and Sissy. I keep my head down like I been told to do. A
skinny stable boy leads the pigs out of the cart.

I ladle water out the bucket for Cato and Sissy to distract

them, and Nana sits on a tree stump with youngins in her lap. They just learn to walk like Cato and Sissy. Nana's too old for field work, so she tends to little ones, like I do till I'm tall enough to hold a hoe. Nana don't talk much; she mostly sings. She's the oldest one on the plantation, been here the longest. Cato and Sissy were born one after the other. They attached to each other like vines winding around the same fence post.

Cato's plump pink lips slurp water from the metal ladle. Sissy puckers her lips and takes her turn. Faster than a fox in a henhouse, that white man grabs Cato and Sissy's arms—the rest of their bodies dangle like the rag doll the young Missus carries. She holds the arm, pays no attention to the rest, lets that doll drag in the dirt. I make my dolls out of corn husk and sticks and dig a secret hole in our cabin under a scrap of burlap. I hide them where no one can get to them or hear them pray.

That white man don't give them no time to flee. He winds a rope around their tow cloth shirts till their legs and arms can't move and tosses them in the cart. He swings his leg over the horse. Sissy and Cato cry out for Ma. I get up to go to them; Nana holds me back.

Crows caw, pigs squeal and Cato and Sissy holler so loud, I push and pull trying to get to them, but Nana has her arm around me tight. He spits one more time, the horse's hooves kick up dust, and Nana hums. Cato and Sissy been sold for those pigs.

That's why Ma flees again. This time I don't want her to come back and get whipped, tied to a tree with a pot of hot pepper and salt waiting to be scrubbed into her lashes. I want to find Ma, escape with her. Ma, why you don't take me too?

Auntie and Nana whisper at night in our cabin. I pretend to be asleep, catching their voices here and there between the crackling fire.

Auntie shakes the cowrie shells she hides in a hole under her pallet. They are the white shells from the old folks. Nana sucks her corncob pipe; sweet tobacco fills the air. Auntie pokes a needle with black thread into red cloth. She's making mojo bags for protection. I seen Auntie slip one of them to the house cook. They sing real low: a lament and prayer at the same time.

Auntie is older than Ma. Grey hair pokes through her head scarf. She's too old to bear youngins, and her eyes are hard as nails, like what she seen in her life made them that way. She has conjuring powers from Africa. He leave her alone. Auntie ain't scared of him and He knows it. Someday He's gonna get his. Someday. All the bad He done in the world gonna swirl around his body and squeeze him till He has no more breath. Auntie is the most feared woman on the plantation. She's the only one that look at him straight in the eye—He don't want no spells from her. Nobody crosses Auntie. They come to her when they sick; she gives them roots and herbs she picks in the woods.

Cato and Sissy play under the oak tree. Auntie rattles shells in her hand, opens her palm; the shells are small and egg shaped with teeth on their edges and open mouths. I turn to tickle Sissy and Cato but they gone. I can't find them no more. I dig a hole in the dirt thinking they dug into the earth and escaped. There at the bottom of the hole are my corn husk dolls.

"Cato! Sissy!" I shout. The horn blows, time to get up. It was a dream. Time for breakfast, I eat a little hoe cake and bacon. Auntie rushes out with the other field hands. I gather the little ones with Nana and set them under the tree. Mothers suckle their babies and drop them in Nana's lap. Lucy kisses baby Indie, passes her to me and sets off to the field.

What a strange feel here today in the air. Clouds swirl, wind rattles the leaves on the trees, babies fuss. The house cook fetches water at the well. Nana and her nod at each other like they know inside each other's thoughts. It's a foreboding. The wind sends its warning.

The field hands drag their limbs back for supper. They dot the land with their tuckered out bodies. The overseer on his horse trots ahead of them—eager to get to his meal, I suspect. He's a mean one, and I stay away from him; he just as soon whip you for looking at him the wrong way.

Back at home, Nana sends me to the woods to gather kindling. Maybe I'll find Ma. I run to the river. I bend over, pick up branches and put them in my sash. "Ma!" I shout turning in every direction. Woodpeckers tap on tree trunks; bushy-tailed grey squirrels hurry up trees. I swat mosquitos as fast as I can before they get me. The river gurgles. Ma says the river sends you sweetness if you pray to her.

Water rushes over my feet. "Thank you river." I scoop some in my hands, splash my face, cup my hands and drink. I know my way in the dark, and I better get this kindling to Nana. Hunger pains in my stomach make me run faster. The kindling sways in my sash as my feet thump on the ground.

I drop the branches next to the hearth. Auntie flicks a rock and flint stone together and catches a spark with a piece of cotton. She lights dry leaves and carefully places kindling on the flames. I wish she was Ma, 'cause then I'd hug her and take in her scent of tobacco and saltwater. Ma holds me even when she's too tired. Nana sits on a stool sewing red bags, humming. Her voice reaches deep inside me; I start humming, too. I wash the yams in the water bucket and hand them to Auntie. She puts them down in the ashes to cook.

I want the fire to rush and get that yam done! But I don't fuss. I know Auntie don't like fussing. Sweet syrup oozes down the side of the plump yam. Auntie spears the yam with a stick and puts it on my plate. I blow on it, can scarcely wait for the sweetness in my mouth.

Cato and Sissy, y'all wondering why I'm not sharing? I lift the burlap cover and pick up my dolls. I feed them some yam. Cato and Sissy, I don't forget you. See, I don't ever forget you.

My belly is full for the first time in a long spell. I kiss Cato and Sissy and place them next to me on my pallet. Nana and Auntie's soft voices fade in and out as I struggle to keep awake.

Ma was right, the river sent me something sweet: that yam.

Soft lips on my forehead, the smell of salt water and tobacco —Am I dreaming?

"Shhhh." She put her finger to my lips. "Sleep now, Eliza."

She lifts the blanket and cradles me with her strong arms. Ma you came home, Ma. Ma rises as usual, like she never been gone. Her and Auntie whisper.

"Put this under your skirt."

Auntie hands Ma a little red bag. Ma nods and ties it on her waist. Auntie and Ma rush out to join the other field hands before the overseer whips them for being late. Harvest time is almost over. Oxen pull carts of big bundles of leaves to the tobacco barn for curing. The leaves hang from the ceiling like bats; it smells so strong in there, makes me dizzy.

Nana and I walk to the oak tree. Nana sits on her stump with her corn pipe in her mouth. We wait for mamas to drop off droopy-eyed babies and join the others in the field. Lucy hands me baby Indie. Indie smiles at me when I take her. I smooth out a blanket on the ground and set her down next to me.

I'm waiting for Him to come out of the big house like usual, whip in his hand—scouring faces, shouting "Clara, Clara, you best come here now!" ready to tie Ma to the tree. The tree that held her cries with each lash of that cat-o'-nine-tails, the tree Sissy and Cato played under, the tree Nana sits under and hums her songs. This tree sees it all. If it could talk—I wonder what it would say?

I keep watch of the wood-carved door with the iron black knocker. I touched it once, when I was too young to know better than go up there—the Missus came out and knocked me clear across the yard for approaching the front door. Never did it again. He don't come down the porch steps with whip in his hand and revenge for Ma. Tree branches sway and chills run down my spine.

Clink-clank of metal and moans like a cow bearing a calf startle Nana. Her back shoots straight up.

"What is it?" I ask her. The creak of wagon wheels and moans gets louder. And way over yonder, you can make out a trail of men chained two by two, women following behind with sacks on their heads and children in tow like a long line of marching ants.

A white man on a horse with a pistol and whip leads the group. A boy carrying a fiddle jogs to keep up with him. I seen these sorrowful coffles before on their way to be sold down the river to the sugar plantations south. They say in Mississippi and New Orleans they work you to death down there. They sound so mournful, I cover my ears so it don't enter me—all that sadness.

Nana grabs my hand. "You stay close to me now, Eliza."

I squat next to baby Indie. Indie kicks her blanket off her; I toss it over her again. She smiles. I know it's a game she likes. Her stubby legs kick the air; I tickle her. Nana sucks her corn pipe. Crack of whip—I hold my breath.

"Stop that whining, you hear!" the white man on the horse shouts. "How's about a nice song like *Old Virginny*! Boy, start that up on your fiddle."

Whip cracks. Babies cry. Wheel creaks. Dust flies. Cling clang the chains sway.

"'*Den carry me back to Old Virginny, To old Virginny's shore . . .*'"

Fiddle plays high and joyful, but the way they sing is the way folks sing when we put someone to rest. Where does the line end? I can't see the end of the line.

The wagon driver pulls the reins. "Ho!" The coffle comes to a stop.

Nana prays, "Lord have mercy, mercy, mercy. Lord have mercy . . ."

The wood-carved door swings opens, and there He come out the big house: black coat, tall hat, white shirt, boots and a crooked grin.

Indie kick her covers off again. She wants to play. My heart pounds. The fiddle music races through me; I hold my head. Ma and Auntie run from the fields, gripping their skirts; others race in front of them. The overseer trots behind them on his horse, saying, "Git! Git, now! Git!" His whip flies in the air.

It's too early for them to be coming back for dinner. Indie starts to cry. I cover my ears. Nana hums, rocking back and forth. Ma rushes to me, says "Get your things." We run to our cabin, leaving baby Indie and Nana at the oak tree. Folks scatter about like chickens; mothers grab their babies from under the tree and tie them on their backs.

All I got is my blanket and my dolls. Cato and Sissy, I'm leaving you here. That way, when I return, I know where to find you. I kiss the dolls and put them back in the hole, cover it with the burlap sack and say goodnight.

"This is his revenge on me, this is his revenge." My ma ties her bundle together.

"Ain't no use worrying about that now; this was bound to happen one day." Auntie wraps the scraps from breakfast: pieces of hoe cake and a bit of egg.

"We never coming back?" I ask them, "What about Nana?"

"Eliza, come here." Ma opens her arms. She takes a knife and cuts off some of her hair, opens a tiny crimson bag attached to a cord and puts it in there. "Eliza, you always be my baby, always be my Eliza. Wear this round your neck." She puts it over my head, and I hide it under my shift. "We always be together, always."

Bang bang on the door; the overseer shouts, "Now git! Time to git out!" Auntie rolls her bag of special shells, roots and herbs in a cloth and hides them in her bundle. Auntie is like a cat ready to pounce. She hands me a leather string with a round piece of metal attached to it. It is a scrap of iron from the blacksmith hammered down into a circle. She ties it around my ankle. "The path be clear for you, Eliza." It feels cool against my skin. We run out of our cabin to the coffle.

"My baby! My baby!" Lucy bolts through the crowd like an ox busting through a fence. Four men stand between Lucy and baby Indie. Indie is on her back kicking up her feet like a beetle in the sun.

"Now here, wench, stop kicking up a fuss!" The trader whips Lucy to stop her bawling. Nana, slow-like gets off her stump, shuffles to Indie and picks her up off her blanket. Nana and Indie are the only ones left. We don't say goodbye. Nana hums in that low voice—the voice that enters through me and around me: I hold it inside.

Dust flies behind the men and boys in front. If they don't walk fast enough, the traders on the horses whip them. I try and keep up with Auntie and Ma, though my feet are cracked and bleeding. I wish I could sit on the cart stretched behind us. Sweat runs down my neck and my red mojo bag is damp against my chest.

Lucy lags, her shirt torn open from the lashes. She has a look that scares me—the same look Ma had when He sold Cato and Sissy, and she ran to the woods. Lucy won't run anywhere. She can barely pick up her feet. The slower she goes, the more they whip her.

Lucy tried to get to her baby. Indie kicked up her soft pink heels in the sun wanting to make her little arms and feet crawl, to get to Lucy's arms. Nana's holding Indie under the tree, humming the song that's inside me.

Lucy stops like she's listening for something. Ma urges her on. "Lucy, come on, Lucy. You got to keep on." Ma grabs her hand. Lucy don't move. Ma tugs her arm. The trader whips Lucy on the head. She drops to the dusty ground.

"Git up!" He whips her again; his face is like a ripe tomato.

Red streaks drip down Lucy's neck and back. She don't move. She has become a stone— no matter how many whips— still. A man from the front trots over on his horse; he yanks the reins and halts next to the red-faced trader with the whip. He takes out a gold pocket watch, points to it, says something to the red-faced trader and trots back to the front of the line. The red-faced trader coils his whip, turns his horse, and orders us to move on. We walk around her, some step over her. She don't get up.

Lucy don't move. Cling clang the chains sway . . .

Lucy still don't move.

Campfires light up the field like fireflies at night. A river flows nearby. The women set up tents and men lie on the ground in chains. Ma wraps my feet in wet rags. Women whisper around me:

"She rather die than keep on—"

"Just left her there—"

"Who gonna bury her?"

Auntie burns a bundle of herbs on fire: bay leaf, rosemary and sage. She raises her arms. Ma joins her side, adds tobacco in the fire. Others come making a circle. I squeeze in next to Ma and a young woman we call Pretty Betty. We pray quietly. We don't want the traders to hear us. "Lucy," Auntie whispers, placing the herbs in the fire. Sizzle, pop, the fire says. "Least she won't be sold down the river." Auntie's words hang in the smoke.

My eyelids are heavy. I struggle to keep awake to listen to the women whispering around me.

"That's where we going?" I make out Pretty Betty's soft voice.

"Down the Mississippi to cotton fields and sugar cane. Unless you lucky and get sold in Tennessee." Auntie says.

The women get up and leave before the traders come and make them. Auntie puts out the fire; Ma carries me to our tent passing a white man standing in front with his pistol in hand. Women lie down with their babes in their arms, fixing blankets, and braiding their children's hair. Ma takes the wet rags off my feet, finds an empty space on the ground, and spreads a blanket down for us to sleep on. Auntie comes in covering her herbs in a cloth, humming. I lie down. Tennessee. I wonder, how far is it? I fall asleep; the smell of tobacco and rosemary wraps around me.

She sounds like a bird when you get too close to its nest, but louder. Ma tells me if they catch you, don't fight, make your body stiff, like playing dead. If you fight, they might kill you. I crawl out of Ma's and walk to the front of the tent. I lift the flap and peek out; the moon stares back at me. I step out onto the cool grass, feels mighty nice on my sore feet. At Betty's tent a few tents down, there's a line of men in front of the opening. A man relieves himself on the side while he waits his turn. There's hollering and cheering. Betty's cries turn to whimpers, like a puppy. Bottles clink. Did she fight? Or is she still alive?

"I told you to stay put." Auntie scolds me. She opens her bundle that smells of damp earth and pine needles. I follow her back into our tent. Auntie breaks off the stem of a plant. She ties a string around it and puts it around my neck.

"Stinking gum keep you strong." She says, patting my chest. The sharp smell stings my nose. Creek creek creek goes the frogs and crickets—the whimpers are softer now; I can barely hear them.

At sunrise we are up again, packing the tent, Ma ties rags tight around my swollen feet. We get ready to line up, Pretty Betty is surrounded by other women, helping her walk. Auntie passes roots down the line. "For Betty," she says. The women pass it carefully. "So she won't have no babies."

Amherst, people say we heading to Amherst. My stomach growls. We haven't stopped for food yet. Step step, sun beams down, wagon wheel creaks, horse hooves stomp, sun beams down.

The Pen

Amherst, Virginia

The walls are so tall, the tips of trees peek over like they watching us. Smells like a stable:

sweat, cow dung and lye. Except there no cows in here, just people. Clatter of wagons and horses seep through brick walls; there ain't no windows, but you can still hear them.

Men and boys walk freely about the yard. Some boys return to their mamas, others wander like ghosts looking for a place to sit. I stay close to Auntie and Ma. Auntie gives me a root to suck on for my hunger pains. A woman comes over and asks for help. Auntie carefully unwraps her bundle, smooths out a cloth on the ground and throws the shells. She gives the woman a bag and puts in a nail, dust and the same kind of skunky-smelling root she put around my neck. The woman thanks her and in return gives Auntie a bit of corn mush wrapped in a cloth. More people gather near Auntie, some don't have anything to give, but Auntie helps them anyways.

Heavy iron doors creak open. Auntie quickly gathers her shells and roots and ties them up in her red cloth. It's the man with the golden watch, and behind him are two black men, carrying pistols and chains. The man with the gold watch glances over the yard. He points to a boy huddled near his family and two other men standing nearby. He tells them to step forward and form a line. The boy whimpers; his ma begs the man with the gold watch to take her too, to please take her too. Guards shove her away. They march through the iron gate and are never seen again. Wind blows, trees sway, clank, the gate closes.

At night, they crowd us into stables, the same kind back home for the horses. Men in one, women and children the other. During the day, they send us to the yard, sometimes to do exercise, though plenty of us too tired to move; still we do, else they crack the whip. More folks join us, and some get sold in the yard by the man with the gold watch. I'm still here with Ma and Auntie 'cause my protection bag is strong.

We set out to walk again—people stare as we line up and take up the whole street. The man with the gold watch leads the way with the little fiddle boy behind him. Men drag feet heavy with chains while we walk behind them carrying what we can; the little ones sit in open carts in the back. We move like one long, slow snake. This time they say Abingdon, we going to Abingdon.

My feet toughen up, but I'm always hungry. Some drop—can't walk no more and sink to the ground. They make the men dig ditches on the side of the road and throw the bodies in there—no funeral, nothing. Auntie says their spirits won't rest because they weren't buried proper, and the spirits will roam the land and spread their unhappiness until they buried right. I ask, "What about Lucy?" She wasn't even buried; she was left for the vultures circling above.

"She gone back to baby Indie. She won't leave this world without her." Auntie says. I wonder if she flew. How I'd like to fly, fly back, and sit under the tree with Nana and Indie.

Auntie sprinkles tobacco in the air, brown specks dance in the wind.

RATTLESNAKE

ABINGDON, VIRGINIA

What a sight we are! Rags, dirt and sharp bones. Men halt their horses—dogs run by us sniffing and yelping. We pile into the yard; it's smaller than the one at Amherst, though same tall brick walls. Least we get to rest. I keep my eye on the iron door for the man with the gold watch.

Ma, Auntie and me sit in the shade against the wall. Two men in straw hats greet us. They take their hats off respectful-like. One says, "Mam." He's tall and his ankles are red with pus coming out from wearing chains. Ma nods shyly; Auntie gives her fierce look. "I hear we are heading to Tennessee," he says.

"That so?" Auntie says, watching him like a hawk.

"This is the resting place. May we join y'all?" Auntie nods. Ma looks down. "I suspect you all might enjoy some of this cornbread here." He takes a cloth out his pocket and unwraps it. My mouth waters.

"Why yes, that's mighty generous," my ma says and motions me to take some. I break off a corner and shove it in my mouth.

"Not so fast, Eliza. You bound to get sick." Ma scolds me and slowly breaks off a piece for Auntie.

"I'm Isaac, and this here is Gabriel." His friend stretches himself along the ground; he smiles at Ma.

"Where you from?" Auntie asks.

"We come all the way from Maryland to here. Been mighty long." Isaac takes the last scrap of bread.

"That's the truth." His friend Gabriel says. He is skinnier than Isaac.

"I hear you got the curing powers?" Isaac asks Auntie.

"What you heard is right," Auntie says.

"I suspect you can help me with this here ankle." It is swollen. He moves his foot to show her. Auntie unties her bag and sorts through her plants and roots. She takes two big leaves and puts them around his ankle.

"Leave it on. It will help."

"Why thank you, Mam, thank you very kindly." Isaac stretches his big body next to his friend and covers his hat over his face.

Up before sunrise. Men are chained up in front. Isaac is the tallest of them, Gabriel is chained next to him. Only here in Abingdon for a spell, got to move on to Tennessee. The damp ground travels up my body. I shiver, fearful of the sun rising like a wolf coming at you in the forest, baring his teeth. The rays burn my head, my skin, sting my feet. I pray for clouds.

New faces join us; I don't hardly recognize anyone from back home. They all been sold. Where's my home now? I ask Ma she shakes her head. Even the men on horseback are droopy, tired. A trader shoots his rifle towards the ground. "Damn rattlesnake!" I jump, thinking they shot someone for trying to run. We freeze for a moment, the bloody snake writhes in the dirt like a headless demon. We walk around the blown-apart snake. Auntie stops and quickly picks up the bulging head, blood dripping from the neck, and shoves it in her satchel. They don't see her, and no one says nothing. What if that snake decide to wake up and bite her? I watch her satchel in case it comes out and strikes.

We walk until sundown, then set up our camp. Auntie takes the snake head out and squeezes the jaw, dripping venom into a little vial. "For what?" I ask. "We may need it," she says and tells me to sleep.

At sunrise, we wrap up our belongings, ready to march again. I want to know when we will stop. I want to know what I can call home.

Pit pat pit pat pit pat on our tent at night. The sky rumbles angrily. "Lightning's a-coming." Auntie and Ma gather cups and bowls to catch the rain outside. Auntie's right. The lightning and thunder keep me up.

"Don't be scared. That thunder is drums." Ma kisses my forehead. Auntie and Ma dip rags in the lightning water and wash me from head to toe. They wash themselves. Auntie says it will protect us and give us power.

Mud squishes between my toes. Sometimes my foot gets stuck, and its hard to get it out. The line moves as slow as a turtle. They don't bother with the whip. Can't move quick in this mud. Wagons get stuck in the back. We wait till the men haul it out the mud. A woman points ahead: you can make out an outline of houses and buildings.

"That's Nashville." She wipes her forehead with her sleeve. She wears a red headscarf and has a gap in her teeth.

"They sell you there?" A thin woman asks.

"They sell you anywhere. After Nashville is Memphis, and that's the last stop." "Then what?" the thin woman asks. My ears perk up.

"Then they put you on a floating bed and down the river you go to the crossroads: Natchez, Mississippi. There your fate decided, sugar or cotton, either one they will work you to death. I ain't going down there, I'm looking to stay here with my husband in Tennessee, I'm looking to stay right here." She takes a piece of long grass and puts it between her teeth and fixes her red head scarf.

"How you know all that?" the thin lady asks.

"I listen to the traders; they don't know, but I'm listening." She smiles at me, pats my head. "You've been listening too, haven't you, little one." I smile back at her, maybe that's where Ma, Auntie and I will stay too, all together in Tennessee.

Way back they still trying to get the wagon out the mud. Purple bell blooms dot the side of the road. I walk over and pluck some flowers. Auntie comes beside me. "Foxgloves are poison, Eliza. You be careful now, don't eat them."

"Yes, Auntie," Sure are pretty. How can something so pretty be poison? Auntie clips a bunch and slides them into her red bundle. Wagon finally rolls; we tread along towards the outline of buildings to Nashville.

Show Room

Nashville, Tennessee

We line up at another brick building, walls high as a tree. Men go one direction and women another. The feeble and sick, they are sent in yet another direction. Ma, Auntie and me huddle in a locked stable with bars on the window. It's night-time; I can't stand no more. We find a corner, and I fall asleep in Ma's lap.

Splish splosh splish water spills out of the basin they place in the middle of the room. The sharp smell of lye stings my nose. We told to strip and wash. Each of us given new clothes to wear. They call them stewards, the two black men wearing silk vests and pantaloons dressed like gentlemen. They turn their backs to us so we can wash and change. Are they free? I wonder if they dressed like that, maybe they free.

I button my pretty calico dress. I never had a dress like this. Women start asking the stewards questions:

"Where we heading?"

"We being sold?"

"Who's buying?"

"Will it be in Tennessee?" I recognize her voice from the line when the wagon was stuck, the woman with the red headscarf.

One of the stewards, the older one with a grim look to him, explains.

"Yes. You going to a showroom to be sold. And you all best do what the trader tells you or there will be hell to pay." He holds up a wooden paddle covered with spikes that look like thorns. The room freezes as if no one knows how to move or breathe anymore. The woman with the red head scarf falls to her knees, praying. I wipe my damp hands on my dress.

Auntie throws the shells again.

"How can this be?" White shells splay all over the cloth like fallen flower petals.

"What does it mean, Auntie?" I crouch beside her. She sucks in her breath then gives me a foreboding look, like a storm's coming. Auntie picks up the shells and wraps them in her red cloth. My skin itches in this new dress; I want to take it off.

Swirls of gold cream and blue fill the walls. Chandeliers hang from the ceiling, sparkling like icicles. The men from the coffle are dressed in top hats, fancy black coats and white pantaloons from tallest to shortest. I spot Isaac in the front; Gabriel is a few heads after him. Their faces are downward, shoulders slumped a bit like their clothes weigh them down.

Women line the opposite wall with colorful head scarves and long white gloves. The stewards grease our lips and shine our skin to make us look like we just ate meat, they say. They blacken grey hairs with shoe polish, and the sickly they stuff with extra clothes to make them look fat.

I stand with Ma and Auntie. The trader with the gold watch whispers to the older steward. They point to Ma. The steward takes off his hat and approaches us.

"I hear you both have scars. And you best tell them when they ask you why you got them lashes and that you learnt your lesson and you a faithful negress now, understand?" Ma nods her head slowly. "If you don't get sold here the next stop is Mississippi. You don't want to end up down there, do you now?" He bends over, his breath smells foul. "And you, little miss. If they ask do you cook, you say yes, and if they ask do you clean, you say yes, and if they ask can you make shirts, you say yes. Understand?"

"Yes, sir," I say.

"You all stick to the story I tell you. If you don't, they'll be a flogging, and you don't want that." He pats the back of his paddle.

"Any chance we be sold together?" Auntie asks the steward.

"You keep to the story. Just keep to the story." The steward puts his hat on and moves on to the next group.

Ma's palm is warm on my cheek. "Eliza, now you listen to that man and say what he told you so we all can be here in Tennessee together. You hear?"

"Yes, Ma." I put my arms around Ma's waist as tight as I can.

They all come in all at once: top hats, long beards, fancy canes. White fingers poke and prod the men across the room. On the stand in the front of the room, the crier shouts,

"Strong buck field hand, seven hundred dollars . . ." Then he talks so fast I can't understand him. The crier points his finger, "Sold to the gentleman in the back!"

A woman rushes to the platform where the sold man stands with his chin up; she grabs his feet. They pull her off.

She drops to the ground like she has no bones anymore and tears at her red headscarf. White men pat each other on the back and smile. The stewards take the woman away, one carries the wooden paddle. She's the one that warned us to stay in Tennessee, the one fixed on staying with her husband, the one with a gap in her teeth, who patted my head . . .

Women are taken to a room on the side, where they check their backs, make sure they clear. Ma and Auntie's backs are crossed with scars from the cat-o'-nine-tails that marked them.

They don't want slaves that run.

They take Ma and Auntie through the side door. I stand with my back against the wall so still. I close my eyes, maybe they won't see me or notice me.

"Here's a young filly." A deep voice booms. I check the side doors for Ma and Auntie. I remember him, the man with the gold watch. Next to him is a tall thin white man with a long skinny nose like a beak and face all shaven except for a short beard under his chin. Make him look like a strange animal. His long fingers wrap around a thin silver cane. His eyes are watery blue like a lake.

Across the room, a man pokes his pale finger in a little boy's mouth. He reminds me of Cato, but a bit older. The boy lets out a yelp and bites the white man's finger. The white man strikes the boy so hard, he flies back and slams against the wall. The boy doesn't get up.

The man with the gold watch pats my back. "She's a good seamstress, and her mother a good breeder. You are viewing a fine investment, sir." The tall man curves his body over so close I can see the hair in his nose.

"That so? Are you a good seamstress?"

"Yes, sir," I say quickly.

"Well, let's take a look." He squeezes my arms and legs,

orders me to walk and jump. Forces my mouth open—like they do to horses—and rubs my teeth with his long fingers. They taste sour; my stomach turns. He takes his hand out of my mouth and wipes his fingers with his handkerchief. "She'll do." He steps ahead of us; his silver cane taps on the ground. The man with the gold watch grips my arm.

"Come on."

"Ma! Auntie!" I holler.

"You best come on if you want to see your ma again." He tightens his hand around me like a noose. The boy who looks like Cato is still curled on his side. Is he dead? Ma comes out of the side door, her dress tore open. She grabs the legs of the gentleman in front of us.

"Please, take me, too! She's my only daughter—please, I beg you!" The stewards grab her. The gentleman straightens out his jacket and turns slowly to the man with the gold watch,

"You need to get in control of your niggers," he says as he walks around Ma and the stewards.

I shout for my ma as loud as I can. The side door opens. It's Auntie.

"Auntie!" I holler as the man with the gold watch pulls me to the front door.

"Eliza! Eliza! The path is clear for you!" She tries to break free; two men grab her. They shut the door behind me.

Up and down, up and down, packages and barrels thump against the cart on the bumpy road. The driver tied my wrists to the side of the cart.

"In case you try to run," he says. In front is the carriage with fine wooden panels, smooth like glass.

We ride all night. How will Ma and Auntie find me now? I keep a watch carefully so I can remember the way back to them. Trees line the road like soldiers; the moon above keeps watch.

Tallow candles line the road to the house; they give off a rotten smell. I pinch my nose. And there it is: the big house with white pillars in front—much bigger than the one back home. The carriage halts; the cart turns around the back.

"Ho!" The driver pulls the reins and hops off the cart. Servants dressed in white and black unload the packages and barrels.

"Who's this?" a woman with a dark, round face asks the driver.

"He bought her in Nashville. Clean her up for the missus."

The woman unties my sore wrists.

"There, there, little missy. What's your name?"

She reminds me of Ma.

"Eliza, I am Eliza."

Drip drop drip, tears like rain in a bucket. Ma, Auntie, how can I get back to you? She takes my hand and leads me to a small brick house next to the big white pillar house: the cook house. Her hand is warm and rough at the same time. Heat and oil hang in the air, servants rush about unloading boxes. I look for something to eat.

"Now we need to wash you up, you a mess." She clicks her tongue and takes me to a small room past the stove and helps me out of the calico dress. My red mojo bag is now dark red, like blood. I squeeze it tight in my fist.

"Eliza, you can keep it, but don't let the missus see it or you likely get a whipping. She don't stand for none of that voodoo, you hear?" She wipes my face. "Now wipe your feet off and put on these stockings and shoes."

Her palm rests on my head. "I'm Ester. Best you do what I tell you, that way you won't get a whipping."

The stockings itch. And the shoes—I never had a pair like this, so fancy with strings. I shove my foot in, but it don't fit.

Ester laughs, "Come here."

She picks me up and puts me on a chair. "Now Ester will show you once how to put shoes on so pay attention."

She opens the boot; I slide my foot in and she shows me how to lace them up. She takes my hand. "Come now, we don't want to be late."

A mirror hangs above the fireplace. Blue is everywhere. Blue walls, blue curtains, blue rug, and tiny blue drapes decorate the ceiling: like they painted the room with the sky. The tall man with the silver cane from the showroom sits across from a white woman. Blond curls spring from her head. Tiny black boots peek out the bottom of her wide, straw-colored dress.

"Caroline, darling, let me present to you an early Christmas present." He points his silver cane to me.

"I daresay you've outdone yourself, Mr. Ralston!" She squeals, clapping her hands. "You shouldn't have, darling."

Crackle spit, crackle spit, the flames from the fireplace leap. I wiggle my toes; the shoes pinch my feet.

"She is a strong filly and a seamstress." He points to me.

The missus embraces him; her wide skirt swallows his thin long body. Ester stands by the door with two girls in white caps and aprons. They are light, even lighter than Cato and Sissy.

"Ester, make her a pallet at the foot of my bed where she will sleep."

Ester leaves. I stand between her shiny dress and his long legs, afraid to move or speak.

"I paid a good price for her. Of course, this is a trial. If she is not to your liking, I will send her back." He leans on his cane.

To the pen? To Ma and Auntie. I shift in my shoes.

"I'm sure she will be delightful! Won't you?" She peers into my face; her breath is sweet like rum.

"Yes, Ma'am." My shoes leave tiny marks on the rug, like bare feet in sand.

"Well, well, go along now to bed; Tinty will show you the

way." One of the girls at the door leads me out of the blue room. Shoes click clack all the way up the stairs.

"Where are we going?" I ask her.

"Shush," she says, her eyes hazel like a cat's. "Don't address me until I address you."

She shoves me in a room.

"Don't know why they let one as dark as you in the house."

She slams the door. The walls are sunset pink. The bed is pink, too, with lace trim, like a pink cloud I could sink into. At the end of the bed is a blanket made from sewn-together rags on top of a pallet. I untie my laces, pull off my boots, and crawl underneath the covers.

Side doors open and close. A boy with a fiddle plays a fast song. Auntie tosses shells in the dirt that scatter in opposite directions. Ma's crisscross scars bleed. I run to her, and a man with a thin silver cane stops me; he picks up a pail of salt and red pepper. Ma disappears through the side door. A little boy wiggles and stands upright. It is Cato. Cato! I shout, Cato! But he don't hear me . . .

Poke, poke at my side.

"Clear that chamber pot before she gets up."

Tinty pulls my covers off.

Tinty and Tone are sisters. They are older than me and lighter. Tinty belongs to her and Tone to him. Tinty is mean. I try and be nice, but she's still mean. Tone's quieter than Tinty and has light brown eyes. They say Tinty and Tone are his children. And the Missus got angry and sold their mama. Tinty and Tone think they better than everyone else on the account that they got his blood. I don't care. I don't want none of his blood anyhow. I just want my Ma and Auntie.

Smack! Tinty slaps my face.

"There you go daydreaming again!" She throws a rag at me. "Missus says we need to polish the silver. Well go on, get to it."

Silver forks, knives, platters, cups, and kettles spread over the long table. I never polished silver before. I copy Tone: wash with soap, dip in a bucket, and rub with a linen towel. Tone don't look at me.

Clack clack clack, her shoes slap the ground as she walks toward us. I hold my breath, Tone keeps her head down, I copy her.

She squawks at us like an angry chicken, "Make the silver sparkle! I am entertaining a special guest for tea, and it must shine. Tinty, go on and tell Ester to prepare sandwiches. And Tone, be sure the polishing is done properly."

"Yes, missus," Tone says with her head down. Swish swish, Missus' dress sweeps the floor as she leaves the room. A soap bubble rises then pop—disappears. Dip dip, the silver tray in the bucket—the same kind of bucket Ma and I prayed over. The water is dirty, but I pray to it anyways.

My fingers are wrinkled, my hands sore. I don't stop until we're done. Servants rush about dusting, sweeping, and mopping. Tone and I carefully place the polished, bright silver back in the cabinet shelves and drawers.

Missus' dress is dark blue silk: tiny white flowers dot her sleeves and hem. Blond curls hang along the sides of her plump face. White, smooth stones drop from her ears like little moons. Ester and Tinty carry silver trays past us.

"Now, Tinty, make her presentable for my guest." She flits her pink lace fan; curls bounce around her neck.

Tinty grips my arm and yanks me past the long wooden table and cabinet of silver, out the side door, and into the cookhouse. I breathe in the sweet smell of burnt sugar and molasses. Tinty shoves me in a room in the back.

"Take off your shift and put this on and scrub. You're dirty, and you smell."

Tinty drops the bucket, water spills—is that you Ma?

Ding dong, ding dong, we line the hall for the guest. She's thin with small lips pinched together and a long white face. Her hair is dull brown, and she has two pale grey stones for eyes. Her dress is the color of a sunflower. I wish I had a dress like that. I stand next to Tinty, careful not to move, like I'm her shadow.

"Katherine! So delighted you could make it!" Missus clasps her hands together. "Come to the drawing room for tea."

We follow the yellow and blue dresses down the hall. I stand at the side of the blue-sky room—the first room Ester took me to. They sit as straight as trees. White fingers curl around delicate teacups. On a table, silver trays are covered with tiny colorful pastries. My tummy growls.

"I must tell you how surprised I was by the most generous gift my father-in-law, Mr. Polk, sent me." The grey stone eyes lady nibbles her sandwich like a mouse.

"Oh, please do tell, Katherine." Missus takes a sip of tea and sets it down so carefully, I don't hear a sound.

Grey stone eyes lady smiles. "Well, a little boy dressed as fancy as you can imagine comes to my door. Shoes, pantaloons, and even a fancy hat, mind you, not a speck of dirt on him, not one. I assure you he was the cleanest-looking nigger. To my utter surprise, he came with a carriage and a mule. A fine bred mule at that. You must take a proper look outside to see what a fine gift Mr. Polk bestowed upon me. So thoughtful of Mr. Polk. I shall cherish him always."

"How very generous of your father-in-law. And I must show you my latest acquisition. Mr. Ralston traveled all the way to Nashville to acquire her, an early Christmas present. Eliza, come show yourself to our guest."

She wants me? Tinty shoves me. I wobble over to the white

women in dresses so big they cover their chairs. My legs quiver, the smell of sugar and molasses from the silver trays makes my stomach growl again.

"She's quite dark, isn't she?" The woman in the yellow dress leans forward.

"Mr. Ralston says she is an investment and an excellent seamstress. Isn't that right, Eliza?"

My knees shake.

"Go on, Eliza, go." Missus shoos me with her fan. "She's going through seasoning time, you know, needs to get acclimated."

Acclimated, acc-lim-at-ed, what does that mean? I want to grab one of them pretty cookies so bad—but I don't dare. I go back to my place next to Tinty.

"Of course. What a munificent gift from Mr. Ralston." She lifts her chin up, her lips form a tight smile.

"Yes, I believe so. Please, you must try a pastry. Ester baked them fresh."

"Oh my! They look scrumptious!" The woman in the yellow dress chooses a pink and white pastry from the silver tray, taking tiny mouse bites. When do we get to eat? I drop against the wall. Tinty pinches me; I straighten up. Teacups click; my stomach rumbles.

"Katherine has outdone me again! The nerve of her bringing hers to the house. I knew about it; it was in the papers!" She fans her pink face.

I pick up a tray to take to the kitchen. Who is she talking to?

"Showing me up again. I thought for sure this time . . . Get her out of my sight! I don't want to see her, such a disappointment."

Her blue silk dress flops over the chair; she has her face in her hands, weeping. Tinty shoves me out of the blue-sky room, down the hall—I almost drop the tray, she grabs it from my hands, hissing, "Look what you've done now, you've upset her!"

In the cookhouse, Ester is busy cleaning dishes. When do I get to eat? Why is she crying? What did I do? I don't know what I did, I want Auntie. Auntie and Ma—

Tinty slaps my face, "You stop that crying! I knew you were too dark for this house!"

Ester raises a wooden spoon. "Tinty, we'll have none of that nonsense in here. You let her be."

Tinty runs out of the kitchen.

"Come now, Eliza, you set here, and I'll bring you a biscuit." Ester's arms are warm, almost like Ma's. "You don't pay her no mind, that one got the devil in her."

"Tinty! Get me out of this dress; I can barely breathe! And bring me my laudanum."

Missus is sobbing and crying and carrying on so loud, enough to shatter the glass windows. What did I do? Ester hands me a biscuit. I'm so hungry I want to put it all in my mouth. But just like the lady with grey stone eyes, I take little mouse bites to make it last.

Weave Shed

Bra-da-da-da-dum, her bare feet pump the wooden pedals. Da-dum goes the loom. A tub of wool soaks on top of the black stove. A woman sits in front of the spinning wheel as she feeds it wool, turning it to grey yarn.

The candle's glow makes shadows on the walls. Time to sew the winter clothes: one shirt, one pair of pants, and one coat for men and a linsey-woolsey dress for women. Cut-out cloths of shirts and jackets lie on top of a long table, the same kind of clothes we wore back home. Tinty holds the lantern for the Missus, she's not crying any more, but her voice still sounds like an angry chicken.

"Eliza, sit down and get to work. We must get this sewn before it gets too cold. You all best finish today or you'll be up all night till it is completed. There is so much to do. Tinty, I must have time to prepare to attend the party tonight."

Missus wraps her grey shawl across her chest. Tinty leads her out the weave shed.

I suck in my breath. Nana, Ma, and Auntie sewed plenty of mojo bags and quilts. Sometimes, they made dresses and shirts when they could get the cloth. I once made tiny shirts and dresses for my Cato and Sissy dolls out of scraps.

I sit at the long table with women in white headscarves bent over, their nimble fingers pushing needles in and out through the cloth. I pick up a cut-out jacket laying on the table in front of me: it is itchy against the skin, grey and black with streaks of white. Push needle, pull thread, push needle, pull thread—the spinning wheel whirs. I sew as fast as I can.

A rooster crows. The sun fills the room slowly, and we blow out the candles.

"Best get this done quickly," the woman next to me says, twisting a thread into a knot. "Where you from?"

She slaps the table with her hand. "I asked where you from?"

I didn't know she was talking to me. "I come from Richmond."

"Huh, you too young to be a seamstress." She picks up a cutout of a dress and threads her needle. Ma told me to say yes. Yes, I can sew; tell them yes. Ma and Auntie, maybe they close by—maybe they in Tennessee and will come get me soon. I sew as fast as I can.

Ouch—I poke my finger with the needle. I put my finger in my mouth. Tinty walks in the room. She snatches the jacket from the table.

"Why Eliza, these stitches are all crooked! I knew you

wasn't no seamstress. I knew it. You just wait till I show this to her, and what a whooping you'll get!"

The blood from my finger tastes salty. Women around me click their tongues, the spinning wheel whirs. Bra-da-dum the loom sings.

I trail behind Tinty out of the weave shed, across the yard, past the maple tree to the servant's door, then to the blue-sky room. Missus dress is shiny and green as a leaf in sunlight. The jacket lies across her lap. I want to touch her green dress, wonder what it feels like? Tinty stands beside her; she sticks out her tongue at me and smiles.

"Well, what do you have to say for yourself, Eliza?" Missus holds up the half-stitched jacket, threads dangle from the bottom. I wiggle my toes; I don't look at her. "Do you know, lying is a sin?"

Drip drop drip, can't stop tears.

"Honestly, what am I to do? Mr. Ralston assured me you are a seamstress, as indicated in the advertisement. I was so pleased to acquire a skillful negress and now . . . I may need to sell you off, put you up on that auction block out front—you hear?"

She dabs the corner of her eyes with a handkerchief. Send me back? To Ma and Auntie? Thump thump thump goes my heart. I want to go back to Ma and Auntie, away from Tinty's mean green eyes and this cold house.

"Oh, what shall I do? Poor Mr. Ralston went through all the trouble to get you. And Katherine—oh, I can see the glee on her face when she hears I had to send you back!" She squeezes her hands together so hard her knuckles turn pink. "No, she shan't have the satisfaction. Eliza, you must be punished for lying. Oh, how I hate to do this. It is from the goodness of my Christian heart to teach you the righteous path. May God forgive you. Tinty, go on and get a hickory switch."

Tinty skips out of the room.

.   .   .

The bell rings, everyone in the house is called to watch. Leaves on the maple tree are a burnt orange and yellow. Ground is damp, almost winter. Send me back, send me back, how do I get back? Tinty shoves me on the ground and ties my wrist to a stake and my ankles to another. I turn my head in the grass, Ester stares back at me. Auntie, what do I do? Auntie?

"Lying is a sin. Let this be a lesson for all of you. Tinty, hand me the switch." Her voice is like a mean chicken now.

Smack! The branches sting the back of my legs. A cloud drifts above. I pray to the wind; she lifts my body, and I float up, looking down at tiny dots as I fly far, far away.

I come to on a wooden bench in the kitchen. Ester wets a cloth and dabs the cuts on my legs. They sting and are swollen, raw, red.

"I'll clean this up good, Eliza."

She takes a long cloth and wraps one leg and then the other. She helps me up, saying, "Now Eliza, I heard word that they marched a coffle to Nashville and about now, they already boarding the skiffs to be sold to Mississippi or New Orleans, far, far away. Eliza, take my advice: you make it right here. You don't want to end up down there in those sugar or cotton fields; you won't never come back. You make the best here."

My legs throb. I want to throw my arms around Ester and never let go. Ma, Auntie, they won't forget me; they'll come back for me.

"Yes, Ma'am. Thank you." I manage to slide off the bench.

"Now go on, get to bed, and I'll check those legs tomorrow."

.   .   .

The maple tree lost all its leaves now, only grey branches remain. I shiver as I walk past it, trying not to think of my body pinned on the ground, the sharp pain of the hickory switch, Tinty's gleeful eyes, and the welcoming sky. Sun's not up yet, I can see my breath. Women wrapped in shawls enter the weave shed. The Missus let me back in. Told me I better watch the others and learn to sew. She said she took pity on me and wouldn't send me back on account of her good Christian heart. She says I must pray to unlearn the evil ways of sinners—that I should be grateful to have her forgiveness and a path to salvation.

The scabs are hardening on the back of my legs. I watch carefully how the women sew. Sometimes they stop to teach me a stitch. They say I pick up fast and that I will be a good seamstress.

My fingers are sore, my neck and back ache. The dinner bell rings. Women sigh in relief, drop their work, wrap their shawls tight around their shoulders, and huddle together as they move out of the weave shed, through the fearsome wind to the back door of the big house. Ester has a pot of stew and cornbread with table scraps on the long wooden table in the kitchen. We're so tired we eat without talking.

Down the hall past the blue-sky room, I lift my heavy feet up the stairs. At the top of the stairs, the door to his room is half open. Creak creak, Tone is laid over his desk with her skirt up. He grunts. Her dull brown eyes are open but don't see me. I suck my breath in and slip into the pink sunset room. Missus is asleep covered in blankets. I reach under my pallet, grab my mojo bag, and pull the blanket over me.

Auntie

Jackson, Tennessee, 1852

No more time. Memphis is our last stop before the death rafts down the Mississippi. The shells say Eliza has her own path, and Clara and I another. Isaac's ankle is healing. Clara, Gabriel, and Isaac agree to the plan. I sneak them powder—they know when to take it.

I swallow my portion. My body jerks and wiggles on the ground till I don't move. Clara wails and women rush over. A trader gets off his horse and takes my pulse. The women dig a shallow grave. Clara makes sure there ain't too much dirt on me.

Bone to bone, gnarled together like a spider web, babies stiff in their mamas' arms, headless skeletons, wails of lost ones. *Bring us home, bring us home . . .* roots coil around my neck, my feet. *Have you come to bury us?* This earth is cursed. I am lying atop a mass grave of murdered Indians.

I thrust my hand through the ground, scratch my way out, coughing and spitting out dirt. Spirits moan. I say a prayer and sprinkle water to honor them. A raven flies overhead; it follows me as I hitch up my skirt and run, looking out for shallow graves.

There she is. They didn't even bother to cover Clara's body. Three vultures circle above her. I set her upright, slap her back. She coughs and vomits. She tears up; I say we don't have time for that, come on.

The sun is about to set—we got to hurry before we can't see a thing at all. Clara takes one side of the road, I the other to make sure we don't miss them.

Long feet stick out the ground—unchained, the traders took them off cause they are too valuable to leave on a dead man.

"Isaac!"

We found him. We claw the dirt off him as fast as we can. Is he dead? Did I give him too much? It takes both of our strength to set him up. He growls as loud as a bear, shaking the dirt off his clothes.

"Let's get Gabriel," he says, taking my hand.

The coffle is sure to stop and camp overnight. A bent-over figure appears on the side of the road. Must be Gabriel. Clara dashes to him and helps him upright. They cling onto each other like we have time for that now.

"Come on."

I hook my arm in Isaac's, and we keep an eye out for campfires.

We hear them first: the usual drinking and carrying on of the traders. We hide in the trees above the campsite and wait till they sleep.

Isaac and Gabriel get the traders' horses, me and Clara slip foxglove seeds in water pots and canteens, enough so they won't wake up after drinking it. Just in case, I add a few drops of snake venom.

Gabriel and Isaac lead the horses, Clara and I creep quietly behind them. When we get far enough away, I mount Isaac's horse, Gabriel helps Clara up on his, and we take off down the road to freedom, to Mexico.

"Why south?" I ask Isaac.

"'Cause they expect us to go north, and I got people in Mexico."

"Well, alright then."

He grabs the reins, and we gallop into the night.

LEFLORE COUNTY, MISSISSIPPI

We ride till dawn and lead the horses into the woods, so we don't come across any patrollers on the lookout for runaways. The men hunt while Clara and I set up shelter, making a lean-to with pine tree boughs atop soft moss. It will do. Clara tends to the horses at a nearby brook. Clara is mournful, rarely speaks, her mind is on Eliza. Only Gabriel can bring a soft smile to her face.

I got to keep my mind sharp, to the future, to freedom. I gather kindling and keep my eye out for the comfrey plant for Isaac's ankle. There they are, a family of plants near a fallen rotted tree. I ask permission to take some and pull up three from the ground, roots and all. This forest is blessed. I head back to our spot.

Here they come, a turkey neck dangles from Gabriel's hand. Isaac's bellowing laughter makes my flesh tingle.

"Eliza, you shoulda seen him chase that turkey!" Isaac smiles.

"Naw Isaac, no more of your jests, I own this turkey, and I get to say who eats it!" Gabriel commands, as he swings the bird, making feathers splay, he caught a big one. "You just jealous cause I'm the one that caught him."

Gabriel pushes Isaac, Isaac falls to the ground his sidesplit-ting, holding his belly. These two, how long they been together? They act like brothers. I set the comfrey plants down;

I can't help but giggle. I reach my hand down to Isaac to lift him up.

"Isaac, your belly is gonna burst!" I say, and his strong arms take me down on top of him. I roll off. "Now, you stop, Isaac."

I slap him playfully, but I can't wipe the grin off my face. Clara comes back with the horses and secures them to a tree branch.

"What is all this fuss?" Clara asks.

Gabriel offers the turkey to Clara, like its a gold crown.

"For you, my lady," Gabriel says, in a mocking tone like a gentleman in a ballroom.

"Why, Gabriel . . ." Clara bats her eyes, curtsying as if she some grand lady. "I shall enjoy plucking every feather."

They carry on acting like white folks do; we all have a good laugh. Isaac stands and offers his hand to me, helping me upright. I brush the dirt and leaves off my dress and pick up the comfrey plants.

"Let me see that ankle," I say to Isaac.

He sits down, leans against a tree, and unwinds the bandage; it is better but still has a little pus. I remove the old leaves and replace them with fresh ones.

"Thank you kindly," Isaac says, placing his hand on top of mine, sending a warmth through my body. I squeeze his hand, then release my fingers from his and put the remaining comfrey plants in my herb bundle.

I start a fire using a flint, rock, and dry leaves. Isaac helps, adding sticks to get the fire going. He takes out his corn husk pipe, packs it with tobacco, lights it, and sits down next to Gabriel. Clara is plucking the turkey, every so often catching Gabriel's smile.

With full bellies, we take a right nice rest on the moss; the men sleep across from us, snoring with their hats over their eyes. Dusk comes and beckons us awake, an owl hoots, the rustle of night creatures skulk about, they must smell the turkey carcass. There is still enough light to make it through the woods back to the road. Isaac and Gabriel lead the horses, and Clara and I walk behind them. We all know it is too dangerous to speak, lest we be heard by some patrollers.

We watch the horses. Any time they get skittish, we stop. Wait and listen. Horses can feel a breeze before it comes, they give us our warnings. Stars are bright enough to make out the edges of the road. It don't matter how dark it is, horses can see in the night much better than we can. Hooves beat the ground like drums, we gonna make it, I'm sure of it.

Our horse slows and suddenly stops. Isaac and I hurl forward, almost flying over the horse's head. The horse freezes like a deer in the woods with his ears forward. He must hear or smell something. Isaac signals us to be quiet. A faint murmur of a cart is coming toward us. We dismount quickly, and Isaac guides us back into the woods.

Sure enough, three white men in a horse drawn cart ride by; they must be patrollers. We don't breathe or move. We wait till we can't hear nothing and get back on the road. Isaac says the best course is to find a swamp to hide in for a bit. I watch the land for signs of marsh water.

McINTYRE SCATTERS, MISSISSIPPI

Horse hooves stick in the mud, they can barely trot. Ground is wet, so a swamp is near. The air is heavier like it is trying to weigh us down. Tall cypress trees sprout from soft green moss —mosquitoes bite something terrible. We veer away from the road towards the cypress trees and come to a small clearing where we tie up the horses.

The swamp water is murky and no telling how deep it is. Clara and I balance our bundles on our heads staying close to the men. We wade up to our waists to a small island. A man groans in pain his leg is swollen. He's dark like an Indian with short black hair. We all climb onto the bank, surrounding him.

"Rattlesnake?" I ask.

He nods. He's near death's door, no time to waste. I suck the venom out of his punctured leg and spit it out. I do it again, then Clara hands me a cloth, and we tie it above the bite to stop the venom from spreading. I set him upright against a tree, keeping watch over him, don't know if he's a friend or foe. Clara searches for food.

Isaac and Gabriel step back into the swamp to hunt. The man stirs, asks for a drink. I hand him my canteen and he slides himself upright, takes a sip.

"I owe you my life."

His name is Felipe, a Tejano guide from Texas. He used to be a bounty hunter, capturing runaways and returning them to their owners. That is, until he fell in love with one of his captives and married her, a negro woman who was a slave. She was with child and Felipe had a plan to escape south to Mexico where their child would be born free, but they were captured. His wife was sent back to her master and he was thrown in jail. He broke out, but it was too late, they already hanged her and cut up her body bad. Cut the baby right out of her. He vowed ever since that he'd help any runaways. I believe him. Got to be careful though; there are accounts of people turning you in for money. We all know we got a price on our heads now.

Clara sets her skirt full of wild berries on a blanket.

"We won't go hungry."

Isaac and Gabriel climb up the bank, with a slain possum swinging between them. More food than any rations. Swamp done us good. The men sniff each other out the way they do. Felipe swears he will lead us to freedom, to Mexico.

"How do we know this ain't a plan for you to sell us?" Gabriel fixes his eyes on Felipe.

"Upon the grave of my wife and child, I swear, I will not deceive you." Felipe crosses himself.

Gabriel and Isaac walk to the edge of the bank, to mull over Felipe's plan.

"How can we trust him?" Gabriel's voice is antsy.

"What else we do? Stay in the swamps? I say we take the chance." Isaac convinces Gabriel, they walk back toward Felipe. Isaac packs his pipe with tobacco, we seal Felipe's promise with a smoke.

The sky darkens, toads and frogs try and outdo each other with their songs. We will leave the swamp tonight. Three men come towards us on a large raft made of cypress logs, branches, and moss. Isaac is ready to attack if need be. Gabriel stands in front of Clara. They just maroons taking refuge in the swamp. They climb up the bank, we share our food, and in return, they carry us on their raft back to dry land where we left our horses. I ask how long they been in the swamp, they say since the winter, and they will stay as long as they can.

"Swamp is freedom, no going back."

The man rowing spits. His body is slim but strong; he plunges the long stick into the water, propelling us forward. Clara's crying, thinking on Eliza. I don't fight what the shells say ever. And two fell together, one alone. She rests her head on my shoulder as the men row us back to the bank.

Felipe says the safest way to escape is for us to pretend we are his captives. He will act the part of a bounty hunter and claims his plan will work because he was known in these parts as a bounty hunter before he changed his ways.

Clara and I mount one horse, he ties Isaac's and Gabriel's hands to a lead rope behind us. Felipe is behind us on the other horse holding his rifle. Our story is he captured us in a swamp and is returning us to our owners in Galveston, Texas. It will take two days to get to Vicksburg where we will cross over the Mississippi River to Louisiana, and then Texas.

. . .

VICKSBURG, MISSISSIPPI

The port at Vicksburg is mayhem: the groans from a slave market fill me with dread. A coffle of women, children, and men in chains are forced onto the largest boat—a steamboat. They moan and wail like they walking to their death. Overseers snap whips, shouting at them to move faster. Could this be the coffle we escaped from?

Clara whispers in my ear, "Maybe we will find Eliza?"

Her gaze scours the crowd; I tell her to keep her head down. All kinds of boats scatter the harbor, canoes, skiffs, and long flat boats. How are we gonna get across the river through that wide mess? Men load barrels from carts onto docked vessels, my horse is jumpy. We pass behind a crowd facing a man standing on the auction block in chains with his head down, fists curled like he ready to fight. A well-dressed white man in a grey vest, black overcoat, and top hat strikes his cane out and stops us in our tracks.

"Woah, where you going, boy, with these niggers?" he shouts, loud enough to draw attention to us.

My gut boils; I want to strike him.

Felipe answers back, "I'm taking them back to their owner, in Galveston."

He lifts his reins, ready to move on. The man approaches Felipe's horse.

"I can get you a good price for them, right now, and you won't have to travel all that way." His voice is a whisper now.

"Kind of you, sir, but we best be going." Felipe tips his hat, the man steps to the side grumbling.

The auctioneer voice rises above street noise: "This here strong buck, worth four hundred, can I hear four hundred . . ."

No point in looking back. No point in trying to save any of

them. I send my prayers to the wind. I hope Felipe knows what he's doing.

Felipe leads us down to a clearing by the river. White men stand on the shore next to a large flat boat with a little cabin in the center and a short fence around the edges of the craft. Fiddle music and laughter spill from the boat. A man dances a jig, waving a scarf, while others chug liquor from jugs. Felipe gets off his horse, tells us to dismount, and stands behind us pointing his rifle. The white men on shore recognize him and greet him. They believe Felipe's story about returning us to our owners in Galveston.

To pay for our passage across the river, Felipe sells his horse. We board the strange boat with the remaining horse. The men stop their merrymaking and sink their poles into the water, steering us to the other side of the Mississippi River. The boat bumps the side of the bank. We hide our relief. I pray, giving thanks; above, a raven circles 'round us. How many more rivers will we need to cross?

We pass cotton plantations always keeping our heads down. Felipe rides behind us with his gun pointed at our backs; he knows many of the overseers, we aren't questioned. At times, we head back into swampland for a rest. Clara and Gabriel are like two peas in a pod. Isaac and Felipe share a pipe every night; I consult the shells to make sure we are on the right path. We walk for seven days until we arrive at the Red River in Shreveport; this is the last river we need to cross, then on to Nacogdoches, Texas.

A flock of birds with long necks and thin legs land on the river shore. Nearby, a skiff secured by a thick rope around a tree trunk floats next to a gangly man smoking a pipe. Felipe bargains with him, offering his horse, the one that gave us a warning by stalling in the road. I scratch the horse's neck thanking it, while the skiff captain drops coins into Felipe's palm.

All of us are too tired to talk. The wiry man is surprisingly strong, thrusting the long pole into the rusty water to Nacogdoches, bringing us closer to freedom. We set up camp on the riverbank; Clara and Gabriel fold into each other's arms, Isaac and Felipe take turns keeping watch. I allow myself some shuteye.

It takes near three days to arrive in Houston. Felipe says the backwoods are a safer route than through the center of town. We rest under hanging trees by the bayou and bathe in the water. At night, we reach the railroad tracks and are about two days away from Virginia Point. There, we will take a boat to Galveston Island, where we'll board a ferry to Mexico.

Galveston, Texas

I've never seen water so blue. Men load bales of cotton onto freight ships. Women twirl parasols, strolling with sweethearts. Children run barefoot begging in the street. All kinds of people and no one pays us much mind.

"This one will take you to Tamaulipas, Mexico," Felipe says and points to a ferry, white with blue trim on the bottom. He approaches a man unloading baggage, they exchange secretive looks. He motions us to come forward, and the man hurries us around the back of the vessel to a separate loading dock. Felipe lingers behind, keeping watch.

I grasp his hands, saying, "You will not be forgotten. The next baby born will be named Felipe."

He nods solemnly and walks back down the plank onto the street.

In the bottom of the ferry, we hide behind large crates on the damp floor. Isaac and Gabriel untie the ropes around their wrists. I set my red cloth on the ground. Clara rests in my lap with her hand on her belly.

ELIZA

A fist bursts through the dirt: fingers stretch up. The raven caws above her. Auntie brushes off dark earth, hooves thunder on the ground—

"Ma! Auntie!" Did I wake Missus up? She's still snoring in her pink and white bed. I wipe the sweat off my face. They left without me. I am alone.

I place a damp cloth on Missus' forehead. She is losing another baby. Tinty told me she had lost many babies that didn't hold. Tone carries fresh sheets in her hands.

"It's all the sinning in this house. Tone! You get out of my sight—out!"

Tone places the sheets at the end of the bed. I can tell Tone has a baby in her, just a small bump, but I can tell.

"Eliza put another log on the fire; I don't want to catch a chill." She is hot and cold, hot and cold—the log catches quick, flames dance around it. "You're a good one, Eliza. Don't you be sinful like Tone, you hear now? Eliza!"

I answer her softly and leave for the weave shed. I almost crash into Tinty carrying a tray with tea. I step aside. I refuse to look at her.

I walk through the kitchen to see if there is a biscuit left over—nothing. Outside, I pass men and women bent over hoes, smacking the soil, planting snap peas, corn, tomatoes, okra, and potatoes. The peach and apple trees have tiny sprouts. In the weave shed, the loom sings the same song. I take my seat, pick up a shirt, and start sewing.

A wail so loud from outside pierces through the walls. We drop our needles and thread; the loom stops. Outside, folks surround the duck pond. I run past the orchard. There's Tinty on her knees at the edge of the pond.

"Tone! Tone! Someone get her. Get her!"

Tone's white dress floats in the water; she is face down like a duck diving for food. But she is not coming back up for air. Tone drowned herself on account of that baby. Ester holds Tinty back from jumping in after her.

He leans on his cane, pipe in his mouth. Everyone shushes —even Tinty stops fussing. He rubs his hand over his beard.

"You all know it is a sin to take your own life? There will be no salvation for her. Let her be an example to you all. She will stay in her watery grave until I say it is time to pull her out. Now get on back to work." He sucks his pipe, lets out one last puff, turns, and walks back to the house.

With Tone gone, Tinty turns more sourer than ever. After a week passes, they pull Tone out of that pond, her face bloated and unrecognizable. We bury her in our graveyard. Tinty lost the only person she loved and the only person that loved her. Tinty stops bothering me cause I grew taller than her.

He starts messing on Tinty, and when Missus finds out, she

whoops Tinty so hard—especially on her face. Now, Tinty walks with a limp and her face is all scarred. Tinty's baby doesn't keep. I suppose Missus is happy about it, that it didn't keep.

Missus is with child again, and the doctor confines her to bedrest until She has the baby. She sure grows fat in her bed. Tinty and I help her squat over the chamber pot, She wobbles so. We wave fans over her for hours. My arm gets sore; if I stop, She hollers: "Stop being so lazy, Eliza! Hot, I'm so hot, keep fanning!"

Tinty and I wash her with wet cloths; She got too big for the tub. Only thing She do is feed herself. And She complains that the eggs aren't to her liking, too runny, or her tea ain't hot enough. Back and forth to the kitchen we go. I'll sure be happy when this baby is born.

I stay clear of him as much as possible. Try and make my footsteps so quiet like I'm invisible. A step creaks, I grab the banister, wait. The usual night sounds of crickets, frogs whir in the air. I step, another creak. He peeks out the door, and He summons me to his room. I wasn't quiet enough, I was too loud, my knees buckle. I walk in keeping the door ajar. His long skinny hand grips my arm, I scratch at his face. He kicks the door, it slams. No way out now. His boney fingers latch around my neck like a noose, and he throws me on my back. He takes me over his desk just like Tone.

Ma's voice comes to me: "Don't fight or they might kill you . . ."

It hurt so bad I had to put my mind somewhere else. I found a corner of the rug: red, blue, and white swirls a bit faded from the sun.

. . .

I made sure I took the stinking gum to stop the baby. No matter how much I take, the baby stayed, like Ma when she had Cato and Sissy—sometimes the babies are stubborn and want to get born. Ma said it is the ancestor's spirit searching for a body to come alive in. I prayed it would die, no kind of life for it here. Who do I pray to?

Missus screams about near shook the walls of the house. But her baby came. She lost a lot of blood, almost died. Pale cheeks, stringy hair.

"I've done it, gave him a son."

She smiles weakly. Tinty applies a wet rag to her forehead. The doctor shoos us out of the room.

My belly swelled, but my prayers were answered: it was born early, dead. Ester took it, a girl, and wrapped it in a blanket. I didn't want to see it. Didn't want to know where it was buried.

Nobody said nothing to me. The next day I was expected to do my chores as usual: lighting fires, clearing chamber pots, serving meals, scrubbing floors, and mending and sewing clothes in the weave shed. By the glint in Missus' eyes, I knew her mind was seeking revenge because He sought me out, She knew.

I put the tea tray down as quickly as possible before She noticed the dark wet circles forming around my breasts.

"Eliza, you are to be Junior's nursemaid," Missus says. She hands me Junior, swaddled tight. I want to smother it, squeeze the life out of it . . .

She points to the rocking chair. "Sit, Eliza, so I can see how he takes to you."

His tiny skull switches side to side trying to find my breast.

"Go on," She commands.

I unbutton my dress; he clamps onto my nipple so hard, I jerk back from the pain.

"Well, looks like he takes to you just fine, Eliza, just fine."

She picks up her teacup, her pinky finger raised with a faint smile on her lips. I've got to find a way out of this hell.

The curtains flutter, a rare breeze comes in—take me, oh please take me, I pray, my eyes fix on the window away from her haughty gaze. I about want to jump in the duck pond like Tone. What if he tries again? I ask Ester about escaping. If I get another of his babies inside me, I will kill myself and it. Ester says to wait, the right time will come, wait.

The first snow covers the ground like a blanket stretched as far as I can see: past the apple and peach trees, the frozen duck pond, the tiny cabins, and the fence where Ester hangs her quilts. We are bundled up in jackets and shawls, tending to horses, feeding chickens, pigs, and sheep, milking the cows, chopping wood, and gathering kindling. I follow the trail of footprints in the snow to the weave shed.

I'm the last one finishing a pair of pants. Ester comes in the weave shed with a bag. She puts her finger to her lips to quiet me and slips a bundle of clothes in her sack. I act like I don't see a thing.

Next morning, Ester hangs a quilt way yonder on the fence. She quickly hides the sack in the bushes. So that's why Ester wants me to be quiet: she's helping runaways.

Old clothes left for servants won't be missed. I won't say a thing about it.

"Won't the excursion be diverting!" She hands me Junior and greets her friend with the long face and stone-grey eyes.

I follow them into the drawing room. Tinty stands by the

table filled with treats and tea. She pours the tea carefully in the dainty cups and hobbles to her station by the door, dragging her bad leg.

"Mr. Ralston has a speaking engagement in Pittsburgh. We shall board a steamboat in Louisville and join others for a gay party in Pittsburgh on a boat! Imagine, a boat!"

The baby wiggles; I set him on the floor.

"Oh yes! My husband informed me he will also partake in the oration, so we shall be joining you." She flicks a crumb from her shiny brown sleeve.

"I am certain Eliza will suffice as the nursemaid." She nods to me.

"Wonderful, I will bring along my daughter, as well." Her friend's lips form a line, so thin you can barely see them. I am to care for two babies on this journey, but I have another plan.

The girl has stone eyes as small as pebbles like her mama, and she won't stop crying. They don't pay her no mind; they ride in the carriage with their husbands. I ride alone with the babies.

Missus' baby is asleep after feeding. He rests in my arms, limp and warm. The other one wails so loud, I want to strike her. This is the road that took me away from Ma and Auntie. Now I am returning to Nashville, same pine trees line the road. I was just a girl, now I am a woman.

Horse droppings and rotting garbage fill the streets, even in the carriage you can smell it. We stop for lodging at a fancy hotel. I stay in the nursery. My room is small with two cribs and a pallet for me. The children are tuckered out from the journey, and so am I.

They come in the nursery in the morning to greet their bawling children. The girl reaches her arms out to her stone-eyed mama. She picks up the girl and walks to the dining room. I trail behind with Junior.

"Eliza, take the children in the kitchen for breakfast." Missus points to a room behind the dining room.

I grab the baby girl who hollers once her mama releases her from her frail arms. My head throbs. After breakfast, servants load the carriages. It will be a long journey to Louisville, close to two days.

The unmistakable scent of lye mixed with droppings, of misery, fills the air. As the carriage moves slowly down the street, we see a line of white men wait outside a gate. It must be selling time. Click clock, click clock, the horse's hooves drum on the ground, past the tall walls of the pen, I pinch my nose till the smell disappears.

Underwater Panther

Louisville, Kentucky

I never been on a boat before. I'm afraid it is so heavy that it will sink to the bottom of the river. But it doesn't. People walk about it, smoking, eating—like it is nothing.

Fiddle music, laughter, and voices greet us at the entrance to the dining hall. The baby's hungry again, he nuzzles his nose to find my breast. The girl clings to my skirt, mewling for her mama. The missus turns to Ralston, begs him to dance, but He refuses and sits at the bar, orders a drink. A gentleman offers her his arm, and they spin around, her silver gown skimming the floor.

"Go on, Eliza, take Junior to the nursery." She waves her fan gaily.

A tall negro servant in a white jacket, black bow tie, white pants, and black shoes shows me the way. He is so tall, he has to duck down narrow stairs. Next to a bedroom is a small room with a rocking chair and two cribs. Are you free? I want to ask the servant. I set Junior in the crib; the girl fusses so much, just hollers.

We dock in Cincinnati, one more day to Pittsburgh. Ester said that is the stop. My heart jumps in my chest—one more stop. With all the babies crying and fussing, I can't sleep. Through the tiny window, black water shines in a stream of moonlight—just one more night, one more.

In the little room, the baby is asleep in the crib; the girl crawls around, drooling. The minute I open the door, she goes and hollers again. I take the lantern and find my way to the stairs, hallway, and sneak past the ballroom. I catch a glimpse of her blond ringlets; she doesn't see me.

I set out to the deck, go around to the north side like Ester told me. I wave my lantern and wait. That baby's still crying.

The tall servant leans over me; I almost drop the lantern.

"I'm getting some air, that's all."

Will he turn me in?

"Don't worry, sister, I know. He'll be here."

He must work with them. Boom boom, my heart about to burst, straining to see in the dark.

Sure enough, a light waves back at me. It comes closer and closer, revealing a man in a rowboat. He rows alongside the ship, and I lower myself carefully off the deck. Even as he steadies me, the boat rocks a bit. I sit down. He swings the paddle in and out, in and out, the baby's cries fading with each stroke. I run my hand in the river— is this what freedom feels like?

We bump against the shore; he secures the boat, tying a rope to a tree branch. I take his hand, hoist my dress up, and step onto the landing. I get a glimpse of him: he's an older man with white stubble on his dark chin. A wide brim hat covers his forehead, so I can barely see his face.

"Come on." His voice is soft but firm, and his hand is rough, probably from the rowing, I imagine. "There's talk of bounty hunters up north at Lake Erie; best we take a different route."

We take the path along the Ohio River on the north side,

the free side. We walk like cats in the dark for miles until the sun rises over the Allegheny River.

"This here is where we'll part." He points down the ridge to a pile of rocks. I wish I had something to give him, my dress is muddy and frayed. I don't have anything.

"Thank you kindly, sir, for taking me this far."

"Go on now, you go, and have a good life. Go to the cave, tell the Captain that the Skipper sent you." He tips his hat, trudges up the trail, and doesn't look back.

I want to run after him. What could be in that pile of stones?

Behind the rocks is a small opening. I duck down to get in. The air is cool, moist with a trace of smoke. I trace my fingers along the rough walls, droplets fall on my head and hands. Click of a pistol. I can't see—a hand grips my arm.

"The Skipper sent me," I say quickly.

"Come."

How can he see in here? The cave curves and turns till we come to an opening where a boy squats, eating by a fire. His clothes are tattered, and his limbs are like sticks. Must be a runaway like me. The man lets go my arm and motions me to sit down. Water trickles down the cave walls. I warm my palms by the fire. The boy offers me some fish. I try not to grab it, but I'm so hungry I forget manners. The man with the pistol squats next to us. Long strands of black hair frame his face. He is Indian. He puts a fish speared on a stick in the fire. The fish is strange, white, smooth, with eyes shut. Tastes alright.

"Where you from?" the boy asks, licking his fingers.

Should I trust him? Is this a setup? How do I know they won't take me back? I am sure there is a price on my head by now. That woman is probably weeping and wailing and cursing me all at once—I don't miss her. Don't miss those babies, or

Tinty. Only Ester—yes, she been like a Ma to me, and I'll never tell nothing to get her in trouble. So, I say Richmond, just in case.

"I'm from Kentucky." He slides a bone out his mouth and drops it on the ground. "I'd die before I go back there."

I nod. Maybe he is for real. The Indian turns his fish over; it sizzles and pops. I wrap my shawl over me.

"Cold?" the boy asks. "Sit closer to the fire."

He lifts his arm and brushes fish bones aside on the ground —he has no hand; only a stub peeks through his tattered sleeve. I scoot forward, and he quickly covers his stub. Is it shame?

"They sold everyone, Ma, Pa, my sisters, and brothers, but nobody wanted me—why would anyone want a one-handed boy? I stole a chicken is all; we was starving. I got caught that time—just a youngin. They cut my hand clean off, a lesson for us all.

"After they sold my family, there weren't no reason for me to stay. I was all set to cross Lake Erie, but word got out the bounty hunters patrolling the border, so now we set to go through New York, to Niagara Falls. You hear 'bout Niagara Falls? To cross it is good luck. I believe so, cause you crossing over to freedom."

He is barely a man, not a trace of whiskers on his chin. I suppose he's a bit younger than me. I reckon I am about sixteen now, don't know my real age for sure. The Indian offers me more fish. I oblige, and before I know it, I fall asleep to the sizzling fire and faint droplets.

She laughs gaily. Her silver dress swish swoosh swishes on the floor. I jump into the river, drop all the way down down—you taking me home? Tone drifts by, her white dress floats around her like angel wings—I sink down, no way up, no way—

"Wake up." He nudges me.

Where am I? The fire, the dampness: the cave. I don't even

know the boy's name; did he tell it to me? He hands me his canteen; I take a sip. Was it a good omen or a bad omen? Tone, the floating angel, is she warning me?

His name is Thomas, and the Indian is Captain. Captain leaves every morning and comes back in the afternoon with some sort of game dangling over his shoulder—that's how Thomas knows how many days he been here, by counting the times Captain comes back. He reckons he has been in the cave about seven weeks. Best to wait to leave till Captain says the woods are clear of white men with hounds. Though sometimes, Captain allows Thomas to hunt with him nearby.

"I'm Eliza," I say, standing up to stretch. Bones crunch underneath my feet. Must have been a lot of folks coming through here, spitting fish bones on the ground.

"Wanna see the lake?" Thomas asks.

"There's a lake in here?"

"Come on."

Thomas grabs a spear and hands me a lantern. The cave walls are green, grey, and brown with icicle-like cones hanging from above. Drawings of bears, birds, and figures hunting appear on the walls. I point to a creature with horns, a long body with spikes on its back, and tail like an alligator or over-sized salamander.

"What's that?" I ask Thomas.

"Captain says that's the underwater panther, lives in the lake. Got to be careful not to take too many fish or it get mad and eat you. Got to ask it first if we can fish. And thank it when we're done."

"You believe him?"

"So far it ain't got me . . ." He shrugs his shoulders, I run my fingers along the side on the rough walls until we come to a black lake as smooth as glass. At the edge of the lake, white fish swim to the surface, then disappear. Thomas mumbles something then jabs his spear.

"Time for breakfast."

He jabs it again. I don't dare go near the water, afraid that panther will get me. A flash of white comes to the surface; he raises his spear.

"Got it!" He caught three fish at the end of his spear now. He whispers his thanks to the lake, the blind white fish, and the terrible water panther.

Captain returns just like Thomas said, with two rabbits slung over his shoulder and kindling in his arms; seems like he appeared out of nowhere. Thomas takes the rabbits from Captain and slaps them on a slab of flat rock to skin. I add more kindling to the fire. Captain rolls out a bear skin big enough for all three of us. He takes out his pipe, sucks in, and blows out smoke.

And there she is: Ma. Her thick arms hold me; I am surrounded by her scent of salt and tobacco leaves. Nana rocks in her chair with a corn pipe in her mouth, and Auntie tosses her shells. Ma's warmth is all around me, inside me like smoke. Ma, Auntie, I made it out of there, that evil house! Made it out!

"Who you talking to?" Thomas raises up the skinned rabbits with his hand, smiling. I come back to the cave—can't see them no more. They faded with the smoke.

I help Thomas get those rabbits on a spit, and we set it on the fire, turning it every so often.

Captain takes his pipe out of his mouth, says, "It is sacred for my people here."

He stares into the fire—is he talking to the fire?

"We come from Manhattan, the Lenape, many, many years ago. Many battles, many people perish, leave. We came here for a vision to take back to our people. There were no more people to go back to. Many left for Canada or were forced to move west. My whole family murdered, gone. I came here to wait for spirit to lead me. In the woods, I see many runaways terrorized by the white man. I hide them until it is safe for them to go.

"They name me Captain of the cave of the ancestors. I wait for the vision, and when it is time to go, I will close this cave, and no man will ever enter it again."

Captain scatters tobacco in the fire. Flames swell as we sleep.

I adjust to the dark like a bat. Captain says we must keep the fire lit until he says to put it out. I count three times Captain leaves and comes back, and three times, Thomas and I go to the lake to catch white blind fish. On the fourth day, Captain comes back empty-handed, no rabbit or squirrel.

"Put out the fire."

Thomas and I smother it with fish bones and rocks.

"It's time."

Thomas hangs his canteen around his shoulder and picks up his spear with his good hand. I wrap my shawl around me.

We crawl out of the mouth of the cave.

"The sun will hurt your eyes at first; keep them half-closed," Captain warns us.

Maybe if we stayed in the cave long enough, we would end up like those fish, blind. I want to stay here in the sun, let it warm my body. Captain points to the river.

"Follow the river north till it meets another river. There you walk east towards the sun to Elmira train station. Go to the yellow house nearby. Jones, he will get you to Canada." He hands Thomas a feather. "Hawk spirit will guide you, Wa-nee-shee."

"Wa-nee-shee," Thomas whispers back, and he hugs Captain, almost disappears in the man's arms, he's so skinny. I thank Captain, and he remains still as a tree as we trudge up the hill to the edge of the river.

"What does 'Wa-nee-shee' mean?" I ask. Thomas stabs the ground with his spear.

"That mean, 'may the way be beautiful for you.'" His lips turn downward a bit, like he about to cry. "Come on."

He jabs the spear in the earth again and sticks his chin out like he's about to face some danger head-on.

A hawk circles above the trees—Thomas says it is a good omen. Thomas can spear a fish faster than any heron. Every so often, he stops by a tree, whispers to it, and scatters tobacco in hollow trunk holes. He says it helps with the visions. Captain turned Thomas into an Indian.

We travel at night, sleep in the day like owls and possums. The cave sure helped with getting used to darkness, nothing to be afraid of at all. At any crack of stick or rustle in a bush, we stop and wait till we know for sure we are safe. It takes two days to get to the river crossing. We rest and dry fish for our journey inland.

The path of the sunrise leads us. We dart behind bushes as folks ride by in carriages and carts. We walk along the steel train tracks. Night falls by the time we arrive at Elmira station. Creeping behind the building, there you are, pointing your gun at us. One shot and we would be goners.

"Who's there?" Your voice commands attention, low like a drum.

Something draws me to you, something I ain't never felt before—like when your feet stand at the shore wading, you feel it try to pull you in.

Was not sure if you'd be the death or life of me. All I know is, that moment I heard your voice, Edward, I didn't feel fear; it stirred me all up inside. And oh, what a great love we had—yes, we did.

EDWARD

LION'S PAW

HARRISBURG, PENNSYLVANIA, 1858
I would have stayed if it were not for those white mobs from the South coming up here to Harrisburg, taking people off the street—men who were free, even—and no way out. The court was rigged, could not testify alone: only a white man could show the evidence you were free.

I have been free all my life. I don't know how else to be. I've never worn shackles, and I do not intend to. My mama is a Harris, born free. She married my pop, who was a coachman owned by a white family; he got a pass to come every Saturday night to visit us. He died when I was a boy, fell off a hay loft and broke his back. Pop always told me to get all the learning I can and follow the ways of the Lord.

Lots of free Negroes in Harrisburg. Started with Hercules Harris, born a slave; Mr. Harris was his master. Story goes that Mr. Harris was about to be burned alive by an Indian across the Susquehanna River. Hercules spotted him and swam across the river almost a mile wide. He spoke to the Indian in his language and convinced him to set his master free. In return, the master set Hercules free, and that's how Harrisburg was born of free Negroes.

My mama inherited a small boardinghouse on Tanner's Alley. Robert, my older brother, and I were both born there. My mama and pop were proud card-holding members of the African Methodist Church. Mama does not approve of my working at the dance house and playing the fiddle. I've "strayed from the Lord," she says. As long as I am no man's slave, I think I'm doing well enough.

As soon as I could walk, I was attracted to the fiddle. The look, shape, and sound of it swelled in my breast, I tell you. I started as a messenger for a dance house nearby, owned by a free Black man. Quite a place. Music every night, I learned by listening and watching. I saved up for my first fiddle, smoother than a lady's cheek. I still got it. When I'm not playing, I work the tables. After folks hear me, they tip me more. Mama says I'm sinning, but I say it is a decent living—yes, yes, Lord, forgive me.

My bow flies up and down, the banjo races with me, the crowd stepping, clapping, and jumping. My brother, Robert, dances with his girl, Ingrid; arms flap like wings, feet slap the ground, and rise up—not a silent soul in here; we all in the music at once.

The crowd stops dancing as folks point to the door behind us. A grey haze rises from under the door. Someone lit this damn place on fire! As quick as a match in a tinder box, flames shoot up. Chairs and tables topple as folks flee, coughing and shouting. Sinister smoke swirls to the ceiling. I grab my case and fiddle; Robert and Ingrid hurry out the door.

We thought they were done trying to run us out of here, but they are never done. No point in trying to save the dance house; it's gone. A group of white men stands to the side of the burning building. They don't even try to hide. White men start asking people for their papers; armed and threatening, they round a group up. We slip behind the crowd unnoticed.

Ingrid escaped from Delaware. She hid in our place, and Robert fell in love with her. Now she is with child. Mama hides runaways, along with renting rooms to boarders. They come up to our place all ragged and torn, barefoot and starving. Mama feeds and clothes them and sends them on their way to the next stop. But Ingrid, she stayed on, and once Mama could see how Robert was getting sweet on her, we took her in as family.

The next morning, what is left of the dance house smolders on the ground. The owner drops to his knees. A group of Black men forms around him with clubs, shovels, and sticks. They start off to the prison, where Negroes are shut up in there. Men pick up beams and poles from the rubble and join the crowd. I search the rubble for a stick, ready to join them.

Robert yanks my arm, asking, "What are you doing, Edward?"

He stands in front of me; he is much taller than me, wider, too.

"I'm about to help those brothers get free." I pick up a sturdy stick.

"They'll lock you up." He drapes his arm over my shoulders. "Ingrid spotted a white man in the crowd last night. He's from Delaware, her former master. He didn't see her, but he will try and take her and send her back. We're leaving tonight. Meet me at the barbershop. Mama already knows. Don't be a fool. Go home and get ready."

Well, I might as well go since my job has been burned to the ground. Roy, one of the waiters, carries a shovel and asks me if I'm heading to the jail.

"Nah."

"These white devils best go back down South—this is free land." Roy spits on the ground.

"Not anymore." I drop my stick and circle behind the crowd to Tanner's Alley.

Mama sits sipping tea, curtains drawn.

"It's not safe for you here," I say, trying not to meet her eyes, so penetrating like an owl's. But she sees right through me. I fill a sack with cornbread and apples. She gives me a bag of coins; I don't let go of her hand.

"My Edward . . ."

"We'll come back and get you."

"This is my home, and I'm not leaving. Go to Elmira, to John Jones; he has a yellow house, south of the depot. He will help you on a train to Canada. Walk along the river until you meet the train tracks to Elmira. Should take three days or so. Do not trust or talk to anyone. Lots of people turn the other way to make a few dollars these days. May the Lord keep all of you safe. Write to me when you get to Canada." She lets go of my hands, unlocks a drawer and slides a pistol on the table to me. I kiss her on the cheek.

"I'll come back for you, Mama."

"Don't worry about me. I am a Harris after all."

I give her one last glance before I slip into the night.

"Stop whistling," Robert whispers, as he leads the way with Ingrid between us.

"Why? Nobody will hear us by the river."

"Never know."

I stop whistling and instead let the melody wind around inside my head. Never been this far upstream on foot.

"Safer to walk," the men at the barbershop said. Owls hoot, possums and racoons scurry in the night. At dawn, we walk up the bank to an open field for a rest.

A low grunting comes from the tall grass and a wild boar charges towards us. Robert spreads his arms to shield Ingrid; these beasts can tear you apart if you give them the chance. One shot of my pistol hit him on his side; another, and his body teeters till he drops.

"Good shot, little brother." Robert prods the beast with his toe to make sure it is dead. "Looks like we got breakfast."

We lug the boar underneath the trees. I help Robert make a fire and a spit. We tie the hog's legs to a thick branch and start roasting. After a bit, I go to the river to fill my canteen. My ears prick up. Goddammit. I rush back to the fire.

"Hounds," I pant, can barely talk.

Ingrid and Robert quickly snuff out the fire. Robert hauls the carcass.

"This will lead them astray. You both hurry to the river and walk through it to clear your scent. I'll catch up with you."

"Wait." Ingrid takes a vial out from her satchel. "For them hounds."

She sprinkles powder all over the boar carcass.

"Gooferdust?" I ask. I encountered many runaways claiming graveyard dust sprinkled in their shoes gave them protection.

"Stronger." Ingrid slips the vial back in her satchel, and we bury the fire, cover it with dirt and leaves, and run to the riverbank.

"They close?" she asks. Beads of sweat form on her forehead. I try and reassure her.

"We'll be OK."

"I don't hear nothing." She stands still.

"You don't have my ears." I offer her my hand, and we continue down the shore.

"Son, stand up and sing the Lord's praises!" My father reaches down and tries to pry my hands from my ears. All the sound crowds in at once: claps, stomps, shouts, the anguish, redemption, hope, and pain.

"Let him be." Mama slaps his wrist.

I slide down the pew and wait for the service to be over. Got to know people's shoes. The ones that were so frayed and barely held together: a boarder. Boots without a speck of dirt, the kind you see in advertisements: wealthy free Negroes of Harrisburg. Those without any shoes at all: the runaways. All these feet step to the same beat—the beat that shook my whole body, that felt like it could split my head open before I knew I had the gift, before I knew what it was.

"Mama, they're coming now."

Horses trot down the street, past the barbershop, the church, at the start of Tanner's Alley. Mama quickly hides the two runaways: a man and his wife from Virginia; they squeeze into the cupboard in the pantry until the officers are gone.

We had about four boarders at a time. Mama cooked, cleaned, and did the laundry. Robert and I chopped wood, butchered chickens and hogs, fished, hunted, hauled water up from the river, and did any kind of errands Mama needed. Runaways came and stayed a bit, then moved on to the next place. Most went north, especially after the Fugitive Slave Law —only free land was Canada.

Everyone counted on my ears. I would hear the boarders in their rooms if they were fixing to leave and skip rent. Mama would make sure they paid up. I knew every sound in the house: every creak on the steps, floorboards, pots clanging, sizzle of the stove, cutting and chopping in the kitchen, and Pa's heavy footsteps when he came to visit every Saturday night.

I earned a reputation as a good hunter, always bring something home to eat: racoon, possum, squirrel, wild turkey—something. The woods taught me how to hear one sound at a time so they would not crowd inside my head and make it hurt. By the time I was fourteen, I could go to church without cowering into a ball. That is about the time I picked up the fiddle.

"Robert's coming." I bend back a branch for Ingrid to pass through. She grips the vial in her fist.

"Why you got that?"

"I'm not about to be anyone's slave again and neither is my baby."

Death over bondage, many fugitives that came through our house preferred death over being a slave again. The hounds are gone, probably jerking on the ground right now, mouths foaming until they drop. Stars are out now; we step up a ridge and rest on the riverbank.

Sure enough, my brother springs down the riverside in long strides like a god arising from the water.

"They won't find us." He leans against a tree; I hand him the canteen. Robert threw them off with the boar meat. That boar sure did come in handy.

We arrive in Elmira at night, as silent as cats. Walking along the train tracks, past the depot, I turn my head to the sound of footsteps.

"Who's there?" I click my pistol and point it towards the

back of the depot. A young man emerges, raises his arms; next to him is a girl in a muddy, tattered dress.

"Please, sir, we come all the way from Pittsburgh." The girl says in a shaky voice. She is young and pretty, with full lips. How young is she?

"Why don't you cross up there?" I don't drop my pistol. Who are they fooling? No point in traveling east, could have gone straight up to the north—

"Guards check at the border up there, so we went east, to John Jones, a yellow house." The young man responds. He is tall and thin as a rail.

Robert says, "That's where we're going. They're OK, we're all going to the same house."

He offers his hand to the boy. The boy drops his arms. He has no right hand; it is a stub.

Robert lowers his arm, asking, "Where you from, son?"

The boy pulls his sleeve over his stump. "Kentucky."

He clenches his jaw. Right hands amputated for thievery, ears cut off, or a branded cheek are common punishments.

"Son, what's your name?" Robert asks him.

"Thomas, and this here is Eliza."

She does not smile. I wonder what hell she has come from.

"Come on, his house is just past this church," I whisper, they join us.

No one in sight, and there it is: the yellow house with a lantern on. I knock on the door. A man opens it, greeting us.

"Welcome, welcome. I'm John Jones."

He has the kind of eyes a man can trust, large and brown that look straight at you with nothing to hide, no deceit or trickery. Two children sleep on pallets by the fire, nestled under their mother's arms. A man sits next to them, whittling a piece of wood. John Jones takes us to the kitchen where his wife is cooking. We sit around the table. I sit next to Eliza.

"You from Pittsburgh?" I ask her. She gazes at the ground.

"No. Tennessee by way of Richmond." Her voice is soft and careful, like she is not sure it is safe.

Something came over me like I have never felt. Sure, I had been with women before—but Eliza, I want to protect, to make sure no more harm comes her way.

Our last stop: the four o'clock freedom baggage car on the Northern Central Railroad to Ontario, Canada. Mr. Jones set up a deal with the porters to take us in the baggage car across New York to the great suspension bridge over Niagara Falls.

Mr. Jones whispers to his wife, praying. I don't disturb them.

"Amen." Mr. Jones kisses her hands.

"Here, Mr. Jones, for our passage." I offer him the bag of coins Mama gave me. He opens it, takes out a dollar and hands me the bag,

"Keep the rest." He smiles and pats me on the back.

Never have I met such a generous man as him. Most men would have taken the whole bag and thought nothing of it. The wood whittler and his wife wake their children and roll up their pallets. We all pack our belongings in silence; maybe we are all praying inside our heads.

We huddle together, Mr. Jones in front leading us to the depot. A porter slides the baggage cart door open, and we hustle in, lifting the women and children first into the boxcar.

A ray of light shines through the slit on the side of the car. Eliza leans against the wall. Is she sleeping? Thomas folds his long limbs, holding his right arm against his chest, his sleeve dangling over his stub. Ingrid rests her head on Robert's shoulder, and the man whittles his piece of wood, which looks like a curved X from here. His wife sits next to him dozing, but every so often scanning the car, as if to make sure we are all still safe, stroking her children's hair as they sleep in her lap.

At stops, no one dares breathe. Shouts and laughter of people rustling about are right outside the car door. The train starts up again, and the air loosens around us as we exhale.

There she is: the great Suspension Bridge over Niagara Falls. We all take turns peeking through the slit in the door. I lift Eliza up so she can see through the opening; I set her back down. Our eyes meet for the first time—she quickly turns away. Over the bridge, I take out my fiddle and start up "The Song of the Free." Who's gonna stop us now? Our voices raise up:

> I've now embarked on yonder's shore
> Where man's a man by law,
> The vessel soon will bear me o'er
> To shake the lion's paw;
> I no more dread the auctioneer,
> Nor fear the master's frown,
> I no more tremble when I hear
> The baying negro hound.
> Oh, old master, don't come after me,
> I'm just in sight of Canada, where colored men
>   are free.

We clap, step, sing as the train crosses the bridge and slows to a halt.

"Take your first step of freedom." The porter assists the women and children out of the car. The husband offers the young porter his wood carving: two broken chains open in the front. It must be an African symbol.

"This means freedom, *fawohodie*, thank you, brother." The husband says. The porter holds the carving up to the sun, the husband embraces his family.

Thomas spits on the ground. "Ain't never going back to that hell!"

Robert embraces Ingrid. Eliza lifts her arms.

"Ma, Auntie, I made it," she shouts and raises a small red bag to the open sky.

Thomas

A Hundred Pounds

ONTARIO, CANADA, 1858
I'm no match to fiddle man. He got her—the moment she saw him, I disappeared. What's she gonna do with a one-hand boy like me? I'm a man. Captain told me I was ready to be a man, gave me the hawk feather, and showed me his people's ways.

If she let me, I would embrace her. I was never too tired for her. But she don't seem interested, her mind set on freedom, not on me. I don't touch her—I watch her sleep, protect her like a man ought to.

Riding over the suspension bridge over the falls felt like I was riding on into heaven. Everyone singing, crying, and shouting. Once I stepped on this free soil, I knew I'd never go back to Kentucky. My family sold South; no telling where they at now.

I never knew anything other than the plantation, but soon folks began slipping away, and I asked where they gone and heard about Canada. All I had was hardship and starvation, and shoot, I'd leave if there was something better. What I got to lose?

All around the border here, they got Negro guards making sure men don't come and try to steal away free Negroes. Once we get here, we free unless we done some crime. Guess the only crime I done is steal the horse that got me to the Ohio River. I'm an easy find with my one hand. I keep my stub covered. It tingles like my hand still there and sometime hurts like hell.

The porter told us to go to St. Catherine's Church where they will help us start our new lives in Canada. I never knew of such kindhearted white people as the Reverend Hiram and his wife. At St. Catherine's Church, they fed and clothed us until Edward found some lodging. After a week of searching, Edward took us to our new home not too far from the center of town. Not much, two rooms: Eliza and Ingrid in one room and the men in another. They let me stay with them on the account of I have no kin. It sure makes me sore seeing Eliza smile at fiddle man; she don't ever smile at me like that.

We all need to work to survive but not much work here. Still better than being owned with no say in nothing. Beggars in the street with barely anything on at all take to the bottle, they free and starving, and when the winter come, freezing. I find my fishing spot down by the springs. On a good day I spear four-five fish. I bring it home, fry it up, or dry it for later.

Edward plays his fiddle at a tavern on Saturday nights. We dance and carry on; sure is a good time. Robert got a job as a porter on a steamboat he says goes all the way to Montreal and back to St. Catherine. I sure want to see more of this Canada I never even knew of, and here I am.

Eliza and Ingrid take in laundry, wringing sheets, hanging

clothes on lines. They tend to the garden on the side of our place. Ingrid's with child and getting bigger; she says the winter is when the baby's coming. I give her extra fish.

Negroes here dress in finery: top hats, canes, and women in silk dresses and ostrich hats. They don't pay any white folks no mind either. They ride in carriages down the street like kings and queens. I'd like to find Eliza a silk dress and ostrich hat, win her favor, I sure would.

Every night, Edward gives a learning. He reads the newspaper to us. I can write my name now. I write it wherever I can. On the dirt, carve it into a tree: THOMAS. He says the only way to get ahead is to learn to read and write, else the white folk take advantage of you. He said a Black man thought he was signing a lease but instead sold himself into servitude to a white man for ten years. We got to learn their ways, so we don't get tricked. Eliza squeals like a little girl when she writes her name for Edward. They keen on each other; not a thing I can do.

I throw another log on the fire and sit down making my snowshoes like Captain taught me. Ingrid sure big now, and Robert is home for a while. He is busy carving a cradle for the baby. Eliza sews pieces of cloth to make a quilt. No one says a word, but I know we all thinking, "How we gonna survive this winter?"

Winters here can kill you. Sure, it was cold in Kentucky, but not like this. We do our best patching up holes in the walls, keep the fire lit. Still the chill bites my skin.

Morning light greets me, I go out to check the snares I set in the woods by our home. Soon enough, I spot rabbit tracks in the snow. Lucky me! Two white coated hares are caught in my traps. I sprinkle tobacco on the ground, give thanks, and cut them down. Wait till Eliza sees them, her eyes will shine at me for once—bringing home food is what a man does, not just playing silly fiddle songs. A cry comes from the house; must be Ingrid. It is the wail of a woman bearing children. My mama used to help them with roots and herbs. Some die anyway.

I sling the rabbits down on the floor.

"Boil water," Eliza tells me, she doesn't notice the rabbits, and pays me no mind. I grab a bucket, scurry outside, and pack it with snow. Robert stokes the fire; Edward plucks his fiddle. Eliza bustles in and out of the room, rinsing rags.

Ain't no baby crying. Eliza carries a bundle; the baby's yellow arm falls out the blanket. Robert rushes to Ingrid. Edward takes the dead baby from Eliza. I go outside to skin my rabbits.

Two days passed since she gave birth. Eliza wrapped the baby in the quilt she made and put it out on the porch. Ingrid don't want to go anywhere near it. Neither do I. Who knows if the baby's spirit is wandering looking for a body to take over? Not mine. Not sure where we gonna bury the baby since the ground is frozen.

I say, "Why don't we try one of the colored churches in town?"

Robert crosses his arms, Edward looks down. What they not saying? Turns out Ingrid has a story.

She lets out a sigh and starts talking: "I knew my mother, though torn from me on the block, and that day I was sold to the most wicked people I ever knew. I was just a girl, but that didn't matter to him—that evil bastard! He took my girlhood and when I became a woman, I bore him two children and both he sold. He abused me and the mistress, and the mistress flogged me any chance she could get. If her tea wasn't hot enough, her bed not made just so, if I let a fly in the house, if there was a wrinkle in her dress, if I looked at her the wrong way—everything was a whooping. Any chance she could, she'd whip till she sweat, she would.

"One day, I had enough. I was gonna get myself to Philadelphia. I heard of a safe place, a woman with a boarding room. But the last thing I do, I get some arsenic when she sent me on errand to the store and slip some in her laudanum bottle. I stow away that night on a ship and land in Philadelphia. And I saved a vial of the arsenic for myself just in case I was caught—they weren't going to bring me back alive.

"And I kept running till I got to Harrisburg on Tanner's Alley and found the boarding home, and you, my love, Robert . . . but you see, she took laudanum every night, and they gonna know I did it and come try and put me in jail or worse . . . We can't bury the baby in a church and leave a record; he will find it. I know I sinned, but I figure they sinned, too, and now we're even."

She lifts her cup and takes a swig of whiskey.

Robert and Edward look at each other like they talking without saying nothing, Eliza stares out the window—frozen, seeing something none of us can see. I whisper her name; she don't hear it. She'll come out of it just like she did in the cave. I keep my eye on her.

Edward slams down the newspaper pointing to an advertisement:

RUNAWAY WENCH.
WANTED FOR MURDER OF HER MISTRESS.
COMELY, LAST SEEN WEARING SERVANT ATTIRE: A
CALICO DRESS AND A MAROON PETTICOAT.

100 POUNDS REWARD TO RETURN HER TO THE
AUTHORITIES.

Robert snatches it from him. "Let me see that."

"There's a price on her head." Edward sucks his pipe.

"I'll think of something. You make sure Ingrid stays put, can't be seen anywhere right now." Robert grabs his coat and hat.

"Where are you going?" Edward asks.

"I'll be back."

The wind comes in something fearsome when he opens the door. I check the paper to see if my name in there. I don't see it.

A hundred pounds is a lot of money, but I ain't gonna betray the people that took me in. Nope. Sure are plenty of folks that would do that—black and white—for that kind of money. I figure they as close to a family as I got now, though Eliza don't love me. Maybe I just ain't found my woman yet.

They trust me to keep quiet, cause I surely got a price on my head, too. They could take me back cause I stole that horse. On free land, you ain't exactly free; we still running.

Robert has a plan in the spring to take the ferry to Quebec and from there, a train to Nova Scotia. One of his porter friends gave him the name of a family. There, Robert says, we'll be safe; they won't look that far north.

As soon as the first snow melts, I go fishing and sell what I can on the street. Eliza takes in clothes to mend with Ingrid, and Edward keeps on playing the fiddle. We save our money for the steamboat passage.

.   .   .

I never been in such fine clothes stepping on the steamboat. Eliza and Ingrid made themselves dresses and for us men, a jacket, vest, pants, and shirt. We don't look like runaways no more. I hide my stump in my pocket or inside my jacket. Robert knows all the porters, and they make sure we're safe and hide us down below till we get to Quebec.

Nobody pays you mind in Quebec. Too many people in the streets to care about you. We get to the depot easy, walking straight-backed like we belong. Another long train ride to freedom. Halifax is our next stop: Halifax, Nova Scotia.

Where the colored people at in Nova Scotia? Robert and Edward square their shoulders back like they got nothing to fear. Right on up the hill is where the colored folks stay. They call it Africville. Blue, pink, yellow houses, set above a cove. I reckon it is a good place to fish with so many people out there with rods and nets. Wind whips around us awfully hard. Robert asks a woman selling vegetables if she know where John Dearing stays. She takes a good look at us, all of us. Robert says Mr. Dearing is expecting us. She smiles, so you can see she ain't barely got teeth and points up the road to a small blue house.

"Go on and knock at that door. Where are you coming from?"

Hmm, what he gonna say? Eliza and me come from a cave near the Ohio River, and Ingrid . . . she done murdered her mistress. Robert's smart; ain't no telling when he is lying. Wish I could be smooth like that.

"Montreal," he replies.

"Well, welcome to Africville."

We plod up the hill to the blue house. I can't wait to set down.

· · ·

We stay in the house of John Dearing, his wife, Sophia Francis, and two children, James and Louisa. John is Negro; Sophia is Mi'kmaq. They speak to each other in her language. I listen and try to recognize words Captain taught me. John is a millwright, works at a paper mill up in Queens County. He has big arms, thick neck—I would say he's even stronger than Robert and much stronger than Edward. Edward, me, and James share a room, and Eliza sleeps in the kitchen with little Louisa. Robert and Ingrid stay in a little shack behind the Dearings' house.

Edward's squealing fiddle takes everybody's attention, especially Eliza's—wish she would look at me like that—and he and Robert call me "son." Is that what Eliza sees me like? Like I'm his son? I snatch a bottle of rum and take off to the shore. Each sip is Eliza's hand on my thigh, Eliza's lips on my lips . . . but she don't love me; the rum makes it all right, makes me forget that my heart is so busted.

Almost damn near drowned, I was so close to the shore, waves came lapping in, as the sun stretched over the sea. Captain said the sun is the Great Father. Never thought I would miss that cave, but I do. And Captain. I had her all to myself then. Best go back up and get my spear before the other fishermen take the good spots.

I keep myself clear away from Ingrid. No telling what that woman will do after killing her mistress. What she gonna sneak in my drink if I done something that turn her sour to me? Her and Eliza are like sisters. They giggle and carry on about what dress or latest hat they want.

Robert dresses up that little shack behind the Dearings' house, hangs curtains in the window.

Ingrid say she wants a red house, so he paints it red! Red spells warning to me. I stay clear away, yes, I do, though I think we safe here; don't ever see bounty hunters here. We blend in with the rest of folks.

It sure do smell. A certain draft brings something awful: the dump. You see, the white folks in Halifax don't want no dump there, so they put it in Africville's backyard. At night, rats scurry around here like they own it. People here don't have much, so they scavenge pieces of wood for fire, or even things they can sell in the market in Halifax. Hah! White people don't know we be selling their own trash back to them.

I peddle my fish with the Dearings' son, James. He is my fishing partner. Robert got a job as a porter on a train, and Edward tends horses in Halifax and plays fiddle wherever he can. We get along. Every night, Edward reads the paper aloud. So far, my name hasn't come up in any notices; neither has Eliza's.

Africville is the closest to freedom I have ever felt. They even have a school for the children. James is learning to read when he's not out with me fishing or peddling. I call him "little man," though he is almost as tall as me. He asks me about my stub, I tell him the truth: that's how bad slavery is and don't let no one tell him any different.

They treat you kindly here, lots of celebrations like back home when we were all together having a Saturday dance. The church here is something. They are Baptist, and every so often, folks that feel their spirit is ready to be given over to the Lord and they march on down to the bay, and baptize you right on the spot. I ain't felt nothing yet.

But Ingrid has. She felt the spirit and started crying and carrying on, Robert right beside her, all dressed in white, singing the Lord's praises. They submerge her in the water, she comes out like a black angel. But I still stay away from her.

. . .

The minute they started shouting war in the States, I wanted to sign up and enlist. Give me a gun I'll go down there and teach 'em right! Oh yes, I would be first in line. Point the barrel right between his eyes. BAM BAM BAM! I'd shoot for all the times he whipped me, cut off my hand, sold my kin, BAM!

All kinds of white folks here support the South. That's right, the South! British soldiers runnin' around here in Halifax, ready to face off northern troops; there's fear of invasion, that Americans are coming to attack Nova Scotia.

Edward say the best thing to do is wait and see what happens. I ask him why he don't go and fight? He says there are men who get thrown in jail here for enlisting with the Americans, a foreign government, and that the Queen won't allow it.

But that don't stop the American crimpers in the street. I spot them easy; they act all friendly, want to buy you a drink. I heard a fellow took a drink and was drugged, tied up, and thrown on a warship to fight for the Union. They come around here looking to kidnap soldiers.

"You be careful, little man," I tell James as we roll our cart of fish to the market.

"Of what?" James shades his eyes with his hand.

"The crimpers. They could take anyone."

He is almost as tall as I am but with a face like a young pup. The cart wheel jams, and he runs to the front and lifts it free.

If I had Edward's two hands, I'd be gone; they wouldn't have to drug me or nothing, I'd be gone. But they not gonna let Negro soldiers fight, especially one-handed Negro soldiers. Wait and see, that is what Edward say, just wait.

Now I know why they call Nova Scotia "Nova Scarcity." Scarcely enough food. Can't grow nothing on this rocky soil. Scarcely enough clothes to keep that winter from freezing you to the core. Sophia takes me and little man James far out on a cove where her Indian family live in a birch tree wigwam. They stay out there till the spring comes.

Smoke rises from the center of the wigwam. I trade them dried fish for a sealskin coat. Sure keeps me warmer than the thin coat I was wearing, sure does.

EDWARD

HALIFAX, NOVA SCOTIA, 1861
"You are a pretty one and strong. Anyone ever tell you that? You hear everything like I do, I can tell when your ears pick up. I know you don't want to go out. And no, I don't have an apple for you today, so stop your nudging."

"Fiddleman, you're speaking to the horse again, are you? Hurry up now and tack her up. I have an appointment to make."

Not one speck of dirt is on his boots. Fancy Boots is British. He calls me Fiddleman; I call him Fancy Boots. I don't mind my moniker; I've got a reputation in Halifax as a good fiddler. My mother would say I was playing for houses of sin, but in Halifax, that is all there is.

Got to make a living somehow, and Fancy Boots is not paying me much. Lots of thin stews and rumbling bellies. Not sure how much longer we can survive here. Robert says wait until this mess clears up in the States, wait.

Satin is what I call her, her fur glistens like satin. My father was a hostler in Harrisburg. I always liked horses, learned from him how to treat them. He helped me get as much learning as I could. I can read and write a bit. Does not do me much good. Here I am, walking in his footsteps; only difference is, I am a free man.

"Satin, you take the bit, and I owe you an apple. I know it must be cold. I will get you a big one in town. Why are your ears back at me? Fussy one today."

I shove the carriage step down and open the door. Fancy Boots is a coal man, sells to the Union and Confederate vessels that stop at the harbor to refuel. He sympathizes with the South, like most people in Halifax. I got to be cautious.

Satin sure is antsy. She trots towards the harbor. Her ears prick up. So do mine. I let Fancy Boots off at a building facing the street. Two skedaddlers from America were caught attempting to escape the Confederate draft and are taken to the jailhouse in chains. A mob pushes against the constables demanding to let them free. Hmmm. Who is running north now? Got to get that apple.

"I tell y'all, if I had two hands . . ." He pounds his good fist on the table, makes the cups jump a bit and spill over some. Eliza startles.

"Thomas, even so if you did, now isn't the time to sign up. Halifax is full of southern crackers. We need to keep our heads low, else they might be rolling."

I try to reason with the boy. Ingrid nuzzles Robert's shoulder. I wish Eliza did that so I could feel her breath on my neck.

John Dearing lumbers in, hangs up his hat and coat. He splashes his face, dries his hands, and sits down at the empty chair at the end of the table. Sophia fixes him a bowl of stew.

"From what I hear on the train, they pay colored soldiers half of what white soldiers get. They give them the worst of everything, clothes, food—they are lucky if they get a pair of boots." Robert exhales rings of smoke from his pipe.

"Brother Frederick Douglass tells us to sign up, but I don't see him enlist." I laugh, take a chug of rum.

"Y'all don't understand. You ain't never been slaves, see; you all be fighting if you'd been one." Thomas crosses his arms.

"I understand," Eliza says softly to Thomas, "why you want to fight. I think I would, too, if I could." Eliza doesn't think I'm brave enough to fight?

"We're fighting now, we're always fighting—you think Robert and I wanted to run? White mobs came and kidnapped any Negro they could to sell him down South. My mother risked her life every day hiding runaways. The way I see it, if you're colored, you're fighting anywhere you stand, anywhere!"

"Calm down, brother, we get your point. No sense in us arguing, won't do anyone any good." Robert puts his hand on my shoulder.

Robert always talks sense into me, ever since we were kids. James leans on Thomas's chair and mimics him, folding his arms across his chest. Louisa crawls up on Eliza's lap.

"What we need to do is think and plan; we don't know how this war will turn out. What if the South wins? What then? I say wait and see what happens, then make our move. I have met some porters from Brunswick, Maine. They say Brunswick is a good place to land, plenty of coloreds live there." Robert is always planning, a step ahead of everyone else.

Everyone retires to their room, except Eliza. I throw another log in the stove. This is the time I can be with her alone, sneak some moments. Can't get too close, she frights easy, like a jittery mare. No telling what she has been through, makes my blood boil. I would take up arms and kill any man that abused her. She thinks I'm soft? 'Cause I won't enlist?

She sits down next to me; her graceful fingers wrap around her cup.

"Ready for a lesson?" I ask her.

Most nights I teach her to read. She yawns.

"Too tired?"

"Yes."

Is that a faint smile for me?

"Eliza, do you think I'm a coward?"

"I don't want you to enlist." She turns her face towards me.

"Why not?"

"I don't want to lose you."

I touch the curve of her chin. The candle flickers.

"Oh, Eliza, Eliza, you'll never lose me."

Our lips meet, and I embrace her like I always wanted to, and she doesn't pull away.

Thomas

We sought shelter from the storm in a tavern, wasn't gonna sell any more fish. Besides, I didn't want to go home to see Eliza so sweet on Edward: batting her eyes—ain't never looked at me like that, not even once. James and I are soaked to the skin, not a dry spot on us. The tavern is dark, set in an alley off the pier.

Sure need a drink, more than one. The rum hits me, feels like I'm in a warm bed. James takes a drink, too. Sailors sing ditties and dance jigs. They're merry, even buy me and James another round.

> *What will we do with a drunken sailor?*
> *What will we do with a drunken sailor?*
> *What will we do with a drunken sailor?*
> *Early in the morning*

Before I know it, I'm asleep, drooling on the bar. Must have been out for a while. The place is quiet now; a few sailors are slumped over tables and chairs.

"James, we best get on now. James?" He is nowhere in sight. "Little man?"

A bar maid clears a table.

"You seen a colored boy about my height?" I ask her.

"They took the darkie to the pier."

I about near plow her over blasting out the door calling for James. I ask an old seaman selling ropes on the dock if he seen a Negro boy. He points to a warship on the horizon.

"They took him aboard, a whole lot of them, bloody Union crimpers curse them all! All of them!" He punches the air with his fist.

They drugged us, those Union bastards, and took James! It's my fault. I should have known. I hunch over retching, wondering how I will face John Dearing and the others.

I open the door, hat in my hand, head hanging down.

"Where's James?" My knees buckle, and I start retching again.

"Where?" John Dearing's voice thunders.

"Crimpers, we was drugged . . . they took him, he's gone on a Union ship . . ."

I brace myself for a blow, expecting his fist. Sophia and John start shouting, they must be cursing me—I must be cursed. I hurl again. John Dearing takes off down the road, as if he could stop the ship that kidnapped James. I know it is long gone.

I don't dare go inside. I stay by the doorway, leaning against the thin walls. Why'd this happen? I ask the stars. It's all my fault, I brought James into the tavern. I should have known better.

"Come on in, Thomas, before you catch a chill." Eliza's soft voice beckons me. Her sweet scent of tobacco and salt makes me long for her touch, her skin.

"It's all my doing, Eliza, I should have known . . ."

"Can't change it now, Thomas. You best stay strong, so you can find him." She helps me to my feet; I barely make it to my pallet.

John Dearing hovers above me. I wake up before his ax hit. The dream is a warning. How can I stay here now? Got to find James, but how? They all get silent when I enter the kitchen. I can tell they was talking about me. John Dearing stands at the end of the table.

"Word at the pier is that ship is a-heading to Portland. I'm leaving today."

"Let me come. I can help find him." My voice cracks.

He stares at me a long time, maybe he is thinking of doing me in—get it over with, if he gonna do it, let him do it.

"No. Stay here. Take care of Sophia and Louisa till I get back."

Sophia embraces him, Louisa starts crying. He mumbles some Indian words; the door flaps open like a mouth that won't close.

John Dearing returns a week later empty-handed. I stay away as much as I can, fishing, selling at the market, and keeping a lookout at the pier for James. I return to the tavern, the place James was taken to see if I could spot one of them crimpers that kidnapped him. And I drink.

"Another one." I lift my mug.

My stub tingles. I shove it in my pocket. No one pays me no mind. I don't ever recall how I made it home, but I do. Sophia and John barely speak, Louisa cries most the time, and Eliza tries to sweeten everyone with cornbread and pies. A sour taste lingers in my mouth, can't get it out.

. . .

Men fire off pistols and women cheer, the streets are brimming with madness.

"We got those bloody Yankees!"

"Confederate win at Bull Run!" A paper boy shouts.

More bad news. Little man, you still out there? You alive?

Edward has a paper in his hand, reading out loud: *"Onlookers came from afar with picnic baskets and eyeglasses, cheering as pummels of smoke shook the countryside. Congressmen, journalists, huckster women selling pies, came twenty-five miles from Washington to view the spectacle, expecting a win.*

"They arrived on horseback, foot, and in stylish carriages, only forced to flee as a stampede of Union troops retreated. The Union casualties exceed 2000, a clear victory for the South at Bull Run."

Edward stops, "A damn picnic, that's what they think war is."

"All we can do is wait for James to return."

John Dearing slams his mug down and leaves. Maybe he's looking for James down at the pier to see if he can get some information.

I could go down to Washington and find James, bring him back. Then everyone would praise me. I'd be a hero, but now I feel more like a villain. Sophia sings softly to Louisa in her lap, Eliza hums along with her.

Something kept me up at night, a knowing in my gut. Just as I was dozing off, he appears at the door in rags, so skinny I thought he was a ghost . . .

"Little man!"

His legs give way, and he crumples to the floor. John

Dearing stomps across the kitchen and lifts James up, carrying him to his room. Eliza puts a kettle on.

James won't speak at all. His little pup eyes are hazed over with a hardness with what he been through. I leave him be. Till one morning, he come with me to fish, like we used to do. He trails behind me and sets down next to me at our favorite spot on the bay.

"James, I sure am sorry they took you that night. I wish it were me, not you."

James scratches a large rock with an arrowhead.

"Not your fault, Thomas. They drugged both of us."

I try not to act surprised at his voice, he keeps on scratching.

"Besides, after what happened I will never have another drink again." James chuckles, and I slap his back. We laugh.

"What you draw, little man?"

His scratches turn into figures on the flat surface of the boulder. I can make out a man and next to it some kind of animal.

"That a bear?" I ask.

James nods and starts talking: "Rolling back and forth in the hull of the ship, in darkness, chained, I had no idea where I was. Thought I was in the belly of some great beast. My mother's voice whispered to me, *mui'nej*, little bear, she used to call me. She would tell me when I was frightened to think of *muwin*, the bear, and he would protect me.

"I awoke to a bucket of cold water thrown upon me by a man with the meanest, nastiest face: ruddy red and one-eyed. He unlocked the shackles, led me up to the deck with a pistol at my back. There were others lined up, too, about a dozen.

"'All you louses are to fight for the Union, you hear?'"

"The ship anchored, and we were forced onto a smaller boat tied to the pier. Crimpers. I knew I was done for; they were collecting bounty for enlistments.

"The pier in Portland was like Halifax but with twice the amount of people. I thought of making a run for it but kept on marching. All I could think of was food, and my thirst was so great that puddles on the ground tempted me.

"We were held in a jail in Portland, forced to sign papers that secured our enlistment. The crimpers were paid a fine sum, I'm sure. Finally, we were given some hard bread and water, though we slept on the cold cell floor. We were stripped of all clothing and given Union uniforms: a grey jacket, pantaloons, boots, and a cap.

"I was sent to Company C. I was the youngest one there, with a few other colored soldiers in the rank. At every opportunity, the soldiers cuffed and kicked me; the captain egged them on.

"I stayed with the colored soldiers as much as I could.

"Boarded a train from Portland to Washington. Quite a long journey. Colored soldiers were forced to ride in the baggage cars. We set up camp on a hill to train. I took so many whoopings, I stopped counting them. Anything I did—a wrong look, spitting, marching out of step, running too slow . . .

"And if the white soldiers didn't get to flogging me, the captain took pleasure in it. My ribs were sore, back tore open with lashes—I was already in battle. All of us colored soldiers were. The only way we got through was sticking together, hunting for game, and tending to each other's wounds.

"We marched through Washington with crowds of people cheering us on to the battlefield. Many onlookers joined us in grand carriages, on horses, foot, huskers selling pies and breads—like we were going to a party. People scattered the countryside with picnic blankets and eyeglasses to get the best view.

"Air was so hot and heavy, my feet sticking in the muddy road. At first it seemed like a victory. Union pushed back the rebels; our company was ordered to cross the river using the fords near the stone bridge.

"We were pummeled by rebel fire, a soldier's face right next to me was blown to bits. I sank in the river, explosions and fires all around me. I swam away from falling bodies, lifted my head above the surface and saw Union soldiers retreating as a mass of rebels came upon us.

"I prayed to the *muwin* and took the shape of a bear—rushed out the bloody river. A stampede of Union soldiers on horses cry out, 'Turn back! Turn back! We're whipped!' Carriages ran over wounded men, soldiers cut horses from their harnesses and fled bareback. Wagons overturned on the road. A fat man in a suit wielding a pistol threatened to shoot any running soldier. Civilians mixed with soldiers on foot, merchants and gentry in carriages collided in a mangled mess. I sniffed the air, hastened away from the gunpowder and blood scent to the dank forest.

"I awoke to faint gunshots, the *muwin* spirit gone. Moving in the direction of the sun, I stepped over many dead. Stripped the clothing off a poor lad who was face down in a field and shed my uniform. It took many hours on foot to reach Georgetown. I steered clear of all regiments and walked to the docks in search for a way home.

"I stowed away on a merchant schooner transporting rum. I recognized the vessel as the same kind in Halifax and took my chances. The sailors were drunk most the time, and I wasn't discovered. When the ship anchored in Halifax, I crept above deck and jumped overboard before anyone could catch me and ran all the way home."

James finishes carving the stone. He etched a figure of a bear rising out of a river.

"I owe the *muwin* my life."

Eliza

Coins

AFRICVILLE, NOVA SCOTIA, 1865

I must be respectable with a ring on my finger. Edward says he will get me one. Until then, I am an honorable woman. Not loose and wild like Ingrid, though Robert don't seem to care one bit; he takes her any way she is. Edward and I enjoy our walks by the bay; his hands are warm, heating my fingers like fine leather gloves. I fit nicely right under his arm, like it was made for me, like we belong together.

Thomas sulks around me now, barely grunts a hello. Wears his hat in the house pulled down over his brow, especially around Edward. I try and soften him with extra servings of cornbread or pie. He takes it but still won't speak.

Edward is late tonight. Louisa is asleep on her pallet by the fire. I move my chair closer to the heat, put another log on. Thomas scuffles in; I already smell the rum on his breath. A breeze surges through the open door, the flames swell.

"Set down, Thomas. I'll make you some tea."

"Bet you wish I was Edward, don't you?" He leans into me; he is much taller than me now but still as thin as a rail.

"Shh, Thomas." I put the kettle on over the fire.

He chuckles, flops his hat down on the table. "Eliza, don't I mean anything to you?"

"Thomas, I—"

"What about the time in the cave? And getting to Elmira? I provided for you, didn't I?"

"Thomas, you always be family to me . . ." I touch his shoulder.

He flicks my hand away. "No pity! I don't want your damn pity!"

He slams his fist on the table, lays his head down between his arms and weeps. I want to stop his river of tears—but know I can't. I watch his back heave up and down, till he sinks into the table.

"Thomas!" I nudge him.

He doesn't move. Edward opens the door.

"What's this?" Edward brushes the snow off his coat, hangs his hat up and places his fiddle case down.

"Thomas is in a bad way."

"Drunk?" He warms his back by the hearth. I embrace him, careful to detect any smell of sweet perfume or spot any red lipstick on his collar; playing in those brothels, no telling what kind of women are there.

"Best I get him to bed. Come on, son." Edward lugs Thomas from his chair.

Thomas's feet slide on the floor, his limp limbs hang on Edward's thick frame.

Second time we used this hog bone for stew. Pray this is the last winter in Africville. People got no money cause of this war. No more laundry to take in, so Ingrid and I make baskets to sell at the market. Misery has entered the house, seeping in corners like an unwanted guest. Thomas and Edward don't speak. Thomas don't speak to me. John Dearing and his wife, Sophia, bicker in their Indian language. Thomas is the only one that understands it. I don't.

Ever since James was kidnapped, the house been in an upheaval. It was better for a while when he returned, but now we all waiting for this war to end so we can go back to the States, or somehow make do here. Last harvest was pitiful; not much came up from the soil: a few dozen yams, onions, and potatoes. We rely on Thomas and James's fish; that is, if Thomas don't peddle it and use the money for rum. Spirits are low. Everyone is hungry, cold, and mean. Barely a grunt at the dinner table, barely a log on the fire, and Ingrid waits wistfully for Robert to come back from his porter job.

Snow turns to slush turns to mud dirtying the hem of my dress, but I don't mind, no—least I am warmer. The door flies open. It's Robert. He tosses his porter cap in the air.

"It's over! Union won!" His grin is wide.

The door flaps open and shut, a gust of air twines around the kitchen, bedrooms, blowing the curtains, in and out of corners, setting the flames higher in the hearth. We all shout at once. Robert takes Ingrid's hands, and they do a jig around the table. Edward plays his fiddle, we bang pots. Even Thomas and I dance, crying, laughing, like we are free all over again, free. I'm never to be the Ralston's slave again! I wish I had the power to curse them, maybe they are already cursed. I hope so. Ingrid, out of breath, sits down next to me. She has a glass vial in her hand, the one filled with arsenic that she carried with her in case she was ever captured and forced into slavery again. She grits her teeth and smashes the vial in the hearth fire. Flames turn wild colors, red, blue, orange, and purple.

We make a bonfire outside; neighbors come and bring what scraps of food to share. That wretched evil slavery is over and done. I can dare to hope, dare to have children, dare. Edward's beard tickles my chin. My heart is full. Ma, is it you? Her soft cheek on mine, salt of the bay, sweet smell of tobacco, Auntie's shells scattering—did I find my destiny?

BRUNSWICK, MAINE, 1866

Edward's brother, Robert, learns about a colored town in East Brunswick on his steamboat route. He secures a place for himself and Ingrid and helps find a place for Edward and me. It is a ferry ride from Halifax to Brunswick to our new life. We settle in a two-room house with a brick hearth next to the Freemans, a Negro family that owns land. Imagine that! There is a lake nearby and a river.

We work for white families nearby. I take in laundry and do whatever mending is needed. Edward tends to the family's horses and plays his fiddle at night. Robert and Ingrid live closer to the center of town in a much larger house. Robert is doing well as a steamboat porter, and Ingrid is with child. Thomas has moved to Malaga Island with his new wife. I'm glad he has found someone. The most important thing is that our families stay together, never to be torn apart again. I listen to the river for Ma and Auntie, sending them messages through the wind.

Folks are kind here, help each other out sharing a chicken or extra potatoes, but the way I see it, the lion's paw is still bearing down on us. No matter where we go, there it is. We're all still working for white folks. And now the refugees come up from the South, starving, in rags. It tears me up, especially the children. I give them food or press whatever coins I can into their hands. But today is a day to celebrate the anniversary of the war ending, not a time to brood.

The Freemans' barn is filled with all kinds. Edward was invited to play his fiddle to commemorate the war veterans. A table is spread out with a roasted pig, squash, corn, greens, and plenty of rum. Children run around adults dancing reels: Irish women with Black men, light-skinned women like Tone and Tinty with hands on their men's arms. Natives come dressed in feathers and deerskin, and my Edward, fiddling up a storm with a banjo player. Thomas grins and struts on the dance floor with his sweetheart, a sturdy mulatto woman. Robert and Ingrid step in time. She is with child, glowing.

A tall, thick-necked dark man that would make any woman swoon stands in the center of the long table, his hand visibly scarred and disfigured. Two younger men stand by his side—the spitting image of this dark handsome man, they must be his brothers. He laughs, slapping the backs of fellow comrades: two Black men and an Indian. They stand proudly in faded blue uniforms and polished boots. Edward stops fiddling and takes my arm; they about to give a speech. The handsome man clears his throat, takes his hat off, and starts rambling.

GEORGE AUGUSTUS FREEMAN

COMPANY M

My hand throbs like it's remembering what it went through. And here we all are at the one-year anniversary celebration: war done, over. Miss my Ophelia—is she here somewhere in the rafters hovering, watching our son, Will? Watching me? Got to give a speech. Where do I start? Thoughts crowd in my head taking me to the beginning.

BRUNSWICK, MAINE, 1862

Fighting's in my blood. My grandfather was a slave in Ipswich, Massachusetts. He fought in the Revolutionary War to gain his freedom and came with his family here to Maine. My father never let me forget.

Me and my buddies, we are ready. Lincoln needs to open the door for us to enlist. Monty, young and full of spunk, points a fake pistol in the air.

"Just give me my rifle!"

Lem fills our mugs. "That's right, soon as they let coloreds fight, I'm in."

Lem is as old as me, but we still got fighting in us. A white man sits at the bar nearby. What is he doing on our side of town? Only a few whites ever come in this tavern. He studies us, listening to our conversation, slides off his stool, and leans in, telling us we should emigrate to Haiti. He's short, stout, probably not worked a day in his life, telling us to go. He is on a mission to get rid of us.

Lem smiles. "Nope, we're staying right here. This is our land. We've been here so long we got roots at the bottom of our boots."

We all laugh, slap the table, drink another round.

"Where are you from?" I move closer to his face so I can hear him.

"Boston," he shouts over the racket in the tavern and continues. "It is my view that the only way to solve the, ah, Negro problem here in America, is for you all to migrate to Haiti, a land where you will be welcome and free." He pushes his spectacles up higher on the ridge on his nose, saying, "May I join you?"

He does not wait for our answer and sits down. Lem slides his chair closer to him, rolls up his sleeves, his fists tight. Oh, no. This could end up in a brawl.

"I am free. My mother is free, my father is free, and my children are free. You are telling us to leave home, sail to Haiti—for what? What will we get in Haiti?" Lem shouts in the man's face.

The white man clears his throat. "You will be with your own kind. America will never claim you as citizens."

"Haiti already won their freedom. Now it's our turn!" Monty lifts his cup, shouting, "To

Toussaint!"

We stand and cheer, "Toussaint!"

"Lincoln, open up the gates so we can win this war!" Lem pounds the table.

"Let's do Haiti here!"

I am drunk, almost sway into the poor fellow. He wipes his forehead.

"What is your trade in Boston?" I ask him.

"I'm a painter."

"What do you paint?"

"Mainly landscapes, nature."

Lem cuts in. "Best you go back to Boston and paint your pretty pictures and let us fight for our country like real men!"

We all laugh, the white man stands.

"I meant no harm in my words. In good faith, allow me to purchase another round."

We cheer, the barmaid fills our mugs, and we close the place down.

Ophelia. My first. Doe eyes, golden skin. Came up from North Carolina with her mistress to vacation in Bath. Found her in a field of sunlight, white bonnet, maid's dress, turning in circles. I was on my way home from hunting with a few skinny partridges slung over my saddle. I trot my horse towards her, she freezes like a deer—acting like she does not see me. She is about as golden as the field. Maybe she sprang from that field. I tip my hat.

"You lost?" Golden curls hide her face. "You running?"

She nods, so fearful as if the sky were to fall on her.

"They follow you?"

"Yes." She barely makes the word out.

"Well, come on, then." I help her up.

We gallop down Old Bath Road by the river to my family's farm. I take the shortcut through the woods—feel her breath on my neck, hands on my waist.

My sisters, Julia and Mary, make a big fuss about her. Draw her a bath. My brothers,

Jacob and Jaden, make cracks at me.

"Can't count on Aug to bring home a decent catch, but he sure can pick up a pretty woman!" They hold up the skinny partridges, doubling over with laughter.

"Shut up," I say, and throw my hat at them. They better not try and make a move on her. This golden girl is mine.

My father always lends a hand to runaways, tells us there is a price for freedom your grandpa paid for, don't you forget . . .

She blended into the family. Except to me, she glowed. Like an angel of the field—my angel.

The ground is damp under my knee, her slender hand in mine, no father to ask permission, no family. Just the river, trees, stone, dirt. That is a blessing enough—and she said yes!

I build our house on my father's plot with my brothers' help. I carry her in my arms, white dress, veil, and a crown of flowers on her head. My mother dabs the corner of her eyes.

"My first born, my Augustus . . ."

Father puts his big bear arm around her. Jaden and Jacob smirk, ready to joke and break me out of my spell. But they couldn't. No, I brought my angel home.

After we buried our third baby under the ash tree, she thought she was cursed. Her mind began to unravel like the baskets my sisters made when they got old—pull one piece and the whole basket goes. Every morning, she placed flowers at the head of each grave—singing to the dirt. Stopped talking to me. Only sang a sorrowful lullaby:

My sweet little babies sold by the devil

buried in the ground, buried in the ground.
My sweet little babies sold by the devil
how empty my arms are now.

"Mama gonna get you back! I promise! I promise!" Ophelia scratches the dirt, pleading it like her babies are still there. I lift her up; her limbs jerk about like a wild animal.

I was in over my head. My sister, Julia, knew of a healer on Malaga Island, known as Aunt Cam, that catches babies and conjures remedies.

Anything to get my Ophelia back.

We leave at dawn, travel by canoe down the New Meadows River. Julia, the oldest sister, is the most sensible of the girls. Takes after Mother, sturdy and stubborn, will challenge anyone who says what she can or can't do.

My hands, tough from farming and pulling ropes at sea, are useless with Ophelia. The wind is in our favor. A blue heron stands at the shore. Mother says herons are good luck. She would say that is our ancestor watching over us.

"You're taking me to my babies, aren't you?" Ophelia drapes her long fingers in the river.

"Shh, shh," Julia whispers.

I drag the canoe up a small shell beach. A loon flaps its wings overhead. Ophelia turns her face up to the loon's flight. Julia hooks arms with her, Ophelia splashes the water like a child. Fisherman launch lines, lobster crates bob in the water. Women bend over large buckets scrubbing garments. Clothes flaps on lines. A man sits in a chair playing a fiddle. We walk up a hill passing small dwellings and come to a little cabin surrounded by pines. A woman stands on the porch; must be Aunt Cam.

Shoulders back, spine straight, big walking stick, Indian and Black like most of us. She motions them in. I know better than to mess with women's conjures. I stay out of it, find a spot under the pines, take a proper rest.

Tap, tap, tap. There she is with her cane, looking down on me like a bird to prey. "This one will live."

She commands it. Ophelia rests her hand on her belly.

"She must take herbs every day."

Julia places the bundles in her basket. I don't argue with the woman. I will do what she says. I offer her a purse of coins, tip my hat, and lead Ophelia to the canoe.

She perked up after that. Stopped singing to dirt and started talking to her belly—the new life in her—the one that would survive? I numbered them, no names, just numbers until I knew they would make it. BABY 1: born blue; BABY 2: worms; BABY 3: fever. Got too much on my mind to worry. Found work in Casco Bay unloading at the docks. Don't want to go out to sea, too far away from her.

We have just enough to get through this winter. Our hog came in handy. The butcher slaughtered it right before the snow, cost a bit but worth it. Julia's the one that caught our baby on a full moon. We named him Will and Smart his middle name. The will to live and the smarts to survive. Though I secretly called him BABY 4, just in case.

She wrapped him around her back and never let him out of her sight. Will caught all her murmurs she sang, danced with him. With Will, she came alive again but had no attention for me.

A man gets restless. I went to sea, a steward this time on a ship to the Carolinas. Got my papers with me, though. Made sure the man that hired me wasn't going to try and sell me down the coast as a slave. My buddy Lem said he was honest, worked for him before. You hear of stories of free men like me sold with no chance of returning. But I trust Lem; we are like brothers.

Came back in six months in time for my boy's third birthday. Aunt Cam was right: this one is going to make it. He is a sturdy boy with thick legs. Had a big celebration at my father's barn: Ophelia doting on his every whim. And there was Lucretia, her eyes teasing me behind her fan. My sister Mary invited her; they work for the same white family in town. Lucretia, hair piled up like a queen and wide hips daring me to try and catch her.

We met in town. I rented a room at the colored boarding house. My whole body trembled when she touched me, even looked at me. Oh, Lucretia. my queen, come put your hips on me.

"Yes, I am a queen, and don't you forget it."

Molasses skin under my dark rough hands but not too rough for her—our bodies rocking all night. Guinea, she says, her grandma was taken from Guinea, sold for fifty pounds to a sea captain in Maine. She petitioned for her freedom and got it. She married a Black man, Peters, a veteran of the Revolutionary War, and they founded a colored town in Maine, Peterborough. Lucretia's skin is not too dark cause her grandma had relations with a German man and her father is mulatto. I don't care what she is; all I know is I can't get enough of this woman.

She soon carried my child, and baby Eleanor was born, my first daughter. Eleanor Freeman. I didn't number her. I kept everyone fed. It was hard, but I did it. I kept the two worlds separate, my life with Ophelia and my other with Lucretia. Though Lucretia says someday she won't put up with this anymore, someday she will leave with Eleanor.

"Where you going to go?" I tease her.

She says she doesn't know, but she will be gone. But her soreness won't last. My touch always brings her back.

Every night, the same dream: Ophelia awakes seething like a snake ready to strike. How did she know? I tell you women are strange and powerful creatures. And yes, I lied. I lied to keep the peace.

"There you go with your crazy dreams again! Only thing I got in my hands is you and the crates I load off the ships. Best you go back to sleep now."

She turns over and curls her body in a tight ball at the edge of our bed.

On market day, we set up at our usual spot. Lucretia saunters by our cart in her fine silk dress and hat. Eleanor stretches her stubby arms to me. Lucretia picks up a tomato, turns it over, then places it back in the cart.

"Not ripe enough." She locks eyes with Ophelia.

"Sinful woman!" Ophelia hisses.

Lucretia pays her no mind, gathers Eleanor from my arms, and strolls off. Will tugs on Ophelia's apron.

"Who's that, Mama?" he asks Ophelia, and she turns to me like a wolf about to bite.

"Augustus, you tell him, you tell him who she is." She unties her apron, hurls it in the cart and storms off.

"Woooooo wooooooo!" I find her howling in the lake.

"Ophelia, come back. You will catch a chill. It isn't anything, Ophelia . . ."

"Wooooo!"

Her howl reaches the stars. Wolves howl back. My boot slides on a rock, got to get her before she goes any deeper. What have I done? What have I done . . .

I grab her tiny waist—she flails, scratches my face, trembling. I carry her to the edge of the lake as she bays to the moon, thrashing like a fish out of water.

Will's hand curls in hers, he refuses to leave her side. Ophelia is feverish. Julia tends to Ophelia with tonics and teas . . .

This my fault? I got to keep providing, she will pull through, she'll . . .

Dying is hard, sometimes quick—the spirit ready to give up its shell. Other times, a long, drawn-out hell. Ophelia refused it, then succumbed to it: an all-out tug of war. She braced herself against imaginary whippings, shielded her face from phantom blows, yowled so loud for babies torn from her, and lapsed into coughing fits. The evils of slavery right there in my angel's limbs, my angel's gut-wrenching pleas . . .

I tell you my blood boiled for all they did to her. Her mind not right—evil too powerful for us to heal.

When she stops recognizing Will, I know it will be soon. Her breathing rattles. Her hand clammy, chest rising and falling, then ceases. My angel of the golden field.

At night, the gale rattles my window so hard I awake and there she is floating, her honey-colored skin glowing in her wedding dress with a crown of flowers atop her long, flaxen curls. I run outside up the hill following the faint white dress.

> *My sweet little babies sold by the devil,*
> *buried in the ground, buried in the ground.*
> *My sweet little babies sold by the devil,*
> *how empty my arms are now.*

"Ophelia!"

At the edge of the lake, she turns to face me, lets out the

most frightful howl, and flies into the water, disappearing far below, her white dress fading in the dark water.

"Ophelia!" I holler once more; wolves howl back to me—or maybe it was her.

Grief can kill a man—but revenge . . . Just let me get my hands on a gun, take out those Confederate bastards. Work dries up at the docks. Got Lucretia, Eleanor, and Will to provide for.

Julia takes in Will because Lucretia will not have him. Ophelia's grave is still damp, and Lucretia warns me I better make her an honest woman and marry her. Don't want to lose Lucretia. My heart is heavy for Ophelia, but she is right. We have the ceremony in front of the justice of peace. Lucretia got her piece of paper before I left.

Penobscot Valley, Maine, 1864

The First Heavy Maine Artillery, an all-white regiment, except for us. Lem, Monty, and I muster in about the same time in January with a few Indians. We're waiting in our tent to be examined by the medics. Damn near freezing in our tent, and the colored tent is the last one to get examined. Old men, well, probably my age, exit the medical tent, backs bent low, hats crumpled in their hands. Too old to fight the Johnnies. I am strong, with fire in my limbs, ready to go. So is Lem; we are the same age; Monty, well, he is younger. We look after him.

Lem and I pass the examinations and enter our tent triumphantly. Lem flexes his muscles, Monty smirks at us.

"Didn't think you old men would pass!" Monty slaps our backs; we huddle close to the
fire.

"Watch it, Monty, or you'll see how hard this old man punches!" Lem sure can make a joke but can't hardly take one.

"Calm down, brother. What's there to eat?" I dip my cup in the pot of steaming coffee, spoon beans and salt pork on my plate.

At sea, you don't know if you will make it back. We all worked on a ship, a squall overtook us, we thought we were done for. The crew held fast, and we made it through. Just like we will make it through this war. Company M, for "make it out alive," Lem says, just like we beat that storm.

Uniforms are four different sizes. I know I'm the largest. We trade until we land the right sizes. Dark blue coat, light blue pantaloons, a cotton shirt, pair of drawers, a belt, cap, and brogans that sure are stiff but not for long with all the drilling we do. We drill with sticks, no guns yet.

They make sure we don't have a shred of civilian clothing stowed away, to prevent deserters. Only thing I have is a lock of Lucretia's hair in a small pouch filled with lavender she gave me for protection.

Equipment arrives: a knapsack, haversack, a box of ammunition, and an old Enfield rifle and bayonet. I keep my rifle clean and shiny, oil it every night, wipe down the bayonet before I slide it back in the sheath.

"You caress that rifle like it's your woman!" Lem snickers. Monty chuckles.

"How many women you got now?" Monty smirks.

"You're all just jealous cause you can't make your rifle shine like mine."

I inspect the rifle one last time before laying it down. The way I see it, this rifle here is going to keep me alive, yes.

We break down tents, load up our knapsacks, and march to the depot station in Bangor.

"You hear that?" I nudge Lem.

"What?" Lem faces forward, doesn't want to get attention

of the sergeant riding alongside us. A howl, a wolf's howl. Ophelia, is that you?

The band leads us; we step in time like one man, one foot. My rifle shiny as a dollar coin, brass buttons polished, brogans wiped clean. The crowd cheers, and I spot my boy, my Will, with Julia, Mary, my brothers, Jaden and Jacob, Ma and Pa, and Lucretia waving her handkerchief with little Eleanor on her hip. Those hips— I turn towards her, but not too much, don't want to lose my footing and slip up. We board the train—my first time on a Pullman—and it's a long ride to Washington. I get as much rest as I can.

FORT SUMNER, MARYLAND

They did not send us here to fight but to dig ditches and clear land. Mostly to set log house tents for officers. When we finish one site, they send us to another. Me and the boys are run down—never toiled this hard, even at sea. And to top it off, the quartermaster is stingy with rations.

Colored women come about our tent selling pies. We trade our catch with them. Saul's the best hunter, he has the magic touch, always catches game. He is a Passamaquoddy Indian from the Old Town reservation in Maine. Some men warn us about the pies and say that they have been sent by the Johnnies with glass in them. I don't care. I eat them anyways. So far, no glass.

There's contraband here, runaways from the South. They help with laundry, cook, even dig ditches alongside us to get a little ration, though it is not much.

Every day is the same drudgery. Dig. Drill. Saw. Haul. By the time we get to fight, we will be too tuckered out, the way they work us. At night, the band plays to keep our spirits up, but if I hear "Tenting Tonight" one more time . . . They need to learn some new songs. Every so often, we kick up our heels with the contraband girls, some keep us warm at night.

Got to be ready for the midnight drills. Any minute, any time—woe to the soldier who is late or misses it all together. Our tent is tight. We don't miss any, not one drill.

Orders to pack up. Hand us forty rounds of ammunition, three-days rations. We fill our knapsacks. My rifle, she is as shiny as ever, not a spot on her. I sling her round my shoulder.

"Augustus, let's see how faithful she is," Lem teases me.

We roll out: march through Georgetown and cross the long bridge over the Potomac River to Alexandria. From there, we board a steamer down the river to Belle Plains Landing.

SPOTSYLVANIA COURTHOUSE, VIRGINIA

Sweat drips from my cap. Wounded pass us in carts or on foot, with bandaged heads, arms in slings, and a chorus of groans. My gut tightens. Sun disappears behind us: no turning back now.

Pop! Pop! Shell fragments fly over us. Air tastes like gunpowder. We advance to the pines and rest until morning. I barely sleep with the shells whizzing by all night.

The air is thick as syrup. Saul lights his pipe, offers it to me. Can't smoke, can't eat. All I can do is wait for the orders. Thunder erupts—or is it cannon fire?

I welcome the rain—take my cap off. An officer gallops to our colonel.

"Fall in, First Maine!" The order we all have been waiting for. Soldiers scramble to their feet getting in line. Saul mumbles a prayer and touches the ground. I suppose it is as good a time as any to pray.

We march on a crest atop a hill. Below us the dammed

Johnnies are tearing up the provision train. Mules are shot dead on the ground, teamsters captured, pork barrels smashed to bits. We are ordered to march on through the woods. And firing begins, smoke so thick can't see a thing, but we keep on firing. Saul gets hit, blood gushes from his leg. I run to get him. Crack! Drop my rifle and drag Saul from the open to the side of the road. My hand! My hand got darn near blown off.

One hour of terrible volleys leaves over five hundred men killed and wounded. Guess I'm one of the lucky ones. Lem and Monty are ordered to move on; Saul and I join the ranks of the wounded. They put him in a makeshift cart made from logs hooked up to a worn-out mule. No room in the ambulances led by horses—especially if you're a colored soldier. Every bump along the road makes Saul wince. Nurses give out milk and whiskey to the wounded, that is, if they don't drink it themselves.

We arrive at City Point: the goriest mess. Men lie on the ground in sweltering heat, flailing about like animals caught in a trap. Sometimes they holler a woman's name, "Nellie!" or "Mary!" Most of the time, they cry for their mothers. A parade of men with bloody limbs and mangled bodies line the country-side. I would choose a battle over this hell. Saul and I wait for a doctor to get the Johnnie bullets out our limbs. They don't see us because we're colored: they pass us by.

The air reeks of blood and death like after a pig is slaugh-tered—more like one hundred pigs. You get to understand the different wails: the amputations begging for mercy, the general moans of injured men, and the feverish young boys moaning for their mothers. Crows compete with them, cawing from trees. What warning they giving?

Saul's laid out on the ground, no blanket, nothing.

"I'm gonna get some help," I say.

He nods, stone-faced as ever. Carnage is everywhere: lifeless faces turn up to the clouds. A colored woman wrings out a bloody towel by the river. Maybe she can help us. I nod. She nods back.

"Your hand need tending to?" Her voice is worn.

"Yes, Ma'am." She is not a tall woman; her hair is pushed back into her bonnet.

"Bullet pieces in here." I raise my bandaged hand. "My friend got hit in the leg. We need a doctor."

"I ain't no doctor, but I can get the bullets out." She places the towel in her bucket. "Take me to him."

I lead her through the trail of the wounded to Saul.

"Don't move now hear? And bite on this."

She gets a bullet from her pocket and places it in Saul's mouth. I hold him down. He jerks, then passes out.

"He'll come to. Here's that son of a bitch." She squeezes a bloody bullet between tweezers.

Using my good hand, I build up the campfire with anything I can find. I ask a young boy to fetch me water from the river. I give him a piece of hardtack in return. He runs off with the bucket. Poor boy. Dressed in rags, not much older than my Will.

"You're next." She points to my hand.

Wonder if I'll be biting the same bullet.

She saves Saul's leg and my hand. I try to find her again before we are sent to Columbia Hospital. I owe that woman my hand. At the hospital, Saul is sent to a different ward. I'm in a ward full of white men. I'm the only colored man. You get meals here. Even a bed with sheets, pillow, and blanket. Everything's white here: white walls, floors, beds. The walls are decorated with evergreens, and a large flag with stars and letters I can't make out hangs from a beam. All white men here except me.

Young amputees sit around sluggish with grim faces—who can blame them? They are so small, couldn't even steer a plow.

My hand is still healing; I can move a few fingers, hurts like hell. There is that poor youngster glaring at me again like he wants to strangle me with his only arm. Got no legs, just an arm. A pretty nurse pushes him around in his chair.

"Don't you look at me, nigger! I fought for you—lost my legs—my arm—what you lose? Huh? What you lose?" He foams at the mouth, spit dribbles on his beard, his one hand curled into a fist.

"Now calm down, calm down. Here, have a drink."

The nurse hands him a cup; he strikes it—bang! Mess on the floor. The whole room of men jolt. Nerves are funny that way after combat. He flails about.

"What I got left? What I got . . .?"

A doctor assists the nurse and restrains him. They wheel him out of the room. Two men play cards like nothing is happening; others stare into space. I got to get out of here.

I thought someone would jump me in my sleep. So, I slept with a pocketknife in my good hand. Not safe in here for a colored man. I asked, "Let me do something," so they sent me to a prison to work.

Could not send me to the front lines, but I could handle carrying a plate and water to prisoners. Anguish can creep into you and turn your mind if you let it. Most of the prisoners are sick and starving. Skin and bones. One meal a day, water, and hardtack. Somedays, they get lucky and get a piece of salt pork, but that is rare. They are given thin blankets, leaky cells, and pallets made of hay.

I am his jail keeper, a blue blood, big deal confederate senator. I deliver his daily meal. I'm sure he had been served by Negros before, but not while in chains, half-naked, and filthy.

Maybe he thinks I will kill him, retribution for all the slaves he abused. He was captured fleeing his estate in Tennessee. My blood boils every time I see him—how many lives did he twist up like my poor Ophelia? Can't look at him most days. He deserves this. He deserves worse.

Slam the bucket down, water splatters, he coughs. You can see your breath in his cell, winter is on its way.

"Boy! Boy!" he shouts and coughs. "A blanket, boy! Get me a blanket! I will expire if I don't get a decent covering!"

I drop the plate. "I'm not your boy."

His eyes are liquid blue, sunken into his skull. At that moment, I see deep into his soul—coldest soul I have ever seen. I could wring his neck with my good hand . . .

Nah. Not a fair fight. Not a fair fight at all. A doctor comes and says he will die if we do not release him. They let this one go. Ralston, a senator from Tennessee, that was his name. That is the closest I ever got to one of them Johnnies and the closest I ever want to get.

My brother Jacob jabs my side.

"Augustus, are you done telling your war stories yet?"

"If we don't stop him now, he's never gonna stop!" Jaden snickers and sends the crowd howling, the bastard.

Lem and Monty slap my back. How long have I been talking? What did I say? I must have fallen into a deep reverie . . .

Lem shouts, "Come on old man, time for a toast."

Saul joins us and lifts his glass. "To Company M for making it through!"

"Three cheers for Company M!" Lem hollers.

Lucretia's hand in mine, the soft scent of lavender in her hair, and full hips. I can't wait to get to her tonight. Little

Eleanor chases after a dark boy; Will, a whole head taller now, hangs on Julia's arm, shy, waiting to join the game.

"Ralston . . .that was him, Ralston from Tennessee!" a petite woman shouts before convulsing and falling to the ground. The fiddler stops playing, rushes to her.

"Eliza, what's wrong Eliza . . ." He sets her head in his lap, her body lies listless on the floor.

I pick up a mug of water, walk around the table and kneel next to the fiddler.

"Does she need some?" I place the mug on the floor. People are mulling about but keeping their distance.

"This happens; she has spells." The fiddler caresses her face, saying, "She'll come to."

Her body jerks, knocking the mug over; water stains the ground.

ELIZA

BARREN

U p the windy road to his estate, Ralston doubles over, panting. His clothes torn, fields destroyed, cabins uninhabited. Candles that once lined the grand entrance gone. Barn burnt to the ground. The duck pond is overgrown and barely visible. She is on the porch, rocking, with embroidery in her hands. Faded dress, hair loose, no curls, no pretty ribbons. He stops at the bottom of the stairs. She drops her embroidery, hastens down the dirty white steps.

"My darling!"

His long frame folds in her arms like a child. She steadies him on the porch steps.

"I came as fast as I could." He struggles for air.

"All that's left here is a barren peach tree and skinny cow," She laments.

He straightens his back. "We'll get back up again. We'll get back up."

She helps him ascend the rickety stairs into the house—the house I was terrified to enter, the house I died in many times, the house that almost destroyed me—and shuts the door.

PART TWO
ELECTRICITY

ELIZA

BRUNSWICK, MAINE, 1893

I'm blessed to live near water so I can feel Ma and Auntie's spirits. Edward and I make our home in our small house in the colored section of Brunswick, close to the Freeman farm. There is a lake nearby said to be haunted by Augustus Freeman's late wife, Ophelia, who tried to drown herself after she discovered he was unfaithful. I stay away from it, her howls send a warning at night; Edward says it is just wolves—but he doesn't dare swim in it, very few people do. She is waiting to take some poor soul down in her depths. Thankfully, it is a short walk to the banks of the New Meadows River where I pray. Ma and Auntie's spirits talk to me there, give me guidance.

Our first-born, Priscilla, is a strong girl. She reminds me of Ma, has a gentleness to her and her smile. Edward was so relieved our second child was a boy. He pressed me for a name, but I was waiting for it to come from my ancestors in my dreams; finally he said, "His name shall be Scott Joplin after the great King of Ragtime." His nickname became King, somehow Scott didn't stick, so our son, we call him King.

Edward took King to all the taverns where he played fiddle —he was sure King had the same gift of hearing as him. I knew it. As a baby, he could hear my thoughts and would hum songs going through my head: this child was destined to be a musician. He quickly picked up the banjo and later learned piano. And then our baby girl, Elmira, was born, named after the town where Edward and I met in New York, where the kind man John Jones led us to freedom over the great bridge to Canada. A mean cough took a hold of our baby Elmira, I prayed to the river, to Auntie and Ma, but Elmira didn't make it through her first winter.

Death comes when you least expect it. The ground sprouts grass, softening from the melted snow and spring rains, a promise of warmth. Priscilla and I pull weeds clearing a patch for our vegetable garden, it will surely do well this summer. Edward and King carry fishing poles and pails down to the riverbank.

"Be sure and bring home dinner!" I call after them.

"Ma don't you worry, I'm gonna get the biggest fish there is!" King shouts back.

An uneasiness tingles up my spine. Clouds move across the sky, wind twirls around the tree by our house, shaking branches and leaves. I stand up, listening.

"What is it Ma? You having another one of your spells?" Priscilla asks. She guides me to the porch. "Sit here Ma, and I'll get you a drink of water."

I can't hear her; the wind is talking to me. Priscilla walks to the water pump in the middle of the yard and pumps water into a pail. Before she can give me any, I run as fast as I can to the river.

"It's Edward! It's Edward!"

Sunlight blinks on the waves, King stands over Edward shouting, "Pa, wake up I caught a fish!"

My love, oh no, my love, my Edward, I cradle his face, kiss his lips, no, my Edward, don't go, don't—

"Ma what's wrong? Why are you crying? Pa is just asleep, I'm trying to wake him . . . Look at my fish Pa, look!" King waves his fish back and forth.

I press my ear to Edwards's chest, listening for a heartbeat—nothing. He must have passed in his sleep. His heart just gave out. My poor Edward, my darling Edward.

How strange to not have my Edward here, his embrace, his warmth, his loving. I had Priscilla write a letter to Edward's brother, Robert, to tell him of his passing. He lives in Portland with Ingrid, still works as a steamboat porter, and I lost count how many children they have. We have a small ceremony, bury dear Edward underneath the tree next to our house.

Without Edwards's help, we can no longer afford the house payment. Priscilla and I take in as much laundry as we can manage. Occasionally, I get a seamstress job. And King is stricken with grief. Thomas paddles his canoe up the New Meadows River from Malaga Island where he lives with his wife, Dee. He visits us frequently trying to cheer up King.

The eviction notice comes like we knew it would. Priscilla yanks it off our door and reads it to me. Thomas says not to worry, he spotted an abandoned house right across the river in Bath, he's sure we can make it a nice home. We have no other choice.

Thomas and his friend James arrive in their canoes to help us move our belongings across the river to our new home. Priscilla tries to be cheerful; my heart feels so heavy in my chest. Saying goodbye to our home is saying goodbye to Edward.

A table, chairs, kettle, dishes, pallets, pillows, broom, glasses, pans, blankets, King's banjo, and Edward's beloved fiddle is all we manage to fit in the boats. The river is calm, so it is not too hard to get across. James does most of the paddling, Thomas uses his one hand to help steer, and Priscilla and I paddle the other canoe following closely behind them.

Bath's shore is shallow surrounded by marshland. A small band of Indians have set up camp. Smoke rises out of their teepees. A woman with dark skin sits in front of the teepee making a basket, a small dark girl in a deer skin dress wearing a shell necklace squats next to her, digging in the dirt using a small stick. A man in native clothes stands in front of us, arms folded smoking a pipe. Will he try and stop us from coming ashore?

Tucked away behind some shrubs and trees is a small, grey shack with missing shingles and a fence in need of repair. James and Thomas push their canoe up a clearing onto the sand. Priscilla and I drag our canoe following behind them. Thomas and James approach the Indian man pointing to the shack, the man nods, and he helps us carry our furniture up to the little shack. King and the girl start chasing each other,

"Son, this is no time for play, go and get the blankets and bring them up here!" I shout.

The little girl joins him and helps King carry blankets up to our new home. This house has been abandoned for I don't know how long. Spiders spun many cobwebs in corners. The chimney is intact though, and there is a big enough hearth. We are squatters just like the Indians; I pray that we will be able to stay here.

The first thing I do is sweep the dust and dirt out of the house and hang Edward's fiddle on the wall. I am sure he is with us.

KING

BONES

BATH, MAINE, 1911
My pa says I have the gift of hearing like him, only the fiddle didn't call me. No, 'twas the sweet black and white piano keys. I learned at speakeasies, watching fingers race over keys, playing the latest rag.

Every so often, the piano player would let me play a few notes and pound along with Pa's squealing fiddle. What I hear I could play. Could not afford a piano in our place. I settled for the banjo at home. Scott Joplin's *Maple Leaf Rag* was the first one I learned, and my favorite. Pa always asked me to play it, and he'd join in with slides and riffs from his fiddle. Crowds loved it! Our music sent feet flying and stomping, ladies twirling, and a fair amount of tips.

That was before Pa died. I was just a boy. We were fishing, Pa took a nap on the grass near the river, like he always did. But he didn't wake up. His heart gave out in his sleep. Now his fiddle hangs on the wall as if he would come in anytime, pick it up, and play.

Ma waited to name me to see what ancestor claimed me. For my first few months of life, I had no name. Finally, my pa put his foot down and said I should be called Scott, after the great King of Ragtime: but everyone calls me King.

From the time I could walk, Ma always telling me, "Hold yourself high, son." She always made sure my spine was straight when I left home.

"They look down at us because of our color—don't let that poison in," she'd say softly, put a bag around my neck for protection and kiss me on the forehead.

She escaped slavery, met my pa in Elmira, New York, and fled to Canada, Nova Scotia; now here we are with my sister, Priscilla, in Bath. My baby sister, Elmira, died. When Elmira was sick with consumption, Ma went to the shore, rosary in her hand, praying to save her. Elmira slipped away from us—didn't make it. The way I see it, Ma's gods are not listening.

I learned my letters from my pa. I can read and figure. Not worth much; no one hires a colored man for anything but a farmhand or servant. Paper mill factories are filled with Irish and Italians: they won't hire coloreds. Everyone fishes to survive. But there is barely any fish left, rivers are poisoned by the paper mills—white men run you off the good spots, hurling stones shouting: "Go back to Malaga!" Malaga, the island inhabited by Negros, Irish, Scots, and Indians. Some kids there are white, Indian, others black or in-between. Headlines fill newspapers about savages on the island with two-headed children, one black head and one white—they just don't want us coming together, don't like it at all.

Malaga Island is across Phippsburg, the mainland, so close you could throw a stone to it. One Hand Thomas lives there with his wife, Dee. Thomas is like a father to me, he visits Ma, checking in on her, and he takes me fishing with his friend, James. James is always with him, he doesn't talk much, but he knows the secrets of the river: when the tide is too low for fishing, or the water is too rough to travel. James speaks to the Indians, knows their language; he says he is Indian, but he just looks Black to me.

It's my birthday, I'm twenty-four.

Ma asks me, "When you gonna meet a nice woman and settle down?"

There she goes again, talking about marriage.

"I'll know when I see her," I answer, and she pecks me on the cheek. I take my last swig of coffee.

"Well, well, happy birthday son, and bring this extra corn-bread to Thomas and James."

Ma, always thinking of Thomas, makes me wonder if she is sweet on him. I put the warm bread in my sack. Priscilla places a piece of cornbread covered with molasses on the table.

"Happy birthday!" She smiles, she knows it's my favorite.

She works so hard, cooking and cleaning all the time at home and taking in white folk's laundry. Her hands are worn, and her face thin. No suitors have taken an interest in her, she has taken it upon herself to care for Ma in her old age.

"Thank you, Priscilla." I take a bite, the molasses sticks to the roof of my mouth: a morsel of heaven.

I ride the steamboat down the New Meadow River to Ridley's Landing in Phippsburg across from Malaga Island. It cost twenty-five cents. I'm saving up to get my own boat. The skiff owned by a Black man came just in time; he always gives me a good deal because I share my fish with him. Drifting in silence, he propels us to Malaga's cove as the sun breaks through the clouds. And there is Thomas waving at me with his good hand, his stump covered by his sleeve. James is by his side holding fish pails, nets, and rods.

I pay the man a dime, jump off the raft, and shout at Thomas, "Ready to catch some cod today?"

"Sure enough," Thomas answers, and James stabs bait onto his fishhook.

Fishermen launch their lines, perched on large rocks along the cove while gulls screech and loons dive, disappearing below the waves.

Above the shore, shacks dot the landscape and a few larger houses. That's where the King of Malaga lives. He is a sturdy Scotsman, loud and friendly, the best fisherman on the island. He is married to a Negro woman who has her own laundry business in Phippsburg, the mainland. They're like us: we all got to scrape by doing something for white people—or starve. Most folks get help from the mainland to survive the winter. If you can get your name on Phippsburg's list, they provide extra clothing, food, and a little money.

James and I follow Thomas to the edge of the small shell beach away from the other fisherman. James sets the nets in the water to trap herring that later we sell as bait. We launch our lines there and wait.

Oh, yes! I got a bite, reel in my line.

"You beat Thomas to it, lucky man."

James is always keeping tabs, who can outdo Thomas. Thomas is like his older brother and is about as old as my ma, but he doesn't look like it. He says his wife, Dee, keeps him young. He is as strong as me—even stronger. Love, it does powerful things to people.

"Not bad, not bad." I remove the cod from the hook and toss it in the tin bucket.

Children scamper down the hill and surround us, singing and clog dancing. It is a joyful jig. They know we'll give them something. I take the cornbread out of my sack and tear off pieces, placing it in their tiny palms. Some utter, "Thank you," before shoving it in their mouths, while others can't wait and gobble it up as fast as they can. So far, none of them have two heads.

It is a good day: four pails of fish and a fair amount of herring. Not bad. James throws a live one back in.

"To give thanks," he says.

We are ready to take our fish to sell in Phippsburg and I'll bring home dinner tonight. Ma will be pleased.

We paddle Thomas's canoe across the river to Phippsburg and haul it on shore to one of Thomas's hiding places. James wheels his wooden cart out from the bushes and we fill it with buckets of fish. I drop my catch in my sack. A car stops across the street, and a woman steps out.

"Pop!" shouts a pretty woman in a golden dress standing next to a car. Something hits me deep inside.

I can't move. Heck, I almost stop breathing. James wipes his hands on his trousers and smiles. She must be his daughter.

"Ma wants you home before dark. And bring dinner!" Her voice has an edge to it. She doesn't notice me.

A man in a tan jacket, thin black mustache, opens the car door for her. She steps back in the car; her long legs and thin ankles tease me.

James lifts the cart and rolls it, tiny bells on the handle jingles. Beside him, Thomas shouts, "Get your cod, bait!"

And I can't get her out of my mind. Found out her name is Vera. Vera, I say to myself at night before I go to sleep—what a birthday gift I received! I wake up with her face in my mind. I feel her; she is my destiny.

I fish with James and Thomas as often as I can to see James's daughter Vera again. Songs of Vera run through my head. I bring my banjo to Malaga plucking out my yearning, and James sings along; his deep mournful voice travels over the waves. James stays mostly at Malaga because his mother-in-law, Lucretia, can't stand the sight of him. His dark skin offends her. Though his wife, Eleanor, pleads with her mother, he can only visit. He is broken up about it and asks me to play my banjo, so he can sing his sorrowful songs about missing his wife,

Eleanor. I feel the same way about his daughter, Vera. But I don't let him know.

Thomas, his wife, Dee, and her father, Griff, have a modest house on Malaga Island with two rooms, a small vegetable garden in front, not unlike Ma's in Bath. Dee and Griff are descendants of the first families on Malaga. Griff is mulatto, and Dee is a shade darker with blue eyes, curly brown hair, a thick figure, and a stubborn sweetness about her. Griff walks with a limp—his leg got shot up in the Civil War. He spends his evenings polishing an old pistol from his army days.

"Can that gun still shoot?" I ask him.

"Don't know, haven't had to use it yet." He lifts the pistol in the lantern, inspects it, and continues rubbing.

Griff is a somber man. His wife died during the measles epidemic a while back. Hit the islanders hard. Buried her on the island. At times, he visits her grave, leaving wildflower bouquets for her. His daughter is his life. His small pension keeps them afloat, along with Dee's earnings as a maid on the mainland. She keeps him fed and comfortable. Thomas helps, too, with his earnings from fish peddling.

Dee looks after her uncle and cousins. Uncle's house is the first you spot from the shore, juts out a bit from the shell beach. Everyone calls him Uncle, he is the kindest man on the island, would give you the shirt off his back if you asked. Kids love him, swarm around him eager for a game or a funny story. Uncle is Indian, his wife a mulatto. They're not doing too well now. Uncle suffers a sickness that makes him too weak to work, and his eldest son, well, got an abscess that damn near has taken out the right side of his face. He is going blind. His wife and daughter do the best they can for the family: scrubbing laundry from the mainlanders, fishing with the men, digging for clams, and caring for their sick. Folks help out by leaving baskets of food and offering all kinds of remedies and prayers. Aunt Cam, well known for her healing ways, brings the family bundles of herbs. No one knows how old she is, some say over a hundred, she walks with a cane and lives in a cabin surrounded by pine trees.

Some speculate the water on the island is making people sick. There are three wells spread out near the houses. Can't tell if the water is bad for sure, but makes you wonder. Other folks say it is the unsettled spirits of the ancestors, especially after a boy was kidnapped by officials from the mainland. He was sitting on a rock sunbathing, a boat appeared, and they snatched him. Mothers tell children to be wary of the main-landers.

We're out early to fish: the sun barely greets the sky. Thomas smokes his pipe; James carries the pails and net; I carry the rods. Uncle and his son are wading in the shore near our fishing spot by the shell beach. A steamboat blows its horn full of tourists gawking and pointing at us.

"Niggers! Savages! Mongrels!" Angry faces holler from the rails of the steamboat, hurling bottles.

"We come out to welcome the sun." Uncle strokes his thick beard propping up his son. His son's face is hollowed into a pit of blood and pus due to the abscess, his eye gone, his other eye barely open. "Then these bastards have to ruin it!" He laughs and coughs at the same time.

He gets a chuckle out of Thomas, which is rare. James, Thomas, and Uncle start talking in that Indian language I don't understand. Sharp sounds roll off their tongues like a drum-stick hitting a rim.

"We'll save you some fish, Uncle." Thomas offers him a small bag of tobacco; Uncle slips it in his pocket. His son groans.

Uncle's wife sticks her head out a small window facing the

bay, screeching like a gull, "Get him in the house before he gets chilled!"

A freckle-faced boy gallops around the yard as his mother hangs clothes on a rope. Fine petticoats, dresses, and skirts flap on the line. Much finer clothes than the dull, worn dress she wears. Must be laundry she has taken in from rich folks on the mainland.

"I better go before I get in more trouble with the Missus." Uncle winks. James drops his pails and helps Uncle and his son up the hill to their house.

It is a slow day; I didn't catch a thing. James caught a few, Thomas one. That's how it is on the river. The tide laps at our boots, coming in further and further. To the left of us, I spot a grey object washed up on the shore. It is a tore up old rowboat. James helps me get it out from the tide. Thomas sucks his pipe blowing smoke out the side of his mouth. He inspects the boat with his good hand.

"We can fix this up nice," Thomas says.

"Look like you found yourself a boat, King." James pats my back.

"Ain't got hardly any fish, but the river brought me a boat." I smile, though I am hungry.

It will be thin pickings tonight. James lifts one end of the boat and I take the other end carrying it to Thomas's house.

Chickens cluck, surrounding Dee as she tosses them scraps, talking to them, "Now you rooster, you let that hen eat, you old, naughty thing!"

We put the boat down. Thomas embraces Dee, she pecks his cheek. Her father Griff sits on the porch staring into space. Dee says he has fits, forgetting where he is, fighting invisible enemies, screaming in agony. He always keeps his pistol by his side. Dee says the nighttime is the worst, when he awakes all a terror, wreaking havoc in their home. She slips elixirs in his drink to calm him. Sometimes it works.

We scavenge pieces of wood and fix up the boat. Dee has a bit of blue paint and offers it to me. Just enough paint to cover all of it. I call it Blue. My boat, Blue.

Blue takes me up and down the New Meadow River. It's a kind of freedom I've never felt before, manning my own boat. I save money, too, no longer need to pay the steamboat fare. I hide Blue in the brush near a short trail to Ma's house in Bath. At night, I play rags in the local speakeasy, though Ma dislikes it and wishes I would attend church with her and Priscilla. Still, she appreciates the tips I bring home. I keep my eyes open for that beauty, Vera, so far, no luck.

The river flows in my favor with the wind on my back down to Malaga. I paddle occasionally to steer Blue away from rocks and other boats. It's chilly today, I'm glad I wore a thick jacket. A white tern circles above and nose dives into the water. I pass the lobster crates near Malaga's shore, two white men in large boat sneer at me.

"Don't even think of stealing our lobster, Malagite!" one shouts and spits in the water.

They're always accusing folks on Malaga of stealing their lobsters or taking lobsters that aren't full grown yet. It is as if they think they own the sea.

Two male ducks and one female swim by me. Which lucky duck will win her affection? I tow Blue over the shell beach and secure her with a rope around a tree. The tide is ebbing, soon it will be low enough for clam digging near Bear Island which is right next to Malaga. I walk up the trail to Griff's house. A melody swirls around my head, I try and conjure Vera's face and those legs, but my recollection of her is dimming. I've got to meet her again somehow.

The air is tight in Griff's house. Not the usual morning clamor of Dee cooking, fussing over Griff while James and

Thomas rinse pails, line rods, and mend holes in nets for another day of fishing. Dee wrings her apron. Thomas rubs his forehead with his good hand. James sighs. Did somebody die? Dee sets a mug of coffee on the table for me.

I sit down and ask, "What's going on?"

Dee slides a chair next to Griff at the head of the table.

She starts talking, "I was at my job cleaning house on the mainland and as I was scrubbing the floor, I overheard a conversation with my employer, Mr. Grant, and another gentleman, I don't remember his name. They were talking about coming to inspect the island and what a burden Malaga is for the mainlanders in Phippsburg and how the island would be best used for a summer resort. They said they are coming tomorrow."

"What they gonna inspect?" Griff's voice is almost a growl, his hands balled up like he is ready for a brawl. "Nothing to inspect here. Our family been here for generations, we're hardworking folks. What they think they gonna find?"

"I don't know, but we better set things as right as we can and tell the others," Thomas says wearily.

Dee goes from house to house, spreading the word about the inspection. Folks tidy up their places the best they can. James and I help Griff cover the drafts in the house with old shingles. After that, we help neighbors fix leaky roofs and broken windows. We eat dinner in silence: the usual jests between Thomas and Dee gone. Dee fills our mugs with the last of the rum. I strum my banjo and James hums along until the fire goes out.

I pluck my banjo at the edge of Malaga's shore dreaming of Vera. She appears from the river in a golden dress floating on waves coming to me. I open my arms, oh, my Vera, I finally see you again. She cackles, I try to embrace her, but she is nothing but air—a rumble of a car engine comes from behind me, a man with a mustache opens the car door for her, she gets in, her laughter spills over the engine spurting and backfiring . . . What is that sound?

I awake to the engine sound getting louder and louder. I put on my boots and coat, alert Thomas, and we take off to the shore spotting a group of officials in a wide motorboat approaching Malaga.

The governor leads his wife over the shell beach like she is a queen. She lifts her fine lace dress, twirling a parasol. Other officials with wives join them. A policeman slaps a baton against his hand, strutting behind a man carrying a leather-bound book.

"We call him Agent P." Thomas points towards the man with the book. "He decides who gets help here in the winter. Sure, the extra money helps some families here. I'm not so sure I'd want to be on the list now, it might work against you."

Thomas spits on the ground, glares at the agent.

They stop at Uncle's house first. Passing through the small yard, the men enter the house, the women close behind. Thomas hustles back home to warn the others. I watch them like a hawk. The women stroll out of Uncle's house, their voices squawking like angry crows.

"What a terrible hovel to live in!" says the governor's wife.

"Oh yes, quite! And that disfigured face—I think I shall have nightmares!" another woman laughs.

"The children—so wretched. Surely some family can adopt them." The governor's wife sniffs the air, raises her chin up.

The governor exits the house, barreling between the women. Agent P writes in his book. Uncle's wife shuts the door.

"Please, ladies, do not stray far. You never know what these heathens are capable of doing," the governor says, steering the group towards Griff's house with the policeman and agent at his side.

I hear every word, even though they are yards away—this isn't a friendly visit. I run up the back trail, a shortcut to Griff's house. Dee, Griff, Thomas, and James stand guard on the porch.

"Step aside! We are here to inspect the premises!" the policeman commands.

Dee straightens her hair back. Thomas tucks his stump in his pocket. Griff stands at the doorway, arms folded. The agent scribbles in his book, then slams it shut.

He points his finger at Griff, spittle shoots out his mouth as he speaks: "You are wards of the state. This is no longer your house; it is presently owned by the state of Maine. Now step aside!"

"Ward? I'm not no ward! This is my home, and I'm not moving," Griff shouts.

Dee stands with her hands on her hip.

The governor bellows, "Get the morons' names, so we can move on!"

"Yes, Governor, of course." The agent's tone changes. He clears his throat and asks, "Now who are the residents here?"

He takes a keen interest in Dee, who rattles on about Uncle's family nearby, how much they need food and medicine.

When she says, "Please, a doctor visit would do them so much good!" he asks her how old she is. She replies, "Oh, about forty, I reckon."

Thomas steps in front of her. The agent is furiously taking notes.

"Best move on. Ain't gonna get any more from us," Thomas warns him, staring daggers at the agent until the man joins the rest of his party.

That night, the wind swirls itself around the island in a frightful howl. Ma would say it was a foreboding—and she would have been right.

. . .

Blue, are you ready to go? I sure hope you bring me good luck today and fill my pail with fish. The air has a bite to it this morning. Once I start paddling. I get warm; clouds crowd the sky threatening snow. Two river otters stick their heads out of their den on the riverbank. They look like large slick rats and can be fierce if you get too close. They nuzzle each other and slide into the water. One got lucky and pops up with a fish in his mouth.

There aren't many vessels on the river only a few fishing boats and a steamboat. It is a lazy morning; I wish I could have stayed in bed. But I need to help out at home as much as I can: winter is here, and food is scarce. Christmas is coming, I want to save to get Ma something nice. I hope today is worth coming out for: you never know what the river will bring you.

It starts to snow gently, like it is hesitant to drop out from the sky. On shore, ducks nestle their beaks in their feathers, hiding their bills. I can barely make out Malaga, it is enclosed in a circle of fog, making it look like a raft adrift in the middle of the sea. A churring of a motorboat and men's voices come from behind me. They pass me, heading to Malaga. I recognize Agent P, the man with the leather book, the governor, and the policemen. I paddle as fast as I can to Malaga's shore. I've got to warn Thomas and Dee. I leave Blue on the shell beach and take off to Thomas's house, past Agent P, the governor, a policeman, and two other officials trudging up the beach in thick overcoats and hats.

I'm out of breath, barging into Thomas's home.

"They are here again, Agent P, with the police, they're heading to Uncle's house."

I can barely get the words out. Dee grabs her coat and Thomas, James, and Griff rush out the door down the hill to Uncle's home.

The policeman whacks his baton against Uncle's door. Dee is panting, breath comes out her mouth like fog.

"What are they doing? Did they bring a doctor?"

Thomas grabs Dee. "Stay here, Dee," Thomas pleads.

She wrestles her arm out of his grip and tears down the path like a horse gone wild. We dash after her; Griff limps behind.

"We, the State of Maine, declare that the residents of this household be committed to the Pineland Institute." Agent P clears his throat and enters the house with the policemen. We follow them inside. "Here are new clothes for your journey. Do not leave any of your own clothing on. These are to be worn now."

Uncle's daughter takes the clothes, her arms limp. "But we don't want to leave our home."

Her freckled child starts bawling.

"We will take care of your family. At the hospital, you will have food and medicine. We have you and your family's best interest. You have fifteen minutes to vacate the premises."

Agent P dangles his silver pocket watch. The policeman cocks his pistol. Dee pushes through the long overcoats.

"What are you doing? Where are you taking them? Why can't they stay here? They haven't done nothing!"

Agent P nods to the policeman, who quickly grabs her from behind and handcuffs her. She kicks him, and he butts her head with his pistol. She slumps forward, bleeding; Thomas swings his good arm.

"That's my wife, you can't take her, that's my wife!"

James and I try and calm him— they might decide to take him as well. By now, a group of islanders surround the house. Thomas is about to blow. Griff leans against his cane and points his pistol at the policeman.

"Let my daughter go."

The gun clicks, he means business. James and I can barely contain Thomas, now Griff is about to get himself killed. Two goons swarm on Griff like bees to honey. He drops his pistol. We are outnumbered and out armed, and we know it.

"You think this old pistol is going to fire?" Agent P picks up the gun and hurls it out the door. The policeman laughs. "We don't want this hussy producing any degenerates. We are doing her a favor."

Thomas fires off every insult imaginable, and James tries to calm him, talking in Indian to him.

They won't let the family take any of their possessions, just the grey clothes they give them that make them look like prisoners. Uncle is skeletal, his son even worse off. They can barely walk. Uncle stops, looks around his home, and says some Indian words, James answers him. The policeman drags Dee like a sack of potatoes.

"I'm coming for you, baby! Dee, I'll come git you!" Thomas cries. James and I can barely restrain him.

The governor faces the crowd gathered in the yard. "All islanders are to vacate the premises by July 10, 1912, or your houses will be burnt down."

One of his goons picks up a can of kerosene and douses Uncle's house with it. We all stand back as he lights the match flicking it in the air. Flames lap the house like a hungry dog's tongue. The goons join the governor plowing through the crowd. Dee's slumped body leaves a trail of crimson drops in the snow behind her.

A gloom sets over the island. Women sweep out their houses fiercely as if trying to dispel bad spirits. Now that the state gave the eviction notice to the islanders, they don't provide the usual rations that used to tide them over the winter months. Folks are desperate. Though some got offered money to leave their houses on the island, Griff got nothing. So, he is staying.

"The spring," Thomas says. "We gonna go get Dee back in the spring when the snow melts."

That's about all Thomas will say—when he does talk. Lately, he's been quieter than ever. And Griff, polishing that old pistol of his, barely says a word, stares into space, seeing things I can't see.

A few families break down their homes and float them across the New Meadows River to Phippsburg. Some get lucky and are allowed on shore. Others are sent away with jeers and stones, sent adrift on their own homes.

The poorest Negro family had the worst fate. Denied entry along the bay, they lived in an old schooner, staying at ports till they were forced out. The mother took ill, and during a fearsome gale, the father set out for a doctor, rowing to the mainland. By the time they got back to her, it was too late—his wife had hemorrhaged to death with her two children huddled next to her lifeless body on the boat.

Vera peeks into my mind at times like a light I can't let go of. I keep my spirits up by playing in speakeasies. I'm staying in Bath to help Ma and Priscilla get through the winter. Priscilla works six days a week as a maid for a white family nearby. She brings home laundry for Ma to wash and mend. Between her job and cooking and cleaning at home, she doesn't have the time to keep the wood pile full.

"I'm the man in the house," I say, "I'll get us wood."

I fasten snowshoes to my boots, bundle up ready to face the cutting air. The snow has a glaze of crust on top and is about two feet deep, which makes it hell to walk in without snowshoes. Thank God I have them. I put my ax down on a sled and drag it behind me heading out behind the house into the woods.

Lucky for me, tree branches sag heavy with snow low enough for me to shake the snow off and strike them with my ax. This will be good kindling. I place the branches on the sled and secure the bundle with a rope. I am on the lookout for fallen logs. My mind pulls me back to Malaga: Dee's screams; Uncle's stoic walk with his wounded son beside him; Thomas's curses

at Agent P and the policemen; Uncle's house lighting up the sky in flames. James and I could do nothing but watch and try to hold Thomas back from being taken with the rest. My heart starts racing in my chest and I am dizzy with rage.

Steady, steady, King. I stop and wipe my brow. Got to stay focused. I hum a tune to keep my mind off Malaga—nothing I can do about it right now. I spot a curve in the snow, hoping it is a log. I clear the snow off, and yes, it is! I drag it onto the sled next to the kindling: at least we won't freeze now.

At night, I sit by the fire and tend to Ma's hands. I rub them with liniment oil. She says it takes away the ache. She asks how Thomas is. I tell her he keeps talking about going to Pineland and getting Dee in the spring when it is easier to travel. James and I agree to join him.

"It is a sinful thing they have done, son, evil." Her eyes brim with tears.

"I know, Ma, I know," I say, massaging her fingers.

I wish she could stop working so hard. I don't want to say too much, don't want to worry her. All we can do is wait for the spring. Ma hums a low melody that coils around the logs sending the flames higher.

The snow melts, streams run into the bay lined by yellow flowers, red-winged black birds, woodpeckers, and chickadees return. We survived another winter. I take Blue out for the first time this year with my fishing rod and banjo, downriver to

Malaga. Thomas, I'm sure, is itching to go to Pineland to get Dee.

A hollowed-out feeling takes me over as I walk up the trail to Griff's house. Rectangle patches of dirt remain where houses were, overgrown vegetable gardens and fence posts scatter over yards. His house is the only one left on Malaga Island. Griff is on his porch with his gun next to him. Thomas sucks on his clay pipe. James sits on the steps mending a net. Thomas greets me and slaps my back with his good hand.

"You made it through winter, King," he says, sucks his pipe, squints his eyes.

"Sure did. I came to see about going to Pineland," I ask.

Thomas turns his head to James, James nods in agreement.

"Yes, we will bring my Dee back home." Thomas turns and walks up the porch steps. "Well, come on now inside, and let me get you something to eat."

James continues to mend his net, Griff nods to me as I follow Thomas into the house.

We decide to leave the next morning. Griff refuses to come with us to Pineland. He doesn't want to slow us down. Thomas says ever since the snow melted, Griff visits his wife's grave every day, clearing weeds, decorating it with shells and flowers while he talks to her. He says some islanders come back to visit to stand on the ground where their houses were, to feel a sense of home. They pay respects to their dead, leaving chipped teacups, tiny bottles of whiskey, and dolls on graves.

Griff offers us his pistol. Thomas sighs, saying, "You know that gun don't work, Griff."

"You can scare 'em. They won't know. Besides, what if they try and lock you up with the rest of them?"

Griff is always thinking like a soldier, like he is still in a war.

"Don't worry, Griff, I'm bringing Dee back," Thomas reassures him and swings his sack over his shoulder, James as usual at his side, and I on the other.

. . .

We paddle upriver, stopping at Ma's in Bath, and she is sure glad to see Thomas. She fries up some cod with collard greens and cornbread. Thomas offers me a bit of his whiskey from the bottle he has hidden in his coat. The liquor gives me courage, soothes the uneasy feeling in my gut. Ma senses it. She feels everything, can't hide anything from her.

"Saint Anthony, please bring them home." She lights a candle.

"Saint Anthony? Who's that?" Thomas smirks.

"He is the saint of finding lost people and things, he will help you." Ma's voice is soft but commanding. She must have learned this from the Catholic Church her and Priscilla go to every Sunday. They keep trying to get me to come, too, but I don't have time for religion, too busy trying to survive.

"We don't have time for this voodoo, Eliza. This is man's work," Thomas teases her.

"Well, I aim to help you all, and this is *my* work." She continues her reverie, undisturbed by Thomas's ribbing.

We say our goodbyes in the morning before the cock crows. There's something hard in my pocket. Ma slipped a nail in it, some kind of amulet. I don't believe her mumbo jumbo, but I keep it in my pocket anyways.

After walking a few miles, we get lucky. A friendly man driving a horse and cart offers us a ride. He speaks a little English with a Portuguese accent. We jump in the back. Thomas offers the man whiskey, and he happily accepts; his mood gets jollier the more he drinks. He stops at the entrance of the long road to Pineland. We thank him, jump off his cart, and head up the hill. At the end of the road, a few birch trees stand in front of a red brick building with white trim, surrounded by a green lawn. I read the sign at the edge of the grass:

MAINE SCHOOL FOR THE FEEBLE-MINDED

"Feeble-minded? They told us it was a hospital."

Thomas straightens his coat and shoves his stump hand in his pocket. We stand at the bottom of the steps, all thinking the same thing: What if they try and lock us up? I suck in my breath as we walk up the cement stairs. Thomas rings the doorbell.

A nurse with pursed lips and a ring of keys hanging from her waist opens the door.

"Are you here to drop off a patient?" She scrutinizes us and doesn't hide her disdain.

"No, Ma'am. I'm here to get my wife, Dee," Thomas says in his most gentleman-like voice.

"And Uncle and his family, from Malaga," I say, trying to hide my rage.

"I see. Just a moment."

The woman closes the door. Then a stout man opens the door. The nurse stands behind him, jingling her keys with her fingers.

"State your name and residence."

Thomas slips up and says he is from Malaga.

The man stops writing in his pad and says, "Malaga is no longer inhabitable. We have suitable accommodations for your sort here where you will be aptly taken care of and no longer a burden to communities."

He places his spectacles on, taking a thorough view of us all. He knits his hairy brows together; he has more eyebrows than he does hair on his head.

"I meant Bath, sir. We're from Bath." Thomas tries to hide his fear, but his voice squeaks. "I came to get my wife, Dee."

"And the others?" The man points to James and me.

"They my brothers, that's all, came to help me."

"Come around the back, and I will see if the nurse can fetch your, um, wife." He slams the door.

"And what about Uncle and his family?" I ask before he turns his back.

He clears his throat as if the words don't want to come out of his mouth. "The father and son passed, they were too sickly, we couldn't help them."

He shuts the door.

Barbed wire surrounds a paddock. But there are no horses. Workers of all ages in grey uniforms tend to chickens, weed gardens, and feed pigs. A barn and a drab cottage stand outside the paddock with bars on the windows. Is that where Dee and the others are?

The nurse marches in front of a skinny woman in a grey dress, held by two nurses on either side. She stops in front of the barbed wire.

"Is this your wife?" she asks Thomas.

"Dee, Dee, baby, it's me, Thomas!" He forgets the barbed wire is there and rushes to her, pressing his body against the wire. Dee's face is turned up to the clouds, so skinny her sharp bones jet out her dress like a scarecrow.

"What did you do to her? Dee! Dee, it's me!" Thomas pleads to her.

Dee's eyes roll back.

He continues, "I've come to get you!"

His arms stretch trying to reach her through the space between the wires.

"Get in control of yourself!" the nurse hisses, steps back pulling Dee away from Thomas's one grasping hand and flailing stub. "Clearly, she does not recognize you. She is sick. It is best she stays here where she can continue to get help. Now I advise you all to leave the premises at once."

The nurse motions two helpers to take Dee back to the cottage. The stout man, along with two others in suits, comes up behind us.

"Get out of here, or we will lock you up with the rest." The stout man juts his chin out.

We don't run. We walk past them. Thomas spits on the ground, regains his stoic face as we walk back down the hill. We rest on the side of the road under a tree. Thomas takes out a bottle, starts drinking.

"Her spirit is gone, left her body," James says.

"They drugged her, my Dee, my Dee."

Thomas finishes off the bottle and smashes it against a tree. This is the worst they could do to Malaga, I thought, but found out later I was wrong.

We arrive in Bath the next day. Thomas is too drunk to walk up the porch steps, he leans on James and me as we manage to get him on the porch. Ma greets us at the door, opens her arms, and Thomas enters them, weeping.

She caresses his back, saying, "Shh, shh, Thomas."

He doesn't leave her arms all night.

A storm is brewing when we set out to Malaga to tell Griff of our futile attempt to bring Dee back home. I dread seeing Griff's disappointed face when we arrive without Dee. James and I paddle the canoe; Thomas smokes his pipe. The sun tries to break through the clouds. No fishermen are perched around the edges of Malaga launching their lines; no children dance happy jigs; no women hang clothes on lines; no Uncle greets the morning sun. We walk to Griff's house, and he's not home. We find him at the graveyard, kneeling by ditches, gaping holes, upturned gravestones, and piles of dirt scattered over the gravesite. Griff, with his hat off, spots us in the distance. He gets up and limps as fast as he can to us. He slows down when he realizes Dee is not with us.

"I should have come with you, brought my pistol, got my baby girl—" He lets out a wail so loud and penetrating, my legs tremor. "Now this, they dug up the graves, my wife gone, they dug out her bones, gone—"

We drop to our knees next to Griff. Thomas cries, pounding the ground. I join him, the wind carries our chorus of sorrow and rage across the river, past the barbwire paddock and neat green lawn into bones piled together in an unmarked grave, shaking the earth, cursing the island. James stands, releasing his arms to the sky.

The next day, we tear down Griff's house, build a makeshift raft, salvaging what we can, securing chairs, a table, and a bed on the raft with ropes. We take our chances and row to the mainland. In Phippsburg, we are met with an unruly mob, angry yet entertained by our plight at the same time: laughter mixed with hostility. A swell in the waves almost sends us all adrift, a chair unlooses in the river— that made the mainlanders howl with laughter pointing and jeering at us hurling insults, without offering us a hand. I wasn't surprised.

We manage to pull the raft up on Bath's shore near Ma's house. It takes us a few weeks to set up Griff's house. Griff is immobile, refuses to talk or move. He passes before the summer comes. Ma says his spirit needed to be with his wife. We bury him with his pistol in the woods behind the house.

We stay through the summer until a white man with two policemen came to our homes telling us we have no business squatting on his land. We leave as soon as we can, breaking down Griff's home once more, leaving Ma's behind, and taking what we can across the river to Brunswick's shore. James decides to stay with his wife, Eleanor, and daughter, Vera, at his mother-in-law's Lucretia's home in Brunswick. Vera, there has got to be a way for me to meet her. She is a flame in me that keeps me going. Thomas, Ma, Priscilla, and I set up our house again near where Pa was buried, and hope for the best.

Brunswick

Boom da dee-ah-dah-dee-dah! Fingers bang the keys, folks' toes tap, hands clap. I feel her before she comes, a tingle in my spine and sweet smell of rum. She claps her hands, stomps her feet, swivels her hips. I tip my hat to her full lips and chestnut skin.

"What's a fine-looking lady like you doing in a house of sin?" I immediately recognize her but don't let on that I know who she is. My Vera.

"Sinners have more fun."

I start playing "Liza Jane," and she belts out the verse, her strong voice takes the lead.

A woman like her got to have other suitors. A dark Negro like me has less chance. Vera stays with her grandma—a don't-ever-cross mulatto, Lucretia, known for her tight purse and keen eye for anyone trying to fool her. She piles her hair high like women from the old days and wears a pendant with a locket of hair from her first husband, Augustus Freeman, a Civil War veteran known in these parts for all the fighting he done and the women he had. He left Lucretia after the war, into the arms of an Irish woman, his last wife. Lucretia purchased a house with the help of Augustus's pension that was due to her. She lives with their daughter, Eleanor, and granddaughter, Vera. Least he didn't leave her in squalor.

Vera agrees to meet me at the lake by her house. I put on my best jacket and shine my shoes, packing a basket of food and a blanket. Ma stops me at the door.

"Be careful, son, you know that lake is haunted. And make sure you bring back the basket, now. It's a good one." She crosses herself and straightens my jacket collar. "You sure look handsome; now act like a gentleman."

"Ma, that is all foolishness, ain't nothing wrong with the lake."

I used to be afraid of it as a child, warned never to swim in it because an unsettled spirit lives there waiting to grab people and drown them. Ma kisses my cheek like she used to when I was a boy; she still can't see that I'm a grown man?

I take the greatest care not to get dirt on my shoes or the hem of my pants, every so often stop on the side of the road to wipe my shoes. I choose a patch of sunlit grass next to the lake to smooth out the blanket. I quickly wipe the perspiration on my forehead with my handkerchief before she sees me sweat. I try and calm my speeding heart as she strolls over in a flared red skirt, every step flashing those legs, and sits down next to me.

"You know this lake is haunted?" Vera plucks a grape off the stem.

"Nah," I smile, envying the grape she places between her full lips.

"My grandaddy Augustus's first wife, Ophelia, jumped in the lake when she found out he was cheating on her with Grandma Lucretia. She caught a chill and died. They say she's looking for a body to take hold of, seeking revenge for all the harms done to her while she was in bondage, a slave in Maryland. It has been said that if you swim in there, Ophelia will grab your ankles and take you down in her depths. You know what they say: misery loves company!" She tilts her head back and laughs.

"That is a tall tale. Here let me."

I place a grape between her lips, the tip of her tongue flicks on my finger. She has a tinge of mischief in her eyes. The breeze picks up trees sway, leaves shiver, giving me goosebumps. A faint song fills the air:

My sweet little babies sold by the devil,
buried in the ground, buried in the ground.
My sweet little babies sold by the devil,
how empty my arms are now.

"Hear that?" I say.

"What?"

"That song."

"Why, King, you look as if you've seen a ghost!"

She cackles, takes out a cigarette. I fumble in my pockets—glad I brought matches just for her. One, two, three times, the wind keeps blowing out the flame. She grimaces, disturbed, as if I should control the air for her. The breeze softens, whirls of circles form in the middle of the lake, a woman with long, hay-colored hair and a white dress rises to the surface and disappears. Is it Ophelia? I shake my head in disbelief. Must be the sun. Last chance with the matches. I strike, and the flame reaches the end of her cigarette just in time.

Vera takes out a silver flask from her purse, and once she starts drinking, her tongue loosens. She starts talking about her pa, James.

"He hangs around that one-hand darkie . . ."

She laughs and puts her cigarette out in the grass. Vera looks down on her pa, James, because he is too "country-like" from Nova Scotia and too dark. The way I see it, she is hating on herself—she is not that light.

"And the smell of fish, honestly, I can't stand it." She straightens her hat. "You know the legend of One-Hand Thomas?"

She daintily sips her flask. "Stole a chicken and his master cut his hand off and he stole a horse and escaped to Canada. Grandma Lucretia will not let him in the house, afraid of what else he will steal. But him and my pa are, well—thick as thieves." She chuckles at her own joke.

I breathe in her sweet scent of rum. I don't mention Malaga and fishing with her pa, James, and Thomas. Nor do I say anything about Thomas living with us and Ma's girlish giggles; so far, he hasn't stolen a thing. Though, Thomas has aged since trying to rescue Dee at Pineland. His chest is caved in, and he walks with a cane. Seems like it happened overnight.

Vera snaps me out of my thoughts—I yearn to kiss her ruby red lips. I try and pay attention to her words, but I am on fire.

"My ma loves my father, as dark and country as he is: Indian and Negro. He says that's where I get my eyes from; they Indian eyes." She bats her eyelashes at me. "Pa is nothing but kind to Grandma Lucretia. Ma says Lucretia will not live much longer, and Ma will inherit the house and have whomever she pleases over. She says not much longer. My pa hates Lucretia and makes no bones about it. Yet, we are under her roof. One big happy family! I want to have fun, drink, sing, dance—and if it's the devil's music, so be it!"

She throws up her arms, laughs, daring hell and heaven at the same time—who wouldn't love this woman?

After my set, I order a rum from the bartender. Vera is talking up some guy, I bet she didn't even listen to my playing. I sit down next to her, put my arm around her. He walks away. She slides her gloves off and sets them on the table. I motion the waitress for another round of drinks. Legs crossed, smirk on her face, reading the room: any suckers? I know her thoughts now; I can hear them like a melody running through my head. Suppose she thinks I'm the only sucker sitting across from her. I unfold my handkerchief and wipe the sweat off my brow.

Vera is the main singer of the speakeasy now, but I know what else she does. Corrupts young women into turning tricks for her. Says it beats being a maid for some white family. She is waiting, but not for me. She's the mistress of a Portuguese man

who can't get his fill of her. All she has for me is an upturned
lip . . .

"Give us a chance, baby, give us a chance . . ." I lock down
my tears.

She flicks my hands away and lights a cigarette. "You live at
home, King. Where you gonna put me?"

"Where you gonna have the baby?" I lean back.

"Don't worry, King, it ain't yours." She blows smoke from
the side of her mouth, checks who comes through the door.

She tries to wound me, so I'll disappear, but I won't; I
won't, Vera, not until you are mine.

She has the baby; her mother, Eleanor, delivers a toffee-
colored baby boy. Vera leaves him in her mother's care and as
soon as she can, she is off to the speakeasy. Her lover won't
marry her: she has given up hope on him. And my arms are
wide open.

Church bells ring the moment my son is born. My ma says it is
a good omen, that he will do great things. Henry, we name him,
after my grandpa. My father would have been proud. Vera is
reluctant to nurse. My ma coaxes her and tells her it will help
keep her figure, so Vera yields. But not for long.

Nothing is enough. It's too hot or too cold . . .

"This room is so shabby, when are we getting our own
place? When? I can't stay in this shack forever!"

"Lower your voice," I command, don't want my mother
hearing her nonsense.

Henry yowls, and I lift him up from the crib. Shh, my
precious boy, Daddy's here.

We move to a small house on Munjoy Hill, the colored
section of Portland. Between Priscilla's work as a maid and my
tips and fishing we manage the rent. I convince Vera that Ma
and my sister, Priscilla, need to live with us to help care for

Henry. Vera shows little interest in Henry, or her other son still in her mother, Eleanor's, care. Ma is getting feeble. She talks to herself about a cave and white fish or asks what the shells mean. Priscilla and Thomas care for her. Thomas and Ma whisper to each other holding hands, dozing in front of the fireplace. I make sure they have enough food. Most of the time, I bring Henry with me to the speakeasy. Ladies dote over him, taking turns playing with him during my sets.

All Vera can talk about is that hat. Sunday—a day of rest—and she insists we go shopping. Vera, headstrong as ever, nags us out the door to buy that new hat. Henry walks between us. Money we can't let go of, yet I can't say no. I'll scrape some up some way . . .

I double over, grip my side, dizzy from the sharp pain. I try and get up . . .

"What's wrong, King? Come on, I got my eye on that hat . . ."

Hat, hat, hat, hat.

"Hospital," I mutter. "Take me to a hospital."

I know she is irritated. My side seizes again, like a knife went through it. She helps me up, and we manage to walk to the hospital. Vera can't hardly hold me up, drags me to the red brick building. We are told to leave, they don't treat coloreds. Back on the street, my side explodes, Henry wails, and Vera pleads to a passerby for help. He ignores her and steps over me. Guess she didn't care so much for the hat after all—faint fiddle music—Pa? My body contorts on the ground below . . .

I have no hands, no face, no legs . . .

This it? Done, dead, gone, bones flesh, rot in earth. Ma's tears and prayers. I flicker the lights on and off. She calls my name.

"King?"

Yes, Ma, I answer. Yes, it is me.

As fast as a blink, my life—gone: appendicitis. I am nothing but rage and light roaming the in-between sky, watching the clouds roll back as the sun wakes up the cobblestone streets that James and Thomas's fish cart rolls down; Dee shuffles her feet behind a nurse down a gray hall; Ma embraces my boy, Henry, singing softly to him in her rocking chair; Ophelia rises from the lake, howling; my boat, Blue, buoys near Malaga's shore; and you, Vera, your every step, my love, I've got to find a way back to you.

Vera drops Henry off at Ma's and never returns. She ends up in Boston, employed as a maid for a white family. She despises them and drinks and carries on at night till despair gets the best of her. I crave the scent of sweet rum on her breath, I make the lights flicker to get her attention, but she ignores me—my Vera, I won't give up!

My son, Henry. Your soul hardens, poor orphan, but what you possess—charm, charisma, brilliance, barrel chest, tall, thick arms— makes any woman swoon. And they do, one after the other after the other—couldn't fill that wound, could you?

Lightning travels from your head to your hands, any opportunity, you seize. You are the first Negro engineer without a degree to work with white men at a Boston shipyard during the war.

Fingers dart over piano keys, over women's soft curves, teaching auto mechanics, building your own cars, writing columns in local papers; publishing poetry, songs, and trade books.

Genius flies in and out of you, around you—inventions sprout from your fingers: the wheel balancer, hover machine. You dream in blueprints and scribble diagrams in the middle of the night.

An expert golfer, chess champion; you can't stop this electricity, and now, white men work for you! My ma was right: the bells ringing at your birth was an auspicious omen indeed.

PART THREE
BRIDGE

HENRY

PORTLAND, MAINE, 1926

I'm sweltering in this suit. Mass is finally over. Women flit fans furiously, men try to hide their perspiration. I wave my hat to make a breeze. People start shuffling down the aisle, the organ swells. I want to bolt. But I let the ladies go first, like a gentleman.

I come to see him, the Father. He's colored, like me, and powerful, like a king, like I want to be. White folks listen to him—well, mostly Irish and Italians—but they still listen. That's power.

They keep coming over here. Portland is full of immigrants, mostly Catholics, and they're hated almost as much as Negroes. I grew up here on Munjoy Hill, with my Grandma Eliza and Aunt Priscilla. I barely remember my mother, Vera, a beauty who loved to drink. All I recall is her red lips and breath: the foul smell of rum. She abandoned me after my father died on the street of appendicitis because the hospital would not take in a Negro man. Rage boils in my blood every time I think of it—like I will explode.

In school, I knew the answer before anyone but didn't raise my hand to test myself against the white boys. I'm just as smart as them. Smarter. A bunch of bunk, this talk about coloreds being imbeciles—just about trying to keep us down, our heads down, yes sir, no sir, heads down . . . Not me! I've got ambition, plans.

Finally able to leave, I cross myself at the bottom of the church stairs and turn the corner, welcoming a slight breeze. I jingle the change in my pocket and cross the street to the store. Have enough for a Coke and some chicken wings I'll bring to my grandma Eliza. She's bedridden with rheumatism; I promised Aunt Priscilla I'd make a visit to her. Bells chime as I close the store door behind me. The Coke bottle is cold and wet in my hand.

And there they are. A whole procession of fools. Pointed white hoods and robes stretch down the street, right in the middle of Portland: the Klan. Look at them, thinking they're so high and mighty because they are white. What did they do to be white? Nothing. They were born white. Like I was born Black, but it's not what color you are born that makes you who you are: it is what you do.

What have they done? Nothing. They secretly feel like nothing and need to cover it up . . . "Pride cometh before the fall." That's what the Father says.

So cowardly to mask their hatred, not man enough to hate openly; I spit on the ground. A white onlooker sizes me up as his son wildly waves an American flag, cheering the marchers. I'd like to hurl the coke bottle at them—instead, I take a long swig. Time to go. I walk south to Grandma Eliza's place.

Next to the stairway is an old boat with faded blue paint. Grandma refuses to get rid of it because it was my father's. It is sound enough to take out, and every so often, Thomas uses it to fish at the pier. I knock on the door. No doorbell or knocker. The screen on the door is almost unhinged, chipped green paint exposes wood. Aunt Priscilla answers the door.

"You are the spitting image of your father, King! Come in, Henry." I hand her the chicken, smile and take off my hat. "She's in her bed, just woke up. I'll cook up these wings for lunch."

A lonesome piano is pushed against the living room wall. This is the one I learned on. Once I heard something, I could play it. Grandma says I have the same gift of hearing that my Grandpa Edward and my father had. She says the powers of the ancestors are speaking through my fingers. Her favorite song is *Maple Leaf Rag*, the one my father used to play. I know it. I sit on the piano bench, lift the dusty cover, and start playing.

"King, is that you?" Grandma Eliza shouts from her bedroom.

I stop playing, get up, and walk to her room. Pillows prop up her tiny frame, grey hair frames the edges of her ebony face, sharp cheekbones, and full lips.

She says, "King, you came home!" She raises her thin arms.

"No, Grandma, it's me, Henry."

"Yes, Henry, yes." The light on the ceiling flashes on and off; she points to it.

"That is King, your father."

Huh? What is she talking about?

"He's here, with you."

What kind of mumbo jumbo . . . She presses her bony finger into my chest. I feel dizzy, I step back.

Sharp scent of lye, tobacco, and salt; a white man with a silver cane forces his finger in my mouth—two men yank me out of the room, a woman whimpers, her back is covered with lashes . . .

I steady myself before I fall, wipe beads of sweat from my

brow, and run out the room, past the kitchen, out the door, down the rattletrap steps, and I don't look back.

The last I heard about my grandma Eliza was that she died peacefully with her friend Thomas curled up beside her.

"You hear that buzzing?" I say, as my whole body vibrates.

She traces her finger down my spine. "What are you talking about, darling? Come to bed."

Oh, this woman could turn a saint into a sinner. Why can't she hear it? Must be inside me, this constant thrum, like an electrical current. Keeps me up at night. Images form in my mind, new ways to improve and design functions of engines, cars, and before I know it, I sketch the image in my mind and work it out the next day at the shop.

"Aren't you coming? I'm awfully lonesome, Henry."

She's my fourth wife, all my kids are grown. I don't budge from my work desk. Her voice fades. She'll leave me be. Not like the others who fussed too much and couldn't keep the babies in tow, so I couldn't attend to my work. Children will get by; after all, I did, an orphan no less. Fourth wife and last wife, yes, she is the right one. She doesn't want children; she says all she needs is me.

My eldest, Margaret, from my first wife, Deliah, shows promise. She receives good grades at Portland High School, and she is well mannered. But her brother, Hank, is quite the opposite, smokes, drinks. I don't touch alcohol; it has brought enough of us down and out. I tell him to stop, but he won't listen. He rattles on about what the world has done to him— but that is no way to get out and make your path. It must be from his mother. She loved the bottle more than she ever did me. I had to leave. I figured she would sort it out.

I warned her, "Deliah, our Indian blood can't take liquor." That's why I stay clear of it.

I don't know if she ever sobered up. I finished my associate's degree at the Technical Institute in Boston and was invited to work at the Boston shipyard during the war. I was the only engineer without a bachelor's degree and the one with the best ideas. They even paid me for them.

MARGARET

CHURCH DATES

MUNJOY HILL, PORTLAND, MAINE, 1958
"Margaret, speak the King's English. That is the
only way to better yourself and be respected."
My father admonishes me for using the word "ain't." I drop
my head in shame. His fancy white convertible that he built
himself is parked on the driveway next to my apartment building. It is the kind of car you see in the movies, driving down an
open road with a handsome actor at the wheel and his pretty
girlfriend nestled beside him wearing a scarf to keep her hair in
place. He opens the trunk to his car and retrieves shiny metal
clubs in a white vinyl case wrapped in a bright red ribbon.

"I'll teach you to play someday. You keep them clean now,
until then."

Yes, Daddy, of course, of course. I am his favorite, right? He
did not buy the others a sparkling new set of golf clubs—did
you, Daddy?

I asked him if he could help pay for tuition for nursing
school. He declined. Perhaps this gift was to lessen the blow? A

goodbye gift. But when will I have time to golf? Will he come to Boston to teach me? Are there golf courses in Boston?

My brother, Hank, smokes a cigarette on the steps to our apartment. Ever since he was kicked off the football team for low grades, my father pays him no mind.

"Be good, Margaret."

Daddy starts the engine. I haul the heavy clubs around my shoulders, wave to him as he drives away.

"Golf clubs?" Hank inspects the shiny knobs. "Why'd he give you golf clubs?"

"Because he's going to teach me to golf." I snatch the case away from him.

"That'll be the day!" Hank laughs and flicks his cigarette on the ground.

He will. He promised. Why else would he give them to me? I lug them up the stairs, into the living room, and knock over Mother's empty gin bottle. Oh, no. I don't want to disturb her. She often gets upset and flies into a fury no one can stop—

Mother stirs and slides herself upright on the sofa staring at the golf clubs in my arms.

"Your father gave you those?" she says, reaching for her cigarettes. I nod, watching her closely; is she going to explode in one of her rages?

"Is that bastard gone?" She lights her cigarette.

"Mother, please don't call him that," I say, softly to not excite her.

"Left us to starve, that one did. Who is he married to now?" She lets out a chuckle.

"He gave these clubs to me as a present, and he is going to teach me to golf when I attend nursing school in Boston."

I hope these words hurt her. At least *he* gave me something before I leave for school. I can't help but say them.

"Now don't get all hoity-toity on me just cause you're going to college in *Boston*." She says Boston in a British accent, or an accent that tries to sound British. She laughs at herself.

"You come from humble people, Margaret. Passamaquoddy Indian and Black, and don't forget the Irish." She points to me with the end of her lit cigarette turning a hot pink red. "What the hell are you going to do with those golf clubs? He's never going to teach you anything."

She slurs her words, reaches for the gin bottle, and fills her glass. I don't answer her. She laughs again. Best to ignore her. Like I ignored the teasing at school when I was a child.

"Margaret the Malagite, Margaret the Malagite!" My classmates form a circle around me, taunting me.

I run, trying to break through their arms, fail, fall into a clump in the middle of the circle on the ground. Mother will be furious when she sees I have ruined my stockings. Where will we get the money for new ones? Slaps and kicks will follow, or if I'm lucky, when I get home, she may be asleep on the couch. My knees are wet with mud. Too late, the stockings are torn and ruined.

They start throwing sticks and pebbles. I am a snail. I have a hard shell around me. Soon they get bored, run off to play on the swings or seesaws. I don't know what a Malagite is. All I know is that I never want to be one. And I am not one. I will show them.

I take off my stockings sitting on the stairs to our apartment, dreaming of a house with a porch, red door, lilac bushes, and all kinds of flowers, so when you walk up the grand steps to the grand house, all you smell is sweetness.

I roll the dirty stockings in a ball and shove them in my school satchel. She will never know. Children can be horribly cruel. Funny I am thinking of that now—stop it, Margaret!

Of course, I discovered what Malagite meant, that on account of my Negro blood, they considered me beneath them. My father always told me that kind of talk was nonsense, that all I had to do was to continue to apply myself in school—so I have.

The children's singsong voices haunt me, as I walk out of the living room and carefully place the clubs beside my bed. Soon, I will be gone from all this in Boston with my friends, nursing school. I will leave all this behind.

BOSTON, MASSACHUSETTS, 1957

He was the only one at the mixer that danced with me, maybe dared to dance with me, the only colored girl there. All the ugliness exploding in this country just because Negroes demand to be treated like human beings. Segregation is illegal now, why can't the South follow the law? It makes me so angry to see the young men and women denied entrance to their only chance for an education, and they are blocked by that awful Governor of Arkansas, Faubus. Nine Negro students caused such a threat to him he called the National Guard to stop their entrance. God Bless the Little Rock Nine!

My ears perk up when he says he is from Arkansas. The band took a break, couples linger on the floor then go back to their tables to smoke or get a drink.

"Arkansas?" I ask him, just to make sure I heard it correctly.

"Yes, but Magnolia, it is quite a bit away from Little Rock."

He has a slight southern drawl. He coughs, shifts his weight; I try not to be drawn into his watery blue, Paul Newman eyes.

"It is awful what they are doing to those students in Little Rock." I wait for his response. He doesn't say anything, so I continue. "You know the only way to get ahead is to secure a decent education."

"Yes, yes, I believe so. That is why I left the South." He takes a sip of his drink.

"To get a decent education?" I ask.

"Yes, the best physics programs are here in Boston. And the southern way of life is just not for me."

He exhales, his breath is alcohol sweet. The band starts up again, it is a swinging tune. I tap my feet; he takes my hand, and we dance all night.

On our first date holding hands walking down Newbury Street in Boston, a passerby hurls insults: "Nigger lover!"

This is the North, why is this happening here? A bottle flies over our heads and crashes on the pavement. R.J. wipes perspiration from his forehead. Wherever he goes, it is blasphemy: dating a colored woman.

"Those bloody bastards!"

His face is red with rage. A group of men glare at us, we duck into the nearest church.

I take his hand. We sit in the pew facing the Virgin Mary. His rapid pulse slows, our breath synchronizes; the Virgin opens her arms, her sea blue cloak and white tunic flows as if she is sending a wave to wash over us, to bless us.

Hail Mary, mother of God, I ask for your protection for R.J., for me, for your guidance. Are we destined to be married? He is not Catholic but is open to the teachings. I gave him my copy of *Imitation of Christ,* and he said he would read it. Please give me a sign, your humble daughter, Margaret. I cross myself.

We no longer attempt to meet in public—only in the church. Sitting on the hard wooden pew, we sneak kisses when the priest is not around. Is there a place for our love? For our future children? We confer endlessly back and forth until he opens his palm and offers me a beautiful gold band.

R.J.

In Boston, there are no "whites only" signs; somehow, you're supposed to see the invisible lines drawn throughout the city. Of course, I didn't notice them until I had Margaret on my arm. We never could predict when it would happen: a snicker, a shout, and one time, a bottle thrown towards us. We ran to the nearest church, a Catholic church no less. But I don't care, I'll sit anywhere with her. Sure, my heart's near jumping out my chest, but next to her everything feels right.

My folks refuse to meet Margaret. I implore them to understand she is light, of an Oriental complexion, that she dated only white boys, has white friends—our children will most likely resemble any other white child. Back home in Arkansas, as in many other states, it is illegal for coloreds and whites to marry; it just isn't done. You knew the rules and the consequences for not adhering to them. It is the way of life: coloreds in one place, whites in another. You don't question it, like you don't question clouds in the sky.

. . .

My pop, usually taciturn, explodes on the phone: "Your mulatto woman and mongrel children will not be welcome in our house!"

Mama in the background tries to calm him, saying, "He's our son, please, stop. He is our son!"

Mama takes the receiver. "R.J., a colored and a Catholic, what are you thinking?"

Thinking? I wasn't thinking at all. With Margaret, all I can do is feel: her warmth, her spirit, and faith in God stirs me more than I can say. To say the least, the conversation with my parents didn't go over very well.

She wanted someone's blessing. Driving up the coast to Portland, Maine, to meet her family, I can't stop looking at her; I must remind myself to keep my eyes on the road.

It is a shabby apartment. We sit in the kitchen. The window is open, the chairs are the kind that stick to your skin in the summer, and the green linoleum floor is worn and splitting. I sip my coffee.

I address her mother. "It is mighty fine to meet you."

Her mother lights a cigarette, doesn't smile. She has a somewhat fair complexion, not unlike Margaret's.

"Oh, Mother, please don't smoke. R.J. is extremely allergic." Margaret's voice is soft and cautious.

Her mother inhales deeply, exhales right over our heads before she grinds the cigarette in the ashtray. She gave me a rather cool reception. We don't stay long, say our goodbyes, and drive on to Margaret's father's house.

It is a decent-sized house with a wide-open porch. Blue hydrangea bushes line the steps. Her father, a dark Negro, is quite amicable. This is the first time I ever shook a Negro's hand. Wasn't something you did back in Arkansas. A Negro could get run out of town for initiating a handshake with a white, or not stepping aside for a white to pass on the sidewalk. Even a white child.

MAGNOLIA, ARKANSAS, 1940

I clutch my penny candy bag on my way home and spot a tall Negro man walking towards me from the opposite direction. I freeze in fear. My mama was terrified of Negro men and did her best to keep clear of them. She told me they were capable of committing terrible acts against white women, things she couldn't say. What about me? What would they do to me, a little boy? He stepped aside onto the street. And I kept on walking. It was the first time I felt powerful.I had a bad birth, came out crooked, and Mama almost died. All the surgeries as a baby paid off, though I do not recall any of them, and as a result, I walk with a limp and I have to think to make my back straight, otherwise my right-side hunches. My limp became almost unnoticeable due to joining the marching band at school. I held my spine as straight as I could, blaring the coronet. I was not an exemplary player, though I did manage to squeak out most songs. My mama said it was good for me, would teach me to walk upright, though we had to save money to pay for the coronet. I wanted to fit in with my classmates, but their favorite term for me on the playground was "hunchback." I came home many a day in tears.

Mama said, "Don't you pay them no mind."

My pop as usual said nothing.

You didn't socialize with Negros after a certain age. I could no longer play outside with them, and when I asked why, Mama said, "It just isn't done." And that was that. She shut the door, wiped her hands on her apron and the two worlds became separated for me more than ever.

Separate wasn't anywhere near equal. We knew it, and we accepted it, that the Negro must be an inferior race as proven by their inferior circumstances. Woe to the colored that misstep his place.

Mama's laughter rings through the house as she enjoys her weekly bridge game; cards slap on the table.

"Imagine that! A Negro driving a Cadillac down the middle of Magnolia Square!"

"Not any of our husbands have managed to secure that model."

"Are you sure he didn't steal it?"

"Quite blasphemous if you ask me."

"Well, you know *they* will take care of it."

"Yes, indeed."

I hear snippets of conversation from Mama and her friends, wondering who *they* were.

"R.J., a car is on fire!" my Boy Scout buddy shouts from the screen door. "Come on!"

I race behind him to the colored side of town, and sure enough a car is aflame in the middle of the street. A group of Negroes surrounds it, some trying to put it out with buckets of water, others watching it burn.

We walk up the hill where a few white men stand with their arms crossed. I spot a red gasoline can next to them.

"That will keep 'em in their place." One man's boots stand firm on the ground; he takes a swig from his flask. "Next time, he won't be so lucky; he'll be in the car!"

His hat shades his face, can't make out if I know him or not. His friend chuckles.

A police car rolls to the side of the commotion below. The

sheriff gets out, nods at the men on the hill. They pick up the gasoline can and take off in their Ford, the car most folks drive, most folks can afford. It is the same kind of car they bring in for my pop to fix and I tinker with at his garage. It was the first time I realized who *they* were, who took care of the Negro that had dared to drive his Cadillac down Main Street—*they* were *us*.

Smoke billows from the car on fire, it burns my eyes.

"Come on, R.J." My buddy jerks my arm, saying, "I got twenty-five cents. Let's get ice cream."

We race down the hill to the drugstore, past the smoking car, the stern Negro faces, and the sheriff leaning against his car. I try and keep up with my uneven gait, but he beats me to the store. I kick him hard in his back when I catch up to him.

"Hey, why'd you do that, R.J.?" He starts crying.

"That's what you get for winning."

That'll teach him. I don't want his damn ice cream.

I earned my keep by helping Pa out in the garage. I can't stand the smell of oil to this day due to all the time I spent under greasy cars. He expected me to make my own way, like he did, like our forefathers.

"You're a descendent of a great Confederate senator. Your great-grandfather from Tennessee!" he would proclaim. "Ralston lost everything in the war, slaves, everything! He survived a Yankee prison and climbed his way back up!"

That is how he responded when I asked him for tuition. As if tuition were something I could beat out of the ground. My mama was the peacemaker.

"Oh, you stop all this fuss," she said to him and gave me what she could at the end of the month after bills were paid, in secret. Not much though, so I left for the Texas oil fields.

Explosions gave me headaches, hurt my ears. I constructed

demolition sites, blowing up the ground at precise times, or I could blow, too.

"That was a close one, Einstein."

That was my sobriquet since I was the only student. The others liked to rib me because I did not chew tobacco like them, it made me nauseous. They spit, drank beer, and talked dirty. Rough guys, glad they liked me. And I was able to pay for tuition. I suppose I did beat it out of the ground.

Pop told me that when our ancestor Ralston returned, all that was left was a barren peach tree and a skinny cow, and he got back up and scraped his way to the top again. He is the only blue blood in the family; the rest . . . Well, not much to talk about.

Margaret's father holds out his hand, and I take it.

"Very much obliged to meet you," I say, trying not to tremble.

Wish I had wiped the sweat off my palm—Too late. His grip is firm, hand large, his white teeth gleam as he smiles.

"Margaret has told me a lot about you R.J."

He does not refer to me as "sir." He is, after all, a northern Negro. He has the darkest eyes I have ever seen. We release our hands; I place my palm on Margaret's back as we enter the foyer. His wife is gracious, and the house is somewhat impressive with antique furniture and paintings on the wall; the couple is certainly more than comfortable.

He is interested in my physics work and is somewhat of an engineer without the credentials and teaches auto mechanics. He is unlike the Negroes that worked in my pop's garage. Pop said they were unreliable thieves with no ambition; he could hardly keep any on. He showed us the car he built, and it is quite remarkable, a convertible. He took us for a drive but didn't say a word relating to our pending marriage.

The next day, I have Margaret all to myself. I insist we rent a boat on a lake in Brunswick. She is a stunner in her bathing suit. I can barely control myself; her shining brown skin and girlish laughter move me so—but my mama taught me to be a gentleman. Margaret is hesitant to get in the boat. She dips her toe in the water.

"It is said this lake is haunted by Ophelia, my great, great grandfather, Augustus's, first wife. She tried to drown herself. She died, most likely of pneumonia. A few people have drowned here. And you can hear her cry at night with the wolves." Margaret shivers.

She believes this nonsense?

"Margaret, I promise you no harm will come to you with me. It is just folklore after all, there is no such thing as spirits." I hold out my hand, and she steps gracefully into the rowboat.

Margaret swirls the water with her fingers, making tiny spirals. For the first time, we are safe, away from the scrutiny of her family or mine. The water holds us and accepts our love.

Margaret makes jokes pretending to spot Ophelia, exclaiming, "There she is! Don't you see her, R.J.?"

"Why, Margaret, I must have just missed her." I play along.

We laugh, she continues the game, and I never want this moment to end.

Our last stop is her brother Hank's place. After the visit, I wish we never came. Hank is despondent about the future for our children. He grips the neck of a beer, his breath rank, swaying in front of his apartment building.

"Our cousin went down South to visit his buddies, and he never came back. He was wearing his uniform, fought in the Korean War. They dragged his body down the road, rope tied to

him. That's what your people do. HE NEVER CAME BACK!
Wasn't the war that killed him, it was your people, and you
want my blessing?"

He's much taller than me; is he going to attack me?

Margaret intervenes. "Hank, stop, stop it now. R.J. is not
like that, please . . ."

He steps back, finishes his beer. "There will be no place for
your children in this country, no place at all."

Hank walks up the apartment steps. Margaret calls after
him. He slams the door. As she descends the stairs, I can tell
she is crying. Her family is as much against our marriage as
mine.

Margaret is quiet all the way home. By the time we arrive in
Boston, it is dark, I park the car in front of her place.

"That didn't go as I had expected," I say reaching for her,
hungry for her touch.

She pats my hand. "R.J., I need some time to think about
things."

"Are you calling off our engagement?" I don't disguise my
panic.

"I need to pray for guidance, to make sure this is God's
will."

Jesus! Is she breaking off our engagement?

"It may be too much to raise mixed children in this country." She says, "Where would we live? Where is it safe?"

I want to say we can find a place, but I have no idea where
that place is. Every time I turn on the TV, whites in the South
show their true colors. Attacking activists integrating lunch
counters, setting fire hoses and hounds on demonstrators, and
in Little Rock, the virulent hatred hurled against the nine
Negro students attempting to integrate the high school. It
doesn't surprise me. I grew up in it, the two faces of the South:
the faithful followers of Jesus and the enforcers of Jim Crow
segregation. It never set right with me, and it never will.

"R.J., did your family own slaves?"

Her face is so full of sadness, I want to take it all from her, make it disappear.

"Why, yes, Margaret, most everyone in the South did."

"My father's grandma, Eliza, was a slave in Richmond, Virginia, and she escaped to the north to Maine."

"What does that have to do with us here and now, Margaret? I love you."

"I need time, R.J." She gracefully slides to the edge of the car seat and opens the door.

Time. I will give Margaret as much time as she wants; meanwhile, I can search for a place where our love can exist.

It was the longest six months I have ever endured. Not a word from Margaret. I inquire about her well-being; her friends assure me she is fine. I even dated another woman but felt nothing, flat, like a soda left out in the sun too long.

I receive a note in the mail from Margaret. I hurriedly tear it open—she wants to meet at the same church where we had our clandestine dates. This weekend is my chance to win her back, to show her I will provide for her, protect her. Oh, Margaret, let it be true!

I wipe my sweaty hands with my handkerchief. The church is empty except for a priest. He nods politely to me. My pulse quickens; will she show up? I choose a pew in the second row to sit in. The priest's expression changes to contempt because I didn't cross myself before sitting down, and I will not. Let him seethe. He can't make me, and I don't care because today could be the happiest day of my life.

Oh my, here she is, more beautiful than ever; she has a white scarf on her head and red lipstick. I almost can't contain myself and want to kiss her right there in front of the priest.

"R.J., I've done a lot of thinking and praying . . ." Her voice is measured. "And I am certain, with our love and God's blessings, our children will be happy: our love will make up for any unpleasantries society may heap on them. My father has told me he will walk me down the aisle. But R.J., you must accept that your family may never come around, that you and I may never be able to return to the South together. Are you willing to sacrifice family ties?"

Oh, my Margaret, to have anything precious in this world, one must pay. And I had no intention of living in the South again, even before I met you.

"My life is with you, Margaret," I respond, not caring that tears flow down my cheeks.

We face each other, our foreheads touch, my palms are warm against her cheeks, and we kiss, unaware of the priest or anything in the world against us.

"Shame, shame! Shame on our family name. I will have no part in this, R.J. This is all your doing!"

My pop's last words on the phone boom through my head as my Margaret walks down the aisle towards me with her father, as the organ music swells to a crescendo, and my heart is in my throat. What does it matter what my pop says? He never talked to me anyhow. To hell with everyone—all a bunch of hypocritical ass—

She glows like an angel on her father's arm. We couldn't get married in the church because I'm not Catholic, so we have the ceremony in the small rectory. I don't care, I'd marry her anywhere.

HENRY

Bridges

Bells ring as we walk down the aisle, each step bringing her closer to her destiny. R.J. is puny, yet handsome in a boyish way. He shifts his weight, straightens his back —oh yes, Margaret, he is quite taken by you. He will provide for you—that I can be sure of. The rest, well—she says she loves him.

I made sure he knew I was not the kind of Negro that kowtowed to anyone, not a step-and-fetch-it or a brutish illiterate. My wife was aghast that I allowed a Southern cracker in our house. I tell her the more bridges we can make in this country, the better off we will all be. And how can I stop Margaret from loving him? You can't stop love: it is an undeniable force, an electricity of the heart.

Aren't we something? A Black man walking his daughter down the aisle to marry a white man, a southerner no less. Who would have predicted such an outcome? Somehow love manages to shine through all the hatred in this country, yes it does.

PART FOUR
SKY

Love in
A few words
Is in a few hearts
—Scot William Terrell

R.J

BOSTON, MASSACHUSETTS, 1962

It was the damn banging from the impudent child downstairs that made us move from our apartment on Newberry Street in Boston. Banging at all hours of the day—early in the morning! What in the devil's name are his parents giving him to play with? A hammer? For God's sake that insolent child needs to learn some manners. I've told the parents many times that their child is causing us a great disturbance. Still, the banging continues. Margaret doesn't seem to be bothered by it at all. She dotes on our first-born Joan and is pregnant with another that I hope is a boy. She spends her day caring for Joan, sewing her dresses, and is insistent that Joan's hair is cut short like Mary Poppins. Joan is fair skinned, but her hair does have a Negro kink to it. Margaret doesn't want to draw any more unnecessary attention to us—we receive enough as it is.

At times, we are not admitted to restaurants; one look at Margaret and the proprietor grimaces: "We don't serve coloreds here." Or walking down the street an onlooker shouts: "Go back to Africa!"

We soon learn the safe routes in Boston and avoid the Irish section of town altogether. Boston Park is our haven. Little Joan likes chasing the pigeons and feeding the ducks and swans. Still, at home the incessant banging continues. I've had it and start looking for a house to rent in the suburbs. Over the phone, the realtor is quite certain we will find a place.

However, the moment he sets eyes on my wife and child, his tone changes: "We don't rent to coloreds here."

Two-faced northern liberals! So far, we have visited three towns and have been denied. Margaret suggests we try the town churches, that surely the Catholic church will embrace our family.

Margaret makes sure we are all impeccably dressed, ironed shirts, creases in my pants, and Joan and Margaret wear identical blue dresses with two gold cross necklaces around their necks. The priest shakes my hand and invites us into his small office. He sits behind a wooden desk, a large iron cross hangs above him.

Margaret speaks, "Father, we are a Catholic family, my daughter has been baptized, I was raised in the Catholic church, and we are seeking a community that will accept us, a place where our family can thrive and practice the Catholic faith."

The priest clears his throat, shifts in his chair, and shakes his head dismissively.

"There are churches for your kind elsewhere. I cannot help you." He stands up, opens the door, obliging us to exit.

Margaret points to the huge cross on the wall, "Would Jesus accept us? I believe he would. What do you say father?"

Margaret is shouting, and this is the first time I have heard her raise her voice.

"Come now Margaret, let's go."

I guide her out of the office, the priest's face is as red as a raspberry. Little Joan starts fussing. Margaret picks her up and sings softly to her.

We almost gave up. It was the Unitarians that came through for us in a colonial town with great sprawling fields, trails in the woods, and old Victorian houses tucked away behind trees. We meet the minister at a large stone parish that must have been built in the early 1800's. The minister offers us hot tea and has a gentle unassuming manner. Little Joan squirms out of Margaret's arm and sits on a tiny wooden rocking horse that creaks as she rocks it forward and back.

I tell the minister of our trials, and Margaret chimes in, "We are looking for a place our family will be accepted, where our children will be safe."

The minister seems as if he will cry and extends his hand to Margaret. "Our parish gladly welcomes you and your family."

He gives me the name of a local realtor and we find a house to rent near an open field and woods. Finally, peace and quiet, I was so glad to be rid of that banging nuisance.

1978

There were too many, one after the other. Sure, they came out light enough, a sigh of relief. Though it is a shame no one inherited my blue eyes. I wanted a son, and she gave me two, and two girls. Not quite sure what to do with all of them. I need quiet when I come home, quiet. Every man deserves that after a hard day's work; besides who else is providing for the family? It is my income that sustains us. Margaret insists on working and continuing her education, but I'm the one that suffers. She has arranged for the children to help with the chores and meals; every child is assigned a day of the week to cook dinner.

Damn commute from Boston was a mess! People don't know how to drive, use a blinker for God's sake. I'm starving—Goddamn spaghetti again! Now that is Margaret's doing: that's all these darn children can cook!

"How was your day, R.J.?"

Margaret sits at the opposite end of the long dining room table. This table cost me a fortune; she insisted we buy it so that the whole family could enjoy meals together. The children sit on the smooth wooden benches. They have no idea how much money they are sitting on.

"Fine. Just fine. Long. I'm tired."

A lugubrious bunch, not a word from any of them. A bit disappointing, none have taken to academics, except Ella; she shows some promise for a girl. She can play the piano decently. The rest, what will become of them? Adam, the eldest boy, is too busy smoking and who knows what else. Claude, the youngest, has strong wit, but none of them show an aptitude for math. Joan, the eldest, frustrated me by asking for help with her homework. Margaret scolded me for calling her stupid. I didn't understand why the girl couldn't grasp an elementary concept. I didn't need help as a child: why should they? A path unfolding right in front of them to take—decent schools, advanced academics. If only I had such opportunities as a youngster, I wonder where I would be now? Despite it all, I still managed to get a PhD in physics, not bad, not bad at all.

Margaret seems to think that they can be whatever they want to be. I don't think we should be putting those fancy thoughts in their heads. How will they make a living?

"Pass the salt."

Nobody moves.

"I said, 'pass the salt.'" How impudent! Don't they hear me? "Pass the SALT!"

"R.J., calm down." Margaret's voice is barely audible.

"None of you will amount to anything, will you? Don't come running to me when you're eighteen. You will all be on your own, do you hear me?"

"Now R.J., stop it!" Margaret stands up.

One of them, I don't know who, hurls the saltshaker down the long table. It almost hits me, slams against the wall.

"Who did it? Who threw it?" I stand up at the end of the table, and they have the audacity to laugh! To laugh at me!

"There's your friggin' salt." Adam, the oldest boy, snickers. "I'm outta here."

He swings his long legs off the bench; the rest follow him. He's gotten taller than me, bigger and stronger.

Well, good riddance then, more food for me. The children have gotten out of control. Margaret stands, drops her napkin on the table.

"Happy now?"

Oh no. I've done it again. Margaret is angry with me. For what? What did I do? I just wanted the goddamn salt.

"Margaret, please talk to me."

She turns the page of her book. Her coffee cup sits at the edge of the side table; she takes a sip. I don't know how she can drink coffee this late at night; she says it doesn't bother her. Her brown skin shines against her ivory night slip—the one I like, that makes her skin glisten.

"Telling the children they won't amount to anything is unconscionable. They are teenagers, you are their father! You deserved to have that saltshaker thrown at you."

"Margaret, I'm sorry, I promise I won't—"

"Do it again? How many times have you said that? When will it stop, R.J.? When?"

"I work hard, and I come home, and I—"

"I work hard, too! And I don't berate the children or *anyone* for that matter. . . . What is wrong with you, R.J.? What?"

I've made her cry again. I hate it when she cries.

"Please don't cry Margaret, please."

It rips my insides. I can't explain it.

"It isn't normal to behave that way."

She turns off her lamp, so I no longer see her satin slip. She curls up to the side of the bed. I can still smell coffee.

Margaret

Cardinal

"You made your bed, now sleep in it."

I hear my mother's voice, first thing this morning. This is my time to be alone, gather my thoughts, drink my coffee in the kitchen. The birds tentatively begin their morning praises before it is time for me to go to that suffocating office.

Yes, Mother, I know. I chose to marry him. Yes, I know you warned me. I thought my love for him could change him—apparently not. He showed little signs of belligerence in the beginning. How was I to know?

Mother's been long dead, passed away from pancreatic cancer; I forgave her in the end. She was awful, an alcoholic, violent—but I put that all behind me. Still, her voice comes to me as if she were here. My father passed, too; only came to see the kids once. Not surprising though: he barely visited me.

A bright red cardinal lands on the grey wooden bird feeder and chases the little birds away. The bird feeder was here when we bought this house. I'm glad we kept it, though it is quite old and leans a bit. I must tell R.J. to reinforce it, to make sure it won't topple over. That's if I speak to him again. Ha! That will teach him!

Keep your chin up, Margaret. Don't let him get to you. My doctor warned me my blood pressure is quite high, and I need to cut out salt, of all things—quite ironic. He can have all the salt he wants. It's the children I worry about; they come home reeking. I know they've been smoking that marijuana . . .

It used to be simpler when I had faith, praying to the Virgin Mary—that was magical thinking. A year interning at an emergency room cured me of my belief in God. Watching little babies die ended it. We die. That is it and no one will save us. Maybe no one can save anyone.

That is another bone of contention between us: he can't stand the fact that I am an atheist now, that I refuse to engage in those fanciful childlike beliefs any longer. I am a realist. What people need are social services: food, shelter, clothing, health care, education. If my mother had help, if she weren't left destitute and had received support, education—perhaps she wouldn't have taken up drinking.

I need to get these kids through high school. College? I hope so because education is the only way out. I got out and so can they. I have my own dreams, too. R.J. has a PhD, and so will I. I am determined. Once I get the children through high school, it is my turn; I will obtain a PhD to create policy that will support women and children.

The cardinal has his fill of seed, clenches his claws around the tiny grey pole at the bottom of the feeder, tilts his head inquisitively, and flies off.

CLAUDE

LONGING

SAN FRANCISCO, CALIFORNIA, 1990
I am the last of four. Wriggling out with a beam of light. Caught by strange arms, in a white room, soon suckled to my mother's breast: home. Siblings surround my crib. You tickle me, I squeal, almond eyes shine.

"Children, that's enough. Your baby brother needs to rest. Go outside and play."

I breathe in her sweet scent of coffee and sugar, my mother. All warmth dried up when you put me down. Wailing, wailing for soft arms and sweet smell.

"Shh, shh, baby," Ella, the smallest one with almond eyes, whispers.

Mom sings sweet songs to me. I sing back to her, and she smothers me with kisses.

"Oh, my special boy."

She straps me in a small seat attached to her bike, and we

glide down the sidewalk; every so often, she stops to make sure I'm OK and tells me we're going to the playground. I listen for her songs. She is a haven for all four of us children: her arms, her songs, her breath, her warmth. With our father, we are like vigilant soldiers trying to predict his next outburst.

Bare feet on dirt, we chase each other in the field by our house, all four of us. Inside we freeze—stop—don't exhale—wait to see what happens—when will it happen?

"Varmints!" he growls, takes off his belt—we fly in four different directions—not a game like the one outside.

My sister Ella takes my hand; we crawl under the bed. Brown slippers smack the floor. We stay there until it's dark and she comes back and brings the warmth back to the house.

"You two, what are you doing under there?"

I crawl to her voice, crying. She picks me up. I melt into her arms. Ella grabs her leg. "R.J., what happened?"

"I don't know." He sharply turns the page of his book.

"They were under the bed, why?"

"Honestly, Margaret, you expect me to keep track of all these children?" His voice sucks the air out of the room.

"Silly children under the bed. Are you playing hide and seek? Is that it?"

Her cheek is warm against mine; I want to stay there forever.

We were the first and only interracial family in town. Got called the N-word at school, and my older brother, Adam, took the brunt of it. He was mercilessly bullied, beaten daily after school, until one day he snapped and almost bit the finger off the ringleader. They left him alone after that, and Ella and I benefitted, cause no one would dare mess with his younger siblings. Without his protection, Ella and I would have been goners.

I was nine when the policeman knocked on our door, accused me of stealing a woman's purse. The officer insisted I matched the description of the thief. Never seen my mother so angry.

"How dare you come to our house? My son has done no such thing, nor would he ever!" She tries to close the door on him.

"Where was he last night at 8:00 p.m.?"

The officer is an older white man. I have seen him around town.

"You have no right coming here, no right!"

She pushes the door against him. My father storms down the stairs. The officer changes his tone.

"Yes, well, we have a description. Your son may have been involved a purse-snatching." He speaks to my father as if Mom is invisible.

"Claude, did you?" Dad asks me. He must think I did it.

"Of course, he didn't, R.J.!" Mom puts her arm around me.

"Let the boy answer, Margaret!" Dad yells.

"I didn't steal anything." I start to cry.

Will he take me away? Put me in jail?

"You have no right coming here accusing my child!" I hide behind her, trembling.

The officer puts on his hat and walks down the stairs to his police car. I wish he would slip and fall on the old wooden steps to his car, but he doesn't.

I got used to my dad being two people: a real Jekyll and Hyde. The southern gentleman and the raging tyrant.

"Get out of my way," he growls at me and my brother, Adam, sprawled on the rug watching T.V.

He kicks us as he passes by. We do not move or flinch, just keep watching TV. Fear and terror, fear and terror and TV. And more TV to numb out. Never knew when he would attack like a rabid dog and tear into us—

Until he turned into the southern gentleman, the one that smiled, asked how I was doing in school, shifting his weight awkwardly. I'd step carefully around him, avoiding his gaze. Learned not to ask him for help with my homework. He'd fly off the handle, call me stupid because I didn't add or subtract correctly; so, I thought I was stupid.

They didn't teach us any real history in school. Glossing over pictures of chained Africans in the bottom of a vessel squeezed together like sardines in a can. Turn the page. They were slaves when they were brought to America, now they are free. The end. Never sat right with me. That's why I became a sociology major. The American narrative was too sterile, too simple, and the victor of the story always white. They taught nothing about Native Americans, though they pushed the Thanksgiving reenactment on us.

The teacher gave us a choice: "You can dress as a Pilgrim or Indian."

I chose the Indian. Made my paper band and stapled a colored feather to it. Sure, a stereotype, but at least it was something, and it was all I was going to get.

Mom said be proud of who you are, of your Black, Passamaquoddy Indian, and Irish ancestry, proud and pass, proud and pass, an impossible task when there is no place to sit in the high school cafeteria, no group to join. She didn't mention Dad's contribution. She was glad she didn't have any English blood, but I got it all swirling inside me, had to make sense of it somehow. Or numb it all out.

I hung out with the leather-clad, pot-smoking burnouts and toked my way through school. I had crushes, one girlfriend, but we ended up being just friends. I was searching for someone, longing. In college I had a few more girlfriends, but there was something missing. The summer after graduating college she came to me in a dream: *I'm rowing a blue boat down a river with the most beautiful woman. She carries a silver flask; her breath is sweet with rum and her voice melodic as any great jazz singer. Her name is Vera, my destiny.*

"King," she says to me, "where are you?"

A peace washed over me when I woke up. That morning, my college roommate called me from San Francisco saying he needed a housemate. The lamp next to the phone flickered on and off. *Maybe this is a sign, this is where I will find my love, Vera.* I was ready for a change and bought a one-way flight to San Francisco. And here I am in the Sunset District starting my life. Now Ella, my sister, is coming to California, too, and I can't wait to see her.

Ella and I, the last two of the children, held each other up, though when we were kids, we beat the crap out of each other, too. We are mirrors for each other, mirrors the distorted world can't give. One glance from Ella, and there I am; I look at her, and there we are.

I take the J train to Embarcadero Station and walk a few blocks to the Mission Street bus terminal, waiting for Ella's bus to arrive. And there she is, carrying a green duffle bag, staring up at the sky. Her hair is cut right below her ears, a different look for her. We embrace. I pick up her duffle bag.

"Ella, I know you are going to love it here," I say to her as we descend the steps to catch the subway to the Sunset District.

ELLA

THREE HUNDRED DOLLARS AND A DUFFLE BAG

NEW YORK CITY, 1990

Claude was the only one that was there for me after my stint at Bellevue.

"It's gonna be OK, El," he assured me on the phone, "because we want it to be."

My goal is to stay out of hospitals. I manage to keep my nose above the tide of emotion that threatens to take me under like a turbulent undertow. *Ophelia tugs my feet, claws my limbs.* I didn't tell anyone else in the family. Once I entered the world of emotional uncertainty—when I could no longer be the child they could hang their hopes on—they wanted nothing to do with me. Oh, well.

Everyone has medicine and poison—got to watch out for people's poison, squash it before it gets to you, gets inside your thoughts, creating a track of misery that is not yours, until it sours your whole body seeking a way out. Misery does that—looks for places to settle. It detests solitude. In fact, solitude can kill it, and it wishes to live.

I need to watch out for my own poison, find the antidote trudging through this land called America, making my own path with my brother Claude right next to me: parallel rivers seeking the same ocean.

We made a pact: we wouldn't leave each other alone on this earth no matter how hard it got.

The last time we went to Maine as a family, I was taken by the lake, moonlight, stars, and woods where the wolves howl— where our ancestors roamed.

Claude paddles the canoe to the center of the lake. I take a swig of beer.

"No matter how hard it gets, I'm here for you." Claude has a serious tone to his voice.

"I know. And I'm here for you, Claude. Always."

"So, no bailing, right?"

"You mean out of the canoe?" I smile.

"Yeah."

"No, Claude, I won't. But you can't either."

I finish my beer. A faint glow of a woman's face appears at the surface, or is it the reflection of the moon? Her mouth opens as if she is screaming, as if she could swallow me whole. My spine tenses.

"Ophelia!" a man's voice shouts.

She twists and turns near the side of the canoe, golden wisps of hair swirl around her face like seaweed. She wears a crown of flowers on her head and a white dress.

"Ophelia!" the voice shouts again.

"Did you hear that, Claude?"

"What?" Claude drops his hand in the water.

"The name, 'Ophelia.'"

"No." He looks around the lake. "We're the only ones here."

The wind picks up, the canoe rocks slightly. That was the

first time I saw Ophelia. Now, no matter where I am, she's there waiting for me, to take me under. The wolves howl. We howl back, our promise seals into the night.

I almost jumped. Got to hold on, hold on.

This city cracked me open, and I'm not sure what to do. I stop auditioning. I see no point when the only role I land is the Latina prostitute, and let's face it, I can only order a burrito in Spanish.

My career as a waitress isn't over. I find another job at a Japanese macrobiotic restaurant.

I like the clean, fresh food, the hardwood floors, and limited alcohol. They only serve beer and sake. Not a lot of drinking here, which is good because I need to stay away from it; it gets me in trouble. I end up with men I'd rather not remember, like the time at Peggy Sue's, a hole-in-the wall bar in the Village. Heartthrob Matt Dillon was performing spoken word with his entourage of gorgeous women hanging on every syllable. I envy his flawless Ken-doll skin.

An older guy in a grey suit and glasses, not part of the entourage, buys me a drink. And another drink, and another, and the next thing you know, I'm scrambling to find my underwear to make a quick escape. I don't remember anything as I face the unbearable sunlight, my head throbbing, walking back to my humble room, telling myself never again.

Goodbye to you, booze that took my ability to choose. I have a hard time with choice—I keep forgetting I have one. So, I say yes, yes to Japanese macrobiotic cuisine, on West Fourteenth Street, hoping they need a waitress. As I walk in, a handsome Japanese man with long hair pulled back rolls sushi behind a bar. I immediately catch his eye.

A skinny Asian woman with glasses and bangs welcomes

me in. I put on my best professional voice and ask if she is hiring. I hand her my resume and give her some story about having to quit my previous job because I went on a vacation. Ha, some vacation. White walls, white nurses, white beds, white plastic ID around my wrist, white pills I refused to take. *Golden tendrils coil around my neck. My limbs flail under the water, tearing at her, and burst through the surface . . .*

I start on Saturday. Leaving the restaurant with a spring in my step, I can't help but smile at the gorgeous sushi chef. He winks at me on my way out.

Steamed squash, kale, brown rice, carrot dressing, vegetarian sushi, tofu pie, and twig tea. This is my new life. I take on the world, one macrobiotic step at a time. One day at a time, one moment at a time, surrendering to some power greater than myself which, by the way, is not a man, definitely not a white man. I need something else to pray to, but all that pops into my mind is Jesus with a beard from my Sunday school coloring book. Though I did feel something when we would all hold hands in a circle, reciting the Lord's Prayer at the end of service. Maybe I need to pray to a circle.

Stars come in as inconspicuously as possible. Elvis Costello sits at a corner table with wide, black-rimmed glasses. I serve him his sushi rolls and miso soup like he's just a regular. It is New York code: never gawk at celebrities. Susan Sarandon waits in line for takeout. Nobody approaches her; she waits like everyone else, in sweatpants, a long jacket, sunglasses, and her hair up. Maybe this is a sign, that I am working here for a reason—my big break, like a Marianne Williamson miracle. I tried to read *A Course of Miracles*, but I admit it, I didn't get through the book.

A thin, tired-looking woman waves me down impatiently

with a grimace on her face. "Yes, I'd like two pieces of sushi, kale, and a spoonful of rice."

Spoonful? Does she want me to feed it to her like a baby? I don't hide the disdain in my face at all; in fact, I am downright irritated.

"I've ordered this before. You must be *new* here."

She stresses the word "new" like she is an old Hollywood movie star, saying it with an affected accent. Is she famous? Frizzy brown hair frames her large round glasses that almost hide her sunken cheekbones. I take her order and go in the back.

My co-worker, Ethan, is the most laid-back guy I have ever met. He is from California, where Claude lives now. Ethan's pace is so slow, he shuffles along in the most hideous pair of wide sandals with thick straps and socks. Sandals in the winter? If Claude starts wearing these, I will slap him.

"A spoonful of rice?" I say imploringly.

"Oh, her." His voice is nasal and dismissive. "Put a little in a bowl with a spoon."

Nothing rattles him as he slides by with bright pink socks peeking out of his sandals. I need to be more like Ethan—not a worry in the world. Or maybe he is just high.

I get used to the regulars, like the parrot guy who requests the tiny bit of sesame seeds left over on his plate, a thimbleful, to be taken to go.

"It's for my bird," he explains.

And there are the models who come in and order one piece of sushi and frown at you when you bring it to them, as if you are the one depriving them of food, the gatekeeper of unwanted calories. This place is a breeding ground for neurosis: macro-neurosis.

They hire a new girl, Shelley, an ex-Mormon from Utah with

pale skin and doe eyes. We hit it off. We work upstairs at night sipping tea waiting for customers.

"Are you still a Mormon?" I ask her.

"Well, not ever since we escaped."

"Escaped?"

"My boyfriend and I planned the whole thing." She lowers her tone as if she is in hiding. "I saved money working as a waitress. My parents hated my boyfriend because he is not Mormon, and they are strict. So, one night after work, he picks me up in his truck, and we left!"

"Here's to getting out!"

We clink teacups.

We imitate customers, making a guessing game of it, "parrot guy" or "repressed model," sending us into hysterics. It gets us through our shifts.

Until the last one. Parrot guy comes in and, after eating, as usual, asks for a few seeds to take to-go. Shelley finds the largest to-go container, scrapes the tiny seeds into the box, and places it in a huge shopping bag.

She hands it to him nonchalantly with the check. His face turns beet red as he fumbles through the bag, searching for his bird's meal. I double over in hysterics, steadying myself by the steaming squash. The manager has a puzzled expression. Parrot man approaches her, pointing to the bag, complaining. I can't stop laughing. At the end of our shift, on our way out, the manager stops us.

"Give me your aprons," she commands.

I turn to Shelley; we both untie our aprons from our waists and hand them to her.

"You two are fired."

"But why?" I ask.

"For laughing too loud."

That is a new one. Shelley suppresses a giggle. I wink at the sushi man on the way out.

OK, this is not the first waitressing job I've been fired from. I can only go up from here. New opportunities await me. I am exactly where I am supposed to be. I cram my head with affirmations to push down the panic rising in my throat.

What I love about twelve-step groups is that public breakdowns are OK. I'm good at them. In fact, people thank me after I share my unemployed status and my ramblings around the city, waiting for something like a character in Beckett's *Waiting for Godot*.

A lady sitting next to me mentions her therapist, my ears perk up. Maybe I'll learn something. Can't afford my own, so secondhand therapy is at least something. I remain in my seat after the meeting. My tears keep flowing. Once they start, they are hard to stop. *She grasps her thin fingers around my leg, jerks me down.* My throat constricts. I need to get out of here, onto the street, I need to sing, to push this out before, before— . . . Too late. She won. *Legs intertwined with mine, bony fingers around my neck, her white dress balloons around me.*

> *My sweet little babies sold by the devil,*
> *how empty my arms are now.*

Her haunting song—

How long have I been on the floor? I don't remember getting home. A heaviness in my chest lingers. Ophelia does it again. Just when I can take a breath, make a joke, feel my own space . . . Maybe it is time to leave New York. I don't want to be an actress anymore; why am I here?

"Ella, you'll love San Francisco," Claude said on the phone.

That's all it took . . . and three hundred dollars and a duffel bag.

"All aboard," the conductor shouts.

I nab a window seat. *"If I can make it there, I'll make it anywhere . . ."* Lyrics to "New York, New York" mock me. Damn. Can't get this song out of my head. Home. This train is my home now. Got my pen and paper, a window seat; here I come, California.

Goddamn it! Why is this guy sitting next to me? There are plenty of other seats. I need to sit and write, to decompress as the train carries me across America to San Francisco, to Claude.

And I have nowhere else to go, so . . . Now, he is staring at me. Shit! I quickly glance at him: thick brown hair, wolf-like blue eyes, and a stocky body like a TV actor, a teen heartthrob. But he is on a train like me, so he probably isn't. I try and ignore him. I feel him fixate on me. Hmmm. Stalker? I start to panic, feel dizzy . . .

"Woah, you OK?" He places his hand on my back.

I flinch.

"What the fuck?" I swat his hand away.

"I'm sorry. I was just trying to help." He raises both hands in the air in retreat and drops back in his seat.

"I don't know you."

I glare at him. His eyes are blue like my father's. The last time I saw my dad, I realized I could never go back home again.

The house sits on the hill in darkness. They must be asleep. I creep in, fumbling my way up the

stairs, to the attic.

"Who's there?"

The light switches on, my father growls in his blue pajamas. White hair sticks out around his head like a maniacal halo.

"Oh, uh, hi, Dad. Just me." I smile weakly.

"You could have called. Now you woke me up!" His brow forms rectangular lines on his forehead as he whispers fiercely in his southern accent.

"I didn't want to bother you."

My bag is heavy. I want to set it down and get in under the covers; that is, if my bed is still there.

"Well, it's too bloody late for that now, isn't it?"

He still uses the term *bloody* from the British comedy, *Faulty Towers*. He loves the actor, John Cleese. Dad says *bloody* with a southern accent, which always cracks me up, so I stifle my laughter. Laughing would make him go off even more.

"It's good to see you, too, Dad," I mumble.

He plods to his bedroom. Home. There's nothing like it.

They showed me off like a prized possession as I played piano for their dinner guests, plucking out Beethoven, Mozart, and Chopin for admiring ears. They attended my concerts, plays, and performances as I sang, danced, and emoted from the stage. I was the golden child, the one that made sense, the one that made it to college. That was until my breakdown; then I became a peculiar unknown specimen they could only prod, observe, and move away from as quickly as possible.

Morning light bounces of the kitchen walls.

"Ella!"

My mom embraces me. Her breath smells like sweet coffee. I want to be held longer by her strong brown arms. I don't want her to see me cry.

"It's time for my walk. You should really get outdoors. The leaves are changing; it is a beautiful time to be here."

She kisses my forehead before she walks out the door.

Words are wedged in my throat. The screen door slams. I stifle a scream. Ophelia's clammy fingers reach for me—

No. No. No Ophelia-drowning-in-her-grief ending for me: the poor fragile woman who can't withstand her emotions, timeworn Shakespearean motif. No. I'm wading this one out.

I barely sleep at night, way up in the attic with the slanted walls I scrawled poetry on. I started doing it in high school, and soon friends wrote on it, and Claude, he wrote a poem for me, too. I take a photo of it with my camera in case I never come back.

I go back to New York tomorrow. This has got to be the day I confront them, so I can move on and create a new story instead of reliving the same one over and over. My guts ache; I steady myself on the banister as I walk down the stairs.

They sit in silence at the chocolate-colored circular wooden table in the kitchen. Dad reads the morning newspaper; Mom reads a book. I grip the ends of a chair for support.

"Mom, Dad, I need to talk to you."

My words rush out, my legs feel rubbery. My brain is a mess. I was a girl, just a little girl. I thought I was ugly, useless, only worthy if a man thought I was pretty, dangling on their ego, trying to fit in their white world, and I need to tell you this, I need you to know this, so I can heal. Do you get it? I'm trying to heal, to heal . . .

My father raises his eyebrows and lowers his paper a bit; Mom has a hint of worry in her face. Her concern makes me want to stop, but I say the words that were stuck in my throat for years, letting them sprout wings from my chest. I don't know it, but I'm crying, shaking, gripping the back of the chair with my hands.

"Chasing us with your belt, we never knew when you

would . . . or what we did. I never knew why you came after us—"

"This can't be true, this can't—where was I, Ella?"

I feel my feet on the ground, anger flushes my face. "I don't know. Where were you, Mom?"

"R.J., did this happen? Did it?" My mother stands up glowering over him like a judge.

He is stunned and angry but answers like a schoolboy in trouble. "No, Margaret, I don't remember any of it."

He picks up the paper and resumes reading.

My mother pauses and, with great composure, says, "I suppose that's it, Ella. You heard your father; it must be something you imagined. Make sure you get outside today, Ella, it is another beautiful day. Now, it's time for me to meditate."

She glides by me, past the kitchen and up the stairs to her room. Water level rises, up to my nose now—lifejacket, anyone? I run out the door, feet pounding on the dirt path, past pine trees, ferns, into the woods.

Thoughts churn like seaweed in a whirlpool I'm caught in . . . What did I expect? A homecoming? I drop to my knees; knobby roots peek out of the grass. I claw at the ground digging, digging. I need to find them, got to find the buried ones, the— . . . What am I looking for? Leaves shudder on the trees. She sings:

> My sweet little babies sold by the devil,
> buried in the ground, buried in the ground.
> My sweet little babies sold by the devil,
> how empty my arms are now.

Her palms press the small mound of a new grave.

"Ophelia," a man shouts, "stop singing to that dirt now. Come on in, or you'll catch a chill."

She keeps singing, and I can't get the haunting melody out of my head.

Where are we? Train whizzes by trees, *her large brown eyes, honey skin, and golden curls reflect in the window*. I shake it off, jerking the seat a bit.

"Are you OK?" he asks.

Am I OK? Let's see, I had a nervous breakdown in New York and flailed about as a wannabe actress. No job, no boyfriend, yet I refuse to go down like some insipid frail woman archetype or tragic mulatto trope because, I guess, I think there actually might be something out there for me, beyond the 'You're so pretty, exotic, why are you sad, you're too beautiful to be sad, smile, baby, smile' bullshit. No, she will not pull me under, into her depths of self-pity and victimhood. I'm writing a different story, a story where—

"Uh, I said, are you OK?" His eyes have a hint of crazy or terror in them, or maybe it is concern. I'm not sure.

"Look, I just need to be alone."

"You picked a funny place—"

"Huh?"

"To be alone on a crowded train?" he says emphatically.

Oh, God. This is gonna be a long ride.

We arrive in Chicago in the morning, and I will transfer trains to California, where I can lose him. I can't sleep, not with him beside me, I just can't. I put on my Walkman and play INXS. I really want a smoke. I get up and go to the snack bar, buy a pack of Camel Lights, and go to the lounge.

"Chicago, transfer to California Zephyr!" The conductor

collects tickets on the back of seats as he intermittently makes the announcement.

Freedom! I quickly reach for my green duffle bag and haul it down, ready to get off the train. The guy is not fazed, has his nose in a book. Guess this is our goodbye. Though I don't want to say goodbye. Hell, I didn't want to say hello. He doesn't stir. The train comes to a halt, and passengers retrieve bags and suitcases from the rack above and fill in the aisle. Careful not to bump the lady in front of me with my duffel bag, I move along, so ready to get off this train and get some air before I transfer to my new life.

I board the next train and find a window seat. Exhale, stretch out my legs. A thump startles me. It's him. He shoves his bag on the rack above, slides down in the seat across from me and folds his arms nonchalantly across his chest. His biceps bulge out from his T-shirt. I try not to notice.

"Looks like we're going to the same place." His face is slightly triumphant.

"California?" I don't hide my dismay.

"Don't worry. I won't bother you. I'm just gonna read."

He takes a book out of his backpack; his chiseled jawline tightens as he reads. Every so often, I check his resolve, quickly scanning to make sure he's not wavering, but thankfully, he reads. He has good concentration. I even allow myself to sleep.

My arms and legs are outstretched like a starfish; silver fish dart under my chins. A whisper—a warning? Too late! She snares my arm, I jerk my limbs around, shriek—no one hears.

I double over, gasp for air—

She's got me. I clutch the side of the seat, the metal bar is cold, reassuring. I steady myself and manage to sit upright.

"I'm fine," I lie.

I feel his body heat, smell a faint whiff of deodorant.

"Let me get you some water."

His pant leg swishes past my knees as he gets up. I'm stupe-fied, still gripping the handrail, for certainty—something solid.

He comes back with a plastic cup of tepid water. I drink it anyways. Damn—now am I gonna have to sleep with him?

"You feel better?" His voice has a sincerity to it, and those biceps—

I wonder what he looks like with his shirt off. No. Ella, no. Stop. Not another man. I'm always falling into them somehow, like a bad habit I can't break.

"Yes, uh, thanks," I say meekly.

"Does this happen to you often?" he gently asks.

"Well, ah, no. I . . . I'm going through something."

"Something?"

"Yeah."

"Hyperventilating?"

"I was catching my breath. Sorry, I don't want to bother you."

Why did I say that? Sorry? What am I sorry for? Sorry for existing, for taking up space, for—

"You don't have to be sorry." His voice is sweet, comforting like warm milk on a cold night.

I shrug my shoulders, smile nervously, and change the topic.

"So, what do you do?"

"I'm a journalist." Impressive, a thinker. "I just got back from El Salvador."

"Sounds dangerous." His lips form a solid line like he's holding something in; I don't

press for details.

"You write, too?" He points to the journal on my lap.

"Ah, kind of . . ."

"You're always writing."

"Keeps the demons at bay."

"Demons?"

"Yeah, demons."

"You don't look like you have demons."

"You don't know me very well."

The train chugs along. We are close to Colorado now; we arrive in California in the morning. I grab my purse, search for my cigarettes. He's watching my every move. How can I brush this guy off when he is being so darn nice?

"Can't you tell me your name?" He extends his hand.

"Ella."

His hand is small but strong with callouses—a hardworking hand, not some freshly manicured pretty city boy hand.

"Mark."

He doesn't let go of my hand, like he's going to kiss it, like we're in some romantic Victorian film. Is that a glint of desperation in his eyes? They turned fire blue, sapphire, like a wolf's eyes. I don't know what to believe, his words or his eyes. I retract my hand and dig in my purse for matches, a good time for a smoke. On the way to the lounge, I check to see if there are any empty seats. Passengers sleep with mouths agape, couples snuggle together. Nope. Nothing.

Massive orange-brown terrain topped with snow surrounds both sides of the train. The train moves gingerly to avoid toppling off the rails. Icicles hang like crystal spears on the edge of cliffs. Steam collects on the windowpane from my breath.

"Beautiful, isn't it?" He runs his fingers through his mane of thick hair.

"Unbelievable."

"Come on. Let's get closer."

He leads me between two train cars. Chilling air rushes in. I almost lose my balance. The Rocky Mountains make my feet unsteady. He hugs me and tells me I'm beautiful. Surrounded by the majesty of the mountains, I almost believe him.

After our Rocky Mountain moment, he is cautious with me, like I'm a feral animal that might bite if provoked. He stays on his side of the seat, reading and snoozing. I'm glad I can finally sleep.

"Next stop, Oakland, California."

Wow. Almost there, entering my new life. Claude is meeting me in San Francisco. Mark helps me get my bag down, and we exit the train.

"That was a long trip." I yawn and stretch my arms.

"Hey, can I get your number?" I drop my duffel bag. People mill about. A father picks up his son, embraces him; the mother, all smiles, balances an infant on her hips.

"I, uh, I don't have a number yet."

Which is mostly true. I have the phone number of the lady whose living room I'm staying in but not my number. He shifts his weight nervously.

"Yeah. OK, no problem."

I pick up my bag.

"Well, see you."

I walk towards the Greyhound bus. He walks in the opposite direction out of the train station doors.

Freeways curve around each other, some on stilts, which makes no sense with the earthquakes here. To the left are huge, grey, metal-like Trojan horses lined up in a row. Crossing over the Bay Bridge sandwiched between the sky and sea, the possibilities are endless. The bus stops at the Transbay Mission Street terminal.

And there he is: my brother, his brown face grinning at me, grey cap on, and above, a brilliant blue sky—the kind from a postcard, not a cloud in sight—and Claude's smile brings me home. We hug, and I pat his back like a horse.

"You're darker."

"California sun."

His brown glow contrasts with my winter yellow complexion. The scar on his cheek he got from the hook accident when we were little is faded.

All four of us are outside playing tetherball. We decide to take off the ball and swing the hook around. The afternoon sun warms the back of my legs; the grass is soft under my feet. We swing the hook, laughing. It snags Claude's cheek and rips his mouth open. Joan, the oldest, cradles his screaming face to her chest.

"Quick, someone get Dad!" she yells above Claude's screams.

My big brother, Adam, dashes into the house. I am frozen—I want Claude to stop screaming. Dad runs out of the house in a thin muscle shirt and shorts; his neck is red like his face. We move out of his way.

"Jesus Christ!" He scowls. "Everyone get in the car now."

We cram into the beige Volkswagen Bug. I sit in the back. I thought Claude was dying, all that blood pouring out of his cheek like red strawberry jam. In the waiting room, the nurse tells me to watch the fish in the tank, to stop my crying. Fat, bright orange goldfish glide by silver fish with blue-striped sides.

"Is Claude going to die?" I ask my sister, Joan.

She reassures me, "No, Ella."

Claude gets stitches that permanently mark him. The scar gives him a tough-guy look in contrast to the lanky, long-legged, curly-haired grace emanating from him without any effort.

"You cut your hair, El."

Yeah. Tired of the long-hair, princess-from-hell look, been there done that. Chopped it off, cut off the part of me that died in that hospital to grow new parts. I pretend to punch him; he fakes a fall. We laugh. We are so close in age, we could be twins: each one predicting the actions of the other from years of playing together. We get each other's jokes before delivering the punchlines.

Claude

San Francisco, California, 1990

There you are again, visiting me in my dreams. I didn't want to wake, I wanted to linger with you. *I'm rowing a blue boat down a river with you, Vera, my love.*

You whisper in my ear, "Take me home."

My heart is blown open. I know we will be together. Just need to be patient.

Time for my morning jog before work. The streets are empty as the sun begins to wake up the sky. Cool air tingles my skin; I take my usual route to the ocean. With each step, I say your name, *Vera,* all the way to the edge of the Cliff House. Waves smash into huge boulders down below. A hummingbird darts in front of me, hovers a moment, and flies off. A good omen?

A sign?

I put my Walkman on and blast Coltrane's *My Favorite Things*; his horn travels through the top of my head, down my torso, out each exhale as my feet batter pavement in time to the drums. Coltrane, every song a prayer, a cleansing, a new beginning. Down the hill, back to the Sunset District, the faint smell of eucalyptus trees lingers in the chilly fog.

If only I could see you. Please know my arms are meant to be around you, precious one. Love is still possible. It can squeeze between the concrete like persistent blades of grass, pushing through like an open fist.

Back home, my roommates are snuggled together on the couch. They are engaged to be married; good for them, they found love. I greet them, still panting from my jog, and down a cool glass of water. We have the usual morning chit chat, but I cut it short, I've got to take a shower before work.

Steam from my shower fogs up the mirror. I wipe it and try to find something to like in my face, to replace the self-loathing. . . .

And all I can come up with is you, your touch, your hands, your lips . . . My love, Vera, it will happen we will reunite— . . . It is your love that makes me go on.

Got to catch the bus, doing a double shift today at the shelter.

JOB #1

Each man guards what bit of dignity the streets can't destroy, that indestructible light in all of us. A man signs his name, hands me back the clipboard, and takes a blanket and pillow. We are at capacity: the maximum is two nights and then back on the streets until there's room again. What a cruel cycle. Some minds unravel, some were already undone, others keep quiet and still like noble kings in an untenable situation.

At night, the place exhales: grey walls, grey floors, grey cots, a slight scent of ammonia. The men's dreams twist and turn around, vying for space in the ceiling, reaching for the sky.

I punch in and punch out of the shelter. My timecard is my ticket out of here. Still, even with a degree in sociology and two other jobs, I need to give blood again this month to make rent.

JOB #2

"Hello, I'm Claude from Lightning Telecom. How are you—"

BEEEP. It is hard to get even the first line out. Last call of the night. I drop my headset and lean back in my chair. Carrie, the bouncy, curly-haired girl next to me, slams her headset down.

"Wanna drink?" she asks me in a tough-guy accent.

Sure. Why not?

A few stars scatter above the streetlights. She takes a drag of her cigarette. She's a 1940s throwback: suspenders, tweed jacket, and mustard-colored pencil slacks cinched at the waist. Her mane of red curls is as lively as she is.

"You make any sales?" I ask, trying to make conversation.

"Nope." She exhales smoke like she is letting out steam.

"Me neither. Hope they don't fire me, cause I gave my last pint of blood for the month."

She chuckles. She must think I'm joking. Her laugh is raspy, like she has been a long-time smoker.

At a bar on Polk Street, she greets people with "Hi, doll," embracing and kissing men in drag, men not in drag, and a few women.

"Carrie!" the regulars shout and raise their glasses.

The bartender, a thick woman with short black hair and black Cleopatra eyeliner, makes a drink and places it on the bar for her as we slide onto our stools.

"Thanks, doll. What are you having?" Carrie asks me.

"A rum and Coke."

She is not anything like you, my love. Your face is still all I see, all I want to caress, all I . . .

The drink is strong and just what I need: a little forgetting. The place is lively. People start dancing to '80s disco. Feathered boas fly in the air as the disco ball sparkles and turns, sending out darts of light. I feel strangely at home.

We make fun of our boss, trying to outdo each other's impressions of him sliding his hair over his bald spot.

"You two stop talking, or you'll start walking!" Carrie imitates him spot on. "Now start dialing, so I can go in the back and try to find my penis."

We bust out laughing into our drinks. Afterwards, on the way to my place, she empties her pockets to the homeless slumped over on street corners and benches. She offers cigarettes when she runs out of change. She can't bear the suffering either. It sinks into her pores like she has no skin.

We creep in quietly, so we won't wake up my roommates. I quickly throw the blanket over crumpled sheets, pick up books and clothes off the floor before I let her in. We kiss and fumble on my bed, throwing our clothes off.

"What are you thinking?" she asks later.

Her curls drape over her shoulders. I draw circles on her thighs. The din of morning traffic breezes through the window.

"Nothing. Glad I met you."

I was thinking of you, my love. I can't stop it. No matter who I'm with.

"Glad I met you too, babe."

We get dressed and go to the neighborhood café for coffee and bagels.

Carrie performs with a local improvisation group. She detests stand-up comedy because it is too lonely. Sketch comedy is her calling, and she is genius. The lights lower, actors enter the stage, engaging the audience, asking for a genre for the opening skit. The audience shouts out randomly:

"Soap opera!"

"Science fiction!"

"1950s musical!"

"Film noir!"

The performers go with film noir. She is a scene-stealer. Her body contorts in and out of characters, and the audience roars.

As the crowd lingers after the show to chat with the actors, I hand her a bouquet of flowers, now a bit withered.

"You were the best one."

"Oh babe, thank you. Give me a minute, I'll be right back."

Actors stand at the edge of the stage soaking up accolades, shaking hands, and laughing. I put my cap on and lean against the front row seats. This is magic; this is where I belong. I performed in a few plays in college. Ella says I'm a natural and that I should keep acting. I miss it. I will start auditioning again.

At night, Carrie chain-smokes, tries to push away pain, her drug-addicted father, her lover dead from a car accident. She dissolves into tears and rage, and I can't help her.

"Don't you love me? Say you love me, babe." She blows smoke out the half-open window, a sliver of the moon rests above the buildings.

"Of course, I love you, course I do."

I do? Yes. No. I don't know. I just want to fucking sleep.

"Why is the lamp flashing?" She is a bit calmer, resting in the nook of my arm.

"It happens wherever I go."

She takes my hand and brings it to her lips. "I've never met any man like you before."

She runs her finger over the scar on the side of my mouth; it tingles.

It is not what you think. You have my heart. You always will. We belong together, don't you see that, Vera? You, my constant longing.

JOB #3

I pick up a shift at a shelter for infants and toddlers. It is a program for young children who are waiting to be either placed in a permanent home or reunified with their parents. I act as the primary caregiver, a surrogate parent until the child is placed. Our staff provides parents with counseling and skills, so they can provide a stable, safe home for their kids. I finish all the necessary training: how to hold and feed a baby, change diapers, and play. And there you two are: golden skin, tight coiled curls, Ilse and William, twins.

Ilse giggles, William sucks his pacifier in the playpen. All they need is patience and love. It is not that hard. I place Ilse on the rug. Almost time for their bottles before bed.

They climb into my lap, sucking their bottles while I read them a story. Ilse and William, I love you. Someday, I will adopt both of you, and we will start a family and create the life we want.

I nuzzle my nose in Will's tight curls. I fill them up with as much light as I can, sing songs to them till they nod off in my arms.

What is so hard about loving? How come my parents couldn't pay me a bit of attention? The last forgotten child, the invisible one. Anger rises in my throat. I exhale, make sure I don't transmit that poison to these babies.

I clock out. Say goodbye to the graveyard shift staff, and wait at the bus stop for the 22 Fillmore. I put on my Walkman, filled with the warmth from the twins and their sweet smell of innocence.

ELLA

I landed in some strange paradise, next to Golden Gate Park, bordered by eucalyptus trees that emit a sharp smell.

Claude set me up with a living room space at his friend's house. My room has a fireplace, a pullout sofa, and a coffee table. I feel like Shirley Temple in *The Little Princess* when she hides in the room in the attic, and no one knows she is a princess yet. And then the magical Indian man transforms her little place into an opulent palace. . . .

Snap out of it, Ella, you are no Shirley Temple. Got to get a job. Money's running out fast. Same old, same old, just a different town with steep hills. I found that out the hard way.

My feet ache as I trudge uphill in heels. I figure I can walk the few blocks and save money. Three blocks in San Francisco are like six New York blocks. Why isn't there a standard for city blocks? I stop at the top of the hill. In New York, I'd pick a direction and stumble across a restaurant, drop off my resume —I always landed a job.

I cross over to Market Street, next to the Muni tracks, and find coffee shops and diners but no luck. They aren't hiring.

I hop on the J train back to the freezing Sunset District. My stomach gurgles. I don't have enough for a burrito. I get off at the corner store, buy a paper, and sit in the closest café.

"Hostess wanted at Neiman Marcus Rotunda Restaurant,"

I circle it, sipping bitter coffee.

The next morning, I wake early to apply for the Neiman Marcus receptionist job. This time, I don't wear heels. I take the J train to Powell Station and ride up the escalator to the street. A drummer punctuates the air, playing plastic buckets on the corner. Cable cars wait for eager tourists shivering in shorts and T-shirts. I put on my New York don't-mess-with-me face as I make my way up Powell Street. Tchaikovsky's *The Nutcracker* blares from a storefront: the clarion call for the holidays.

A tall toy soldier stands at the door of FAO Schwartz toy store. Antsy children with anxious mothers stream in and out of the building. A toddler whines as a flushed mother carries him out the door. The toy soldier walks towards the bereft child—woah, is he a robot? Or is he human? He fooled me. The child screams louder; the toy soldier marches back to his post. I guess he is real—a real man in a toy soldier's tall black boots and bright red jacket. Blond hair peeks out of his black helmet. I detect a faint smile, I nod.

"So, how are you soldier?" Will he break character?

"Good, and you?"

"Aha! So, they let you talk." I pause in front of him.

"If I'm careful." He scans my body. "I'm Todd."

"Ella."

"I'm actually an actor." His chest puffs up with pride.

"I'm a recovering actress."

"Recovering? What are you recovering from?"

"The constant state of wanting."

"We should go out, talk shop. What's your number?"

What the heck? I scrawl my number on a receipt.

He quickly takes it, morphs back into toy soldier mode, and mouths, "I'll call you."

Toy soldier, toy soldier, toy soldier, say that three times fast. Of course, he's an actor— who else would take that job? Never dated a toy soldier before.

Can't be late to the interview. I pick up my pace.

Up the escalator, wafts of perfume assault the air, neon lights clash with the sedate elevator music. Women in blazers, newscaster hair, and perfect makeup stand behind counters. I rise up through the middle of this wedding cake-like store, reminiscent of a Hollywood set from a 1920s Follies production. Where are the dancing girls? At the top floor, walls drip with golden trim and above, an iridescent dome shines with swirls of blue, yellow, and gold: the Rotunda.

I nail the interview. The manager dresses like a politician's wife: short-cropped hair, a skirt with matching blazer, and pantyhose. She scrutinizes my face searching for flaws: I sound as white as possible.

"What a beautiful place! I'd love to work here!"

Too much? Nope. I start Monday.

Heaviness coils in my gut on the way down the escalator. I want to smile; be happy I have a job. A job that pays only seven dollars an hour, but a job. Here she comes, Ophelia the undertow. So, she had to follow me all the way to San Francisco— hah! No matter where you are, there you are. *Golden tendrils tighten around my neck.*

Out the doors, on the street, people are oblivious. I am grateful for their oblivion, that I don't have to explain this strange battle. *You will always be a nobody. You won't ever amount to anything.* Oh, great. Negative self-talk, that really helps. She knows it is her primetime chance to take me under. I pass the toy soldier; he winks.

I grip the rail on the subway. *Reeds bind my ankles and wrists, tighten around my throat* Goddamnit, not again. I exhale, squeeze the metal bar harder. All I can do is surrender and know I won't be submerged forever—I will come up again. I will. Like I always do.

> *My sweet little babies sold by the devil,*
> *buried in the ground, buried in the ground.*

I cover my ears, just want it to stop, make it stop—I make it home somehow and collapse on the floor.

The phone rings, the woman who owns the house knocks on the living room door.

"It's for you," she says.

I wipe my tears and put on my "normal" face; I don't want to scare her. I manage to utter a "thank you" and take the phone receiver. Saved by the bell. I pull myself together. I'm meeting the toy soldier.

Red lipstick, black combat boots, ripped jeans, black sweater, and an oversized tweed blazer gives me a kind of I-don't-give-a-crap look with a splash of sexy, just in case. He sits at the bar in a V-neck blue T-shirt and jeans. His arm is thick from the side view. He must work out. I slide into the seat next to him.

"You made it!" He says.

His smile throws me off: dazzling teeth and perfectly feathered hair flows as he turns like he is in a cutaway from a shampoo commercial. I try to regain my composure from his blast of perfection and order a cranberry and soda from the bartender.

"That's it?" He points to my drink.

"Yeah."

"No beer, glass of wine?"

"Alcohol makes me stupid."

"Oh, I thought that was the point."

"To get stupid?"

"Yes, drunk and stupid." He tries his winsome grin on me once more and motions to the bartender for another drink. "Ella, what brings you to San Francisco?"

"I thought it would be a good place to start over."

"From where?"

"New York City."

"Acting?"

"Yup, then I sobered up and here I am . . ."

"How long were you there?"

"Five years."

"And you . . . you gave up."

Did I? After ending up in Bellevue, I figured it was time for a career change.

"I tell you if I had that opportunity . . ." He grits his perfect teeth.

"What? What would you do?" I cross my arms; this guy has some nerve.

He slams his hand on the bar. "I would have made it, whatever it took."

"Then why don't you go?"

"Now?"

"Yes, now."

"It's not that simple. I have responsibilities."

"Children?"

"What? No! God, no!"

"Then what?"

"I take my roles very seriously."

"Oh, you're in a play? Or film?"

"No, my current role."

"As a toy soldier?"

"It's an acting challenge every day to stay in character. Not everyone can do it. It's the longest run they ever had."

"How long?"

"Almost two years. No one, no one has lasted as long as me." He takes a swig of his beer. "But you, you blew it. Lost opportunity gone; poof, gone!"

He blows air through his fingers like a magician making something disappear.

"What are you, a soothsayer?"

"When will you be able to live in New York again?"

"I broke up with New York!"

"You ran! You failed!"

"Why don't you go? Go and get your dreams smashed! End up with plastic ID wrist band and wondering how the hell you're going to get out—"

"Wait, what? Out of where?"

"Once you get in, they don't let you out."

"What kind of acting class were you in?"

"They won't let you leave, but I got out. I got out!"

"Method? Strasberg?"

I get up and throw a few dollars on the bar.

"Woah, wait you're leaving? Hey, come on, I'm just being honest. You can't blame a guy for that. It's a commitment I made to myself to be honest, say what's on my mind. It's a technique."

"Honesty?"

"Yeah. I'm making a three-month commitment—"

"To honesty?"

"It is helping my scene work. I know it. I will break through to the next level. So . . ." He raises his eyebrows. "Do you wanna have sex? I'm just being honest . . ."

It drizzles, not rain but a fog mist. A San Francisco specialty. I swerve past happy couples. How irritating. Can't they keep their joy to themselves? I guess I am bitter, and according to toy soldier, I "failed." So, what, I failed! I want to shout it to the world. At least I'm still standing on my own two feet, not lying to myself, and expecting some prince to save me. My hair and face are damp with mist, *her clammy fingers send shivers through me.* I step into the Muni car, make it home to my living room, shut the door, and I'm on the floor again. I take out the photo of Claude's poem from my pant pocket, reading his words to help me calm down:

> *Oh, I love you, my sister,*
> *You are me in too many ways,*
> *And I cry too, Ella,*
> *And think of our future days.*
> *A special bond is you plus me.*

I hold the poem to my chest; her current is too strong. . . . All I can do is wade it out.

The next morning, I meet Claude at a café on Church Street. When I tell him about the disaster date, he interrupts me.

"A toy soldier?" Claude stifles a laugh.

"Never mind. It didn't work out."

He laughs loudly.

"Shut up."

I push him; we both start cracking up. We finish our coffee and walk up Market Street and take the Bart to a powwow in

Berkeley. I've never been to a powwow before. Claude says I'm gonna love it.

We follow the sound of the drum. The closer we get, the more I feel it in my chest—an opening I've never felt before.

"This way." Claude points to a park surrounded by buildings.

Booths outline the center of the circle, singers wail warrior cries. All shades are here, from black to white. We find a patch of grass and sit, unable to speak, to translate what is happening inside. Something familiar, something buried rises from our bones—our connection to the earth.

Wafts of sugar and fried bread, mixed with sage and tobacco smoke, hang in the air. Dancers compete in the center of the circle: birdlike, curved spines, soft stepping. We pass by booths selling beaded jewelry in rainbow colors; baskets, stones, crystals, turquoise, and silver rattles. Stoic brown faces stare back at us. We are drawn to a table with shell necklaces and beaded chokers on display.

"You look familiar. Ever been to the Old Town reservation?" The handsome man behind

the table squints at us.

"Nah. What tribe are you from?" Claude asks.

"Passamaquoddy, in Maine."

He is good-looking, long black hair, without a trace of pretension. Claude inhales sharply, and I put down the beaded choker.

"Our mother is from Maine; she is Passamaquoddy—mixed, Black and Irish. We don't know how much Native we are . . ." Claude says a bit dismissively.

"Well, you both look Indian. We could be cousins." He laughs rearranging bracelets on the table.

Claude shrugs.

"That's a long way to come, all the way from Maine," I say, flashing my best smile.

He is handsome; maybe we aren't cousins. His name is Francis, says he's trying to make it in California, get some work painting houses and selling jewelry to send money back home. He says there is not much there, no jobs, and winters are tough; some elders have no heat.

Claude buys a medicine bag and a red and black cross. I choose a beaded shell choker with porcupine quills. A hawk soars above us.

Francis points up. "A message from the ancestors."

Customers crowd his table; we thank him and move on.

Funny, we had to come all the way to California to connect to our Native roots. A dragonfly zigzags in front of us, her translucent wings send out tiny sparkles.

Claude leans against the side of the taqueria under the bright orange "El Faro" sign, headphones on, head bobbing. Across the street, mariachi music blares from a bar. A few men hang out outside, drinking beers. Claude spots me and we walk to meet a realtor to check out a two-bedroom on 20th and Bryant Street in the Mission District.

She stands in front of a door, next to the driveway. Keys in her hand, she turns her wrist to check the time. She is dressed in a green blazer and black dress pants. Her hair is red with grey roots; she must dye it. She folds her arms. Are we late? Claude greets her and introduces me.

"This is a nice unit. You'll like it." Her voice literally sounds like it is coming out of her nose. "And a laundromat across the street—how convenient."

I do not dare look at Claude, or I will burst out laughing. And unit? When did homes become units?

Beige carpet, white walls, open kitchen, and sliding glass doors that lead to an overgrown yard. Two bedrooms, one bathroom, and a spacious living room, everything newly renovated.

"There's a Mexican family who lives in the upper unit. You two will fit right in."

"No, we're not Mex—" Claude tries to explain.

Doesn't she see his Malcolm X cap?

She cuts him off. "You both look Mexican."

"No, we're mixed—"

She cuts Claude off again like she does not have time for us to explain our racial ambiguity. "And El Faro is down the street. It's an exceptional taqueria."

I nod and smile. We exit the "unit" through the dark hallway and back on Bryant Street.

"Muchas gracias," I say to her.

Claude shoots me a look like, "what the heck are you doing?"

"Oh, yes well, you're welcome. Let me review your application, and I'll get back to you."

She opens the door to her black Mercedes and speeds down the street.

We start out slow: a couch from the street, a discarded black-and-white TV, and plastic crates for a coffee table. I work two jobs: the Rotunda in the day and catering at night. I sing as loud as I want at home, compete with the toddler upstairs racing his toys across the floor. I fit in the Mission; no one asks me where I'm from or what I am: I slide by unnoticed. The feeling of belonging, even if false, is comforting.

CLAUDE

LOVE SUPREME

In a long black robe, I'm pulling a rope attached to a blue boat with three men inside carrying fishing poles. One man wears a large necklace with a pendant in the shape of Africa. Another has only one hand and smokes a pipe. The third sprinkles tobacco on the river. They are looking for a place to land. But there is nowhere to land. I keep pulling and wake up sweating with sore arms. Strange dream. Are the ancestors trying to tell me something?

The coffeepot gurgles, light slowly fills the room. I pick up the newspaper and sit on our rust-colored couch. My only day off this week. We are fortunate to have this apartment, even though water trickles into the ceiling in my room, forming bubbles that threaten to burst. We are lucky. We told the landlady about the leak; so far, nothing has been done. Warmth travels up my body through my spine, a calm comes over me. Peace. This is what peace feels like. A whimper, like an injured animal, comes from Ella's room. She bolts out the door, holding her ears.

"Ella, what is it?"

Her whole body convulses; she gasps and falls to the carpet.

"Ophelia . . ." Her breathing slows down a bit.

This is what Dad did to us: we were all victims of his unpredictable rages. I want to slam something. Her shoulders relax. She glances around the apartment as if remembering where she is.

"She's gone. Welcome to my breakdown, Claude." She laughs while wiping her tears.

Who is Ophelia? I don't ask her. Our minds are so fragile, like eggshells. I want to scream, cry, pound my fists at the harm done to her, done to the innocents of the world. When does it stop? Does it ever?

"I know where we should go today, Ella."

We ride the 22 Fillmore bus and get off at Saint John Coltrane Church. It is a small storefront, looks more like a café than a church. Everyone is dressed in white except us; people are friendly, though solemn. If only I could live the way Coltrane plays his horn, communicating with higher vibrations and sending them out.

The bassist plucks strings with long, graceful fingers; each sonorous note enters my heart. The piano—another drum caresses out chords so melodic and surprising, I want to shout! We all chant "A Love Supreme," the hook in part one of Coltrane's suite.

It is everywhere, all directions: flying off the fingers of the musicians, out the mouths of the congregation, through the window, down the street, through concrete, down to the earth's core, rippling in ocean waves, and beyond the stars.

Ella is transfixed. We stay for the second set and afterwards eat a vegetarian meal. We thank the musicians and the church members before leaving. I am always moved by all they give with such grace and power.

"I like jazz." Ella's voice is enthusiastic. "It was like the sound went into my brain and made more space. Like they are speaking a secret language to each other, and we get to experience it, be in it."

My body is electrified from the music, each beat saying now! Now! Now! It's all love, Ella, all of it.

We end up at a club in the Castro. Spiked hair, bare skin, lace, and clicks of high heels saturate the place. My sister takes the dance floor like she owns it. It gets so crowded you have to watch your limbs. Prince comes on, and the crowd goes wild. A figure in black lace and net stockings gyrates towards me.

"You look like him," the figure says.

"What?" I say, trying to keep up with his moves.

He points to the video screen of Prince driving a car. We keep dancing till the end of the song.

"So do you." I smile.

"I'm DonDawn" A tight band holds black curls from his brown face, almond eyes, and faint mustache.

"Like Bon Bon?" I blurt out, confused.

"Don, D-o-n or D-a-w-n, either one is fine with me."

Cool, I get it. We move to the side of the dance floor by Ella.

"You married?"

We laugh.

"No, brother and sister. Guess who's the oldest?" I ask.

"I'd say you." He points to me.

"Nope. Me, I'm the big sister," Ella chimes in.

"It's because my head's bigger than hers, that's why I look older."

My usual response to being pegged as the older one. Ella pushes me; I pretend to fall. We laugh. We all go outside to get some air. The pavement has a metallic shine to it from the rain.

"Grew up here in California?" DonDawn lights a cigarette.

"Massachusetts," Ella says.

"Orphans like me." DonDawn takes a drag, exhales. "So, what are you two running from?"

"Huh?"

I act like I don't know what he is saying. The streetlight above me blinks.

"Everyone who comes to Cali is running from something, something they want to leave behind to start anew."

"I came here to free my hips," Ella jokes.

DonDawn laughs, his own hips curving into a figure eight. We try to copy him.

"Am I doing it?" Ella asks.

"Baby, let go, let go!" DonDawn shouts. "I need take off this damn wig!"

He yanks the band and pulls it off.

"I had no idea that was a wig." I am in awe of our new friend.

"Oh yes, got lots of them. Everyone should have at least three, like pairs of shoes."

We sit on the curb on Castro Street. Most of the shops are closed except for a bar; drunken voices shout singing show tunes.

"The way I see it, we're all survivors of survivors. I am no different. Growing up Black and gay? Child, I'm lucky to be sitting here.

"Did well, in school, liked it. And dancing. Learned from music videos. Stripping got me through undergrad, and a little side hooking. Prostitution is fine if it is done well and safely with condoms.

"My first love, Rob, met him on the dance floor, passion at first step, I moved in with him quickly. I was ten years younger than him. He had HIV. I didn't care, wanted to be with him for as long as I could. We had a good five years, but he was the jealous type and when we fought . . .

"It was the last fight we had, scratched each other up like cats, and that is when I got it.

"I nursed him as long as I could while finishing up my studies. At the end, he was barely there, like an outline of the

person he was, my love. He had no use for his body, he was
done; it was his time."

He snubs cigarette out on the ground. "While I'm here, I'm
gonna make the best of it. Come on. Let's dance."

We go back into the club. The DJ spins Afrobeats, salsa, hip
hop, Gypsy Kings, and takes dance breaks every so often. An
Indian man dances with a scarf, flowing in and out of people.
Ella and I dub him Scarf Man. We laugh, sweat, until we close
the place down.

"DonDawn said I look like Prince."

Ella squints at me. "You know, you sort of do."

It must be 3:00 a.m. We take the 27 bus back to Bryant
Street.

The scar, the sad round eyes, the full lips, and nose I grew
to hate—a poison festering in me. It was a constant battle to
try and see something I could love in my reflection. Prince.
Sexy, outrageous, talented Prince. I pucker my lips and smile.

ELLA

AGOGO BELL

I learned to rock to Michael Jackson, my little ten-year-old hips rigid like cement—creak crick creak—an unspoken rule in New England: don't move your hips or show too much emotion. I already failed at the latter, sang too loud in the car to '70s soft rock, felt too much. I can't stand the music now; whenever I hear it at Walgreens, I cringe.

"I can't live if living is without you . . ."

What kind of co-dependent crap is that?

Once I start dancing, I can't stop. At Third Wave Dance Studio on Mission Street, I take my first ethnic dance class, African Brazilian. The teacher, long-legged with bronze skin and copper curls, leads us in a dance he calls the Mixing Bowl. All the colors, he says, black, white, brown, mixing in Brazil. I churn my body like his, and a blond woman in dreads flails into me. Blond woman in dreads? Isn't that a fashion oxymoron? I am trying to get to my roots here. I want to scream because no matter where I go, there she is, taking up space. Back East, she would look down on me because of my roots; here, she must appropriate them. A Black woman sneers at me—hah, she can't tell I have a Black grandfather? I almost fumble, laughing at the ridiculousness of it all.

I press my feet to the ground, exhale, let go of my jaw, swerve my hips, let it out. Ophelia's poison can't reach me when I dance. The silver, two-toned agogo bell rings, and my arms slice away obstacles like machetes clearing a path.

DonDawn meets me after class in the café downstairs from the studio. It's dark, and a few people with sunken cheeks hide in corners, scribbling away in journals like they are trying to be poets and vegetarians simultaneously.

He hands me a wig. "Let's go."

I tuck my hair underneath long blond tresses, laughing.

We run into a spontaneous party in the middle of Castro Street. House music reverberates off the pavement; sneakers, pumps, and silver glitter platforms step in synch.

"Baby girl, what are you doing for Christmas?" DonDawn shouts.

I shrug. Not about to go back home, can barely keep afloat as it is. My wig flows as I lose myself in a trance, turning in circles.

"Wanna go to Palm Springs?' DonDawn asks, as we hurl down Market Street in his brown minivan.

The city is desolate on Christmas, even mournful. Most people are tucked away with their families, warm and cheerful smiles, and brightly wrapped packages, or out of town.

"Sure."

What do I have to do anyways? Claude is back home, he loves Christmas, a chance to give gifts, show appreciation. I'm glad he can go back. Me? Well, I can't risk another Ophelia episode, trying to stay afloat.

· · ·

I call him DD, he calls me Elly, we laugh and joke about past relationship disasters as he chain smokes down 880 all the way to 5. I bum a cigarette, it's menthol, but I inhale anyway. There's not too much traffic on Christmas.

"DD, why Palm Springs?" I ask, blowing smoke out the window.

"Baby, my dolls are there and all their clothes."

"Dolls?"

"Yes, Sugababes Barbies, they are a collector's item, I've got to rescue them."

"From who?"

"It didn't work out with Bob, I stayed with him a bit in Palm Springs, he got too possessive, you know how that is, Elly."

Yeah, I do. Like that guy on the train, couldn't get away from him. Though he was cute . . .

"DD, who are the Sugababes?"

"You don't know them?" He exhales an irritated sigh. "They're from London, girl, you're missing out."

He expertly flips out a CD, reaches for another, and pops it in.

"Listen baby listen."

We fly down the freeway bopping heads to the beat, DD knows every word.

"Watch out!"

A large box tumbles off the back of a truck slamming onto the road in front of us.

"Too late," DD says casually.

There are cars on both sides of us, no place to avoid the big box. I scream, shut my eyes as DD blasts through it; pieces of plastic fly into the air, glass shatters on the road. Cars honk, drivers swerve, a silver antenna flies onto our windshield. Thankfully, the car is still intact.

"I think we hit a T.V." DD flashes me his impish grin, and we double over laughing.

It's night by the time we roll into the storage place parking lot in Palm Springs and surprisingly cool. DD gets out of the car and walks over to the phone booth to make a call. I stretch my legs, still a bit shaken from the T.V. crash, I chuckle to myself, the absurdity of it, try to figure out the spiritual significance. I tilt my head; stars dapple the sky.

"He'll be here soon." DD takes out a cigarette, lights it, offers me one, I decline.

"Who?"

"Bob, he has the key."

We lean against the minivan, it has a little dent in the front, and shards of black plastic scattered on top of the trunk but that's it.

"That box was something."

"Yes, don't let anything get in your way."

Blast through obstacles to keep moving forward on your path. That must be the lesson. DD drops the butt and grinds it with his sneaker. A guy in a yellow Porsche drives into the lot and parks next to us.

"I hope he's not too pissed," DD says under his breath.

Me too. I'm too tired to deal with drama. I just want to help him get his dolls and get out of here.

"Merry fucking Christmas."

Bob slams the car door, runs his fingers through his blond hair. He is handsome, large blue eyes, wide chest, a little short but stocky, I could see why DD liked him.

"Babe, I'm sor—" DD tries to placate him.

"No! No sorrys! You don't get to say it, you told me you'd give us a chance and 'poof,' one morning I wake up, and you're gone, disappeared—"

"Babe, you knew I was coming back, I'd never leave my dolls."

"That's it? You just want your dolls?" Bob is either going to cry or explode.

"That's not what I meant; can we have a conversation?"

"It's fucking Christmas! I have guests at home, what the hell do you want to talk about?"

"It's just—Bob, I wanted to say I—"

"Nope! You don't get to say it—"

"Want my DOLLS!" DD puffs his chest towards Bob.

Uh oh, this isn't going well, and I don't think I can hold either one of them back. Bob shuffles backwards into his Porsche and slides down to the ground, weeping.

"Don't I mean anything to you? All the time we spent together, didn't that mean anything?"

"Of course, babe, of course . . ." DD sits down next to him.

I don't think they remember I'm here. Gotta use the bathroom, I wonder where one is? I spot a restroom sign at the front of the storage boxes.

"I'm just gonna use the bathroom."

They don't respond, they are in a tight embrace, Bob heaves sobs into DD's arms.

I come back and they are sharing a cigarette. Legs splayed out on the pavement, Bob's head rests on DD's shoulder.

"By the way babe, this is Elly, Elly, this is Bob."

Finally, an introduction. I nod and smile.

"Sorry you had to see that," Bob says.

"Oh, no problem and remember, no sorrys . . ." I say.

Everyone laughs. We pack the dolls into the back of DD's van, they barely fit. Most are enclosed in their original packaging: there's a white, a black, and a beige-skinned doll like me, all dressed in disco outfits. These Sugababes are stunning. I wish I had a beige doll like that when I was growing up, maybe that would have helped, I'd have less issues. Probably not. DD has bins of clothing for the few dolls that are not wrapped in plastic. I want to play with them.

We follow Bob in his Porsche down the deserted roads to a black iron gate that opens automatically. Winding up the long driveway, shouts and a driving beat greet us. Above is a grand yellow mansion, the same color as Bob's Porsche, with cream trim. DD parks in front of the garage behind Bob. Why did DD leave this? A Jack Russell terrier yaps and leaps into Bob's arms. It jumps down and sniffs me, wagging his tail.

"He likes me. Didn't bark." I drop my hand down, so it can sniff me again.

"Oh yes, that's Buster. He's the best." DD pats his back; Buster licks my hand. "He can sniff out any bullshitter, you passed the test."

"Party's still going on."

Bob opens the front door for us, bass blares, a huge Christmas tree with flashing lights stands to the side of a white spiral staircase, wrapping paper and opened boxes litter the floor underneath the tree. It is a disco tree decorated with gold and silver miniature disco balls. Figures move in dim light, mostly shirtless and sexy women—or men dressed as sexy women. Bob leads DD onto the dance floor, I spot a comfy couch with two guys sitting on it, snorting lines on a glass table. I sink into the edge of it, they don't notice me, and I fall asleep—even with the booming beat, I'm exhausted.

The beige doll flies into the air. I'm worried she'll fall and smash to pieces, then I am her, the green glitter gown sailing down, facing grey pavement below, uh oh, this isn't going well, I try to scream but can't— DD holds his palms open, I gasp, just a dream.

"Elly it's time to go sugar."

DD stands over me, Bob is next to him smiling, sunlight fills the room from the sliding glass doors that lead to a pool. Darn, I didn't get a chance to swim. DD grabs Bob's hand as they walk past the disco tree. Sweet, they must have made up, good for them. Bob seems nice, I'm glad for DD.

I get into the van while Bob and DD say goodbye, they kiss, hug, cry, and kiss again. I reach back and open one of the plastic bins, I pick up the beige doll, sort through various outfits until I find a gown for her, not green like in my dream but a sparkling bright red, something that would match the red carpet at the Oscars.

DD backs up the minivan as we descend the driveway through the automatic gate.

"That's great you and Bob are back together again," I say, smoothing the dolls hair.

"Oh no, we broke up."

"It didn't look like it." I'm confused.

"Baby, that's because you have never witnessed a gay breakup."

"You're staying friends?" I ask incredulously.

Straight people scream and curse at each other or give the silent "you don't exist anymore" treatment.

"It's possible, Elly."

Wow. Gay people are amazing.

I hold up the beige doll. "You like her outfit?"

"Yes. But don't get too attached. She's not going home with you, but you can visit her anytime."

"Understood."

We speed down the road to the freeway entrance, I open the window welcoming the breeze.

Margaret

A few more articles to research, and I will almost be done with this section of my dissertation. Almost. A cup of tea would be nice. I fill the kettle and place it on the burner. I must have left my book in my office. I creep up the stairs, careful not to wake him.

There it is. I fold a page over to keep my place. R.J. hates that I do this, tells me it ruins the book. He's given me many bookmarks, but I never use them.

His familiar stomping rattles me, must be up now. Darn. This was my quiet time. I head down the staircase, past the landing with the stained-glass windows that he wanted to replace. I insisted we keep them, though they are quite old and I am sure contribute to the chill in the winter.

Steam rises from the kettle; he angrily turns off the stove and places the kettle on the front burner.

"There you are," he grunts.

"Good morning, R.J." I open the glass cabinet and take out

my favorite teacup and saucer with delicate pink flowers and cream swirls.

"You left the kettle on again." His fingers form a tight fist.

"R.J., I was coming back downstairs. What's wrong?"

"You left it on, Margaret! What if I didn't come down here in time? You could have burned down the house, for Christ's sake!"

"That is ridiculous. I came right down here." My heart starts pounding.

"Stupid woman! Don't you know any better? Never leave a kettle on, ever!"

"How dare you call me—"

"Stupid? You're about to burn down my house!"

"Your house? Your house R.J.?"

"I paid for most of it, so yes, mine!"

I snatch my coat off the chair.

"Where are you going?" R.J. grabs my arm.

"Let go of me," I say firmly.

"You don't have anywhere to go." He grimaces.

"*Your* house, *your* money. You can't take it with you when you die, R.J., you know that? This house is mine just as much as it is yours—"

"That's ridiculous! Who pays the mortgage? The renovation you wanted so badly? Who bought you your new car? Who, Margaret?"

"Take the car back, R.J."

I drop my car keys on the counter and pick up the phone. I'll call my friend. She'll come and get me. I can stay with her; not one more minute here, not one more—

I can't dial. What is her number? My fingers are numb . . . can't feel my left side. I drop the receiver, steady myself on the edge of the counter—

"Margaret!" R.J. catches me before I fall to the floor.

· · ·

I knew it was a stroke. A T.I.A., a mini stroke, a warning. The doctor advises me to avoid stressful situations. That will teach R.J. Now he can tiptoe around me for a change, see how it feels. The doctor is tall, broad-chested, and quite handsome. He has a genuine concern for me. Taking my hand before he leaves, he makes me promise I will be careful.

"Yes, I promise," I say reluctantly, releasing his hand.

Morning rays filter through the front windows along with a faint hum from the cars below, often speeding too fast down the road. I wish they would slow down; the speed limit is twenty-five. Although the school is right across from our house, I made the children walk around the back of the house down the road to where a policeman stood every morning for the very purpose of safely guiding children across the busy street. Cars are dangerous.

Joan, the eldest, was struck, the driver claiming he didn't see her. She had ridden her bike down the steep narrow driveway without stopping, something I had warned them *not* to do. There she was in the middle of the street, forehead bleeding, but she was lucky, minor injuries.

Still, drivers speed.

And our dog, Willy, a black terrier was hit. Killed. The children never got over it, and we never got another dog. Joan, who is quite artistically talented, painted a picture of Willy, running free in a field. Poor dog.

It is pleasant up here in the attic, my own little castle, complete with my desk, array of poems, and piles of articles I must get through today to complete the literature review of my dissertation. I purchased a bright blue kettle—just plug it in, turn it on, and in a few minutes, steam shoots out. I ordered a bed, and painters are coming soon.

· · ·

R.J. is learning to play the cello, I do find the sound soothing, a nice low sound, not like an irritating, squeaky violin. The doorbell rings, he abruptly stops playing.

"Margaret, who are these workers at the door?" R.J. shouts up the stairs.

I come down the narrow attic stairs to the second-floor staircase, gliding my hand down the banister.

"Let them in. They are painting the attic."

"Why didn't you tell me, Margaret?" His hand rests on the doorknob.

"I don't have to tell you everything. Besides, *I* paid for it."

He better not say a word, not a word about it to me.

The walls are a silent, peaceful white. The only thing that is missing is a breadbox, and a small toaster oven would be nice, too. The sun descends through the trees in the back window, exchanging sunlight for night stars.

The children are coming. I need to get the rooms ready, and Claude, my baby boy, is coming, too, all the way from California. Ella isn't coming. She won't speak to R.J. anymore. I am sure it is just a phase. She will come around.

We wanted a boy. I thought she was a boy, so active in my womb, but no, another girl, Ella, the third child. Born in a blizzard, had to take a taxi to the hospital with a plow clearing the way.

Education. I keep telling her to go back to school, get a master's or PhD; that's what I did. She won't listen, won't even talk to her father. She had such promise, good grades, played piano; we gave her much more than I ever had. Well, there's not much I can do. If she won't listen, what can I do?

My facilities are intact after the stroke, but I must avoid another one. My doctor insists I increase my meditation, since studies have shown it to lower blood pressure. He is quite handsome and kind and is genuinely concerned for my well-being, protective like a father. I look forward to our visits—does he feel an attraction for me, too? Oh, Margaret, stop this silliness!

I must finish this poem before my writing group meets. Something is not right with R.J. and never has been, something I tried to fix but can't—it is beyond me. Up here in the attic, I can meditate, write, and be closer to the stars.

Claude

Whitewashed

She wants to come, but I need to go alone. Not this time, but soon, I promise her. She sulks in bed, wrapped in a sheet, comforted by the inhale of her cigarette—and I've told her many times not to smoke in here. Her thoughts rush through my mind like a stream I can't stop. I don't want to disappoint her; I want her to be happy. She is afraid I don't love her, but I do—I mean, I think I do. I open the window, and cool air rushes in.

"But babe, I'll miss you. . . . Won't you miss me?" She stubs her cigarette out on a plate.

Of course, I'll miss you, of course. I try and reassure her; my words don't convince me. *You. You are the one supposed to be in my bed with your smooth chestnut skin, sweet smell of rum. You are the one*—What am I doing? I sit on the edge of the mattress.

She nestles beside me, "One more, Claude, one more time . . ."

She kisses the back of my neck, and I can't resist her.

. . .

Before I leave for Massachusetts, I visit Ilse and William to give them Christmas presents. They giggle as they tear open the packages. Will holds up a red truck and rolls it on the floor and over my legs. Ilse hugs the little brown stuffed dog, making barking sounds, trying to compete with Will. She makes the dog walk over my face, shoulders and back. I can't stop laughing! The joy sticks with me all the way through the flight to Boston.

"Well, I am so very glad that y'all could make it. It certainly is mighty nice to see everyone.

Merry Christmas!" He raises his glass as we all mutter greetings across the long wooden table.

Same hard benches we sat on as kids with Mom and Dad at either end like a king and queen. It is already dark outside, the sun left the sky around four. Books line the wall with titles I remember as a kid still here: *I'm OK—You're OK*, encyclopedias A–Z, and various books on physics. Mom and Dad's collection of classical records lean against the record player on the bottom shelf. I'm sure some of our albums are there, too: Aerosmith, Led Zeppelin, the Who, and can't forget the Jackson 5. Three Christmas stockings hang above the lit fireplace for me, Joan, and Adam—Ella is forgotten.

"Joan, how are your horses?" Mom asks, breaking the silence stretching across the table.

"Good. Got another crazy pony. Nobody wanted it after the owner died. So, I took it. She's slowly coming around." Joan, the eldest, is the shortest but strongest from riding and lifting bales of hay.

"It's not easy. I come home, and she has picked up another stray horse. I mean they're not kittens; it's an expensive habit." Duke, Joan's husband, chuckles.

Joan elbows him in his side.

"If I don't take them, who will?" She sips her wine.

"Where would they end up? Glue factory?" my older brother, Adam, asks.

"Dog food," Joan answers.

"Now, let's not talk about this while we're at the table." Mom's voice is soft but commanding.

"By the way, how is Ella, Claude?" Duke asks in his sharp Boston accent.

"She, ah, she's OK. Got a job as a hostess."

OK, but needs a life raft. OK, but all jumbled up inside.

"That is good to hear, that she has a job." My father's mouth tightens for a moment. "Be sure and keep us abreast of anything you need."

"Claude, have you been in any plays lately?" My mother changes the subject.

"No, not yet, but I signed with an agency."

I can't make out the simultaneous mumbles of congratulations directed at me and miss Adam's joke that got a laugh. That's how it is with big families: you got to fight to get a word in. Sure, we cut each other off mid-sentence, but it's not rude. It's just how it is.

I help Mom clear the dinner plates, and everyone brings their coffee to the living room. I make sure I don't spill any coffee on the new beige couch and carpet. That would set him off. He watches my cup like it has explosives in it that could ignite any second.

"Be careful now." He pats the couch.

"Oh, R.J., they aren't little children anymore." My mom dismisses his comment, continues listening to Adam.

"It's social, Ma, it's all about environment," Adam says. "Got to change the place to change the behavior. We're screwed. Reagan gutted all the mental health services, so now it's a crisis. The streets are lined with homeless—they dumped them all in the streets. And a lot of them veterans."

Adam has a tough-guy way of speaking, with a slight Boston accent, ready to back anything he says with scholarly references. Got to have your stats together if you want to challenge him. He was the most rebellious of us all but ended up following in their footsteps in academia. Now, he's a social worker. Good for him.

"Yes, and mothers and families left to fend for themselves . . ." Mom sighs.

Her sadness fills me. I want to take it all away from her.

"Well, I'm tuckered out. Sure is nice to see you all. Merry Christmas. And turn off all the lights when you leave."

He sends his warning to us, a light left on is highly punishable; you do not want to set him off. We say our goodnights.

"Ma, how's your blood pressure?" Adam asks.

We are all concerned after hearing of her stroke. Joan is curled up on the wooden chair; I can see her reflection in the sliding glass doors next to her.

"Well, up and down. And I think it is time," she pauses dramatically, "to make a move."

Her tone is serious.

"Where, Ma?" Adam's face has a tinge of fear.

"Up to the attic." She waits for our response.

"What? Upstairs?" Joan asks.

"To my own space. I set up my office; my desk overlooks the school playground. The children's little voices bubble up through my window. It reminds me of you kids. I've already ordered a nice bed. That way I will have more control." Her voice is calm and measured.

"Of what?" Adam asks.

"My blood pressure." She places her cup down on her saucer.

"Why don't you get your own place, Mom?" Joan's voice matches Mom's careful tone.

"Oh no, the attic will do. I didn't want to alarm you kids, but it can be challenging here with your father."

Challenging? That's an understatement. Three days max, that's as long as I can stay, all the eggshells I can manage to walk on. It's like a minefield: never knowing when he's gonna blow, always trying to second-guess him. I'm sure my blood pressure is up while I'm here, too.

The attic is Ella's old room where she scribbled poems on her wall in high school including the one I wrote for her. We agree to help Mom move tomorrow.

Adam, Joan, and I cram in Mom's old office on the second floor. It is a tiny room with one large window, a small desk, and shelves lined with books and old photos of us as young kids.

"This lamp and chair can go."

Is that a hint of melancholy in Mom's voice? Maybe this is the first step; in the next one, she'll really move out. As I pick up the lamp, it blinks on and off.

"That turned on . . . unplugged? Claude, you got some superpower?" Adam asks me.

I shrug. It's just something that happens to me. Can't explain it—*that it is a sign from you, my love, Vera, that you are with me*—especially to Adam.

"Mom, what about these golf clubs?" Joan points to a white vinyl case with a faded red ribbon. The clubs are dull silver and have lost their luster.

"Oh, yes, those can go upstairs," she says solemnly.

"Where did you get them?" Joan is always asking the questions we want to ask; we stop, wait for her answer.

"Your grandfather gave them to me," Mom replies reverently.

I never met him, or if I did, I was too little to remember. He didn't come by much. Golf clubs? Don't get it. Mom always says I favor him the most out of all the children. Wish I had met him. Wish I could have known him. Henry, his name was Henry. He was an inventor and played jazz piano, and I guess golf, too.

I walk up the attic stairs to Ella's room. Her poetry wall is painted over without a trace of Ella's words or the poem I wrote for her; whitewashed like it never existed.

R.J

"Margaret, I promise I'll be better. I won't yell—I'll cook for you, Margaret!" She won't come down, stays up in that attic scribbling away.

"No more, R.J.," she said. "No more."

I bring her flowers, lilacs—her favorites, chocolate, tickets to concerts . . . When will she come back down?

It's the children. They talked her into it, helped her move up there—ungrateful is what they are, for all I provided for them. Ella refuses to speak to me. Now Margaret hardly talks to me. At least she's still here, home. I need to be patient, like a heron waiting at the shore, patient.

I rinse my coffee cup and plate and place it in the dishwasher. Margaret still hasn't come downstairs. Well, it is time to practice my cello, pick up the bow, my fingers are stiff. I will master Bach's Cello Suite. Yes, that is my goal. The cello soothes me like Margaret's calm voice; I need to be gentle to make the right note, like her gentle touch. I play for you, Margaret, this is all for you.

She finally comes down.

"Margaret, sit, I'm making dinner. I missed you, Margaret. I'm sorry. I will try harder."

She doesn't respond, sits erect at the kitchen table.

"Have a glass of wine, merlot."

She slightly smiles. Will she forgive me again?

I don't know what happens. I explode at times, can't stop it. We were doing fine until all the children were born; fine, and then it got to be too much. She wanted them. Wanted a big family. I only wanted her. I still do. That's all I want, my Margaret. I reach my hand out across the table, my palm open, and slowly, she takes it. I make a tofu stir fry with low sodium soy sauce for her. We have a pleasant chat about her dissertation and the weather. Oh Margaret, have you come back to me?

She insists on doing the dishes.

"Margaret let me, please."

She ignores me, carefully placing the plates and silverware in the dishwasher. She turns it on, wipes her hands on a towel and walks out of the kitchen.

"Where are you going Margaret?"

"I came down for dinner."

She resumes ascending the staircase. This woman is maddening—

"So that's it, just dinner?"

She continues walking.

"Margaret, please! I miss you; don't you miss me?"

Damn! I am groveling now. She doesn't turn around.

I can barely hear her as she says, "R.J., this is the way it has to be now."

She climbs the stairs, like she's floating away from me— there's nothing I can do, nothing. R.J., you really blew it this time, you really did.

"Margaret! I promise I will change, Margaret! Please come down, please—"

"Leave him there." My pop towers over me.

"We can't leave him on the floor like this." Mama pleads.

"He doesn't remember who we are. Leave him be."

"R.J., honey, it's your mama. R.J.?"

"Those surgeries turned him feeble."

I'm sweating all over, I don't know who these people are. Where am I? Where?

"Leave him be," Pop says.

"My baby, my baby, my baby, what have they done to you?"

Where am I? I don't know where—

I'm crouching at the bottom of the stairs, all aquiver, sweating an awful mess. How did I get here? I sit up against the stair but can't stop trembling. Was that Mama? Was it? I manage to get up and get a glass of water.

"You can't take those dishes! I bought them, not you."

She ignores me, lifting tableware from the shelves. Opens the utensil drawer takes a few forks, spoons.

"That should do it," she says to herself, as if I am not right here in front of her.

"Margaret, put them down. This is ridiculous." She swerves around me. "Are you going to stay up there forever?"

She stops, turns slowly. "You heard what the doctor said. I must avoid stressful situations." Her voice is calm, resigned.

"What about a movie tonight, Margaret? I'll take you to one—"

She keeps walking.

"Margaret, come back down, please come down, talk to me, don't be this way, it doesn't have to be this way." I try and control my voice, so I am not yelling, so I won't agitate her.

No response.

Fine. If she wants it this way, fine. Besides, I'm signing up for the Peace Corps. I don't need her. I've got all my shots.

Planning to go to India with a nice group of people from the spiritual center in Cambridge. Our teacher is our guide. She is Indian. I have one more interview, and we leave in two weeks for two years of service. Margaret will miss me, I am sure of it.

Margaret is reading at the kitchen table when I break the news to her.

"India?" She closes her book. "You can't go to India, R.J."

"I am leaving at the end of the month."

"R.J., they smoke in India, even the children smoke." She closes her book.

"What do you know, Margaret? How do you know this?" What incredible arrogance she has.

"It is a well-known fact, and I can't imagine you could get along there with your extreme aversion to cigarettes and your propensity for bronchitis."

"I am sure our guide knows more than you. She is Indian!"

"Studies have shown that cancer rates are high in India due to smoking." She raises her finger to emphasize her data and picks up her book.

I'll show her! I ignore her and go upstairs to make a phone call to the organizer.

Nobody told me about the cigarette use. You would think they would disclose it before encouraging participation in the Corps. I told them explicitly at the interview that no one was to smoke in my presence. And they rejected me. I cancel the trip and can hardly stand Margaret's smugness.

CLAUDE

ROOTS

Los Latinos Agency sends me out on auditions. As soon as the casting directors realize I can't speak Spanish, they yell, "Next!" It will happen. I need to finish my affirmations in my *Creative Visualizations Workbook*. And it comes, my break: a children's theater tour. *I can save money for you, Vera, my love. Have patience.* Tights, cape, gel in my hair—action! Captain Hydro fighting water-wasters across America! The villain, my nemesis, leaves faucets running and takes thirty-minute showers.

My co-star, Duncan, is drunk most of the time, and I cover for his missed lines. I figure it's good practice, keeps me on my toes. Besides, the boss trusts me with the cash, our budget for six months. He said he could see it in my eyes that I was trustworthy. I carry it in a small black bag. I never lose sight of it.

"You can't get much lower than this," Duncan says, snuffing the cigarette butt out with his sneaker. He staggers, almost loses his balance. "I'm too old for this crap!"

Well, he does not look that old, maybe thirty-five?

"I'm moving to L.A. where the real jobs are, not this babysitting!"

I try and calm him down. "Duncan, first we got one more show to do. Come on."

He runs his fingers through his thinning hair and sighs. He does OK until the last scene: he passes out stone cold on the stage.

Teachers gasp, and I ad lib, "And this is why you should never waste water." I haul him behind the curtain, hissing, "Wake up you idiot! Wake up!"

He does and pukes all over my shoes. After that stunt, he is fired.

"On your shoes?" Carrie laughs so hard she falls to the floor. We both are in hysterics.

"I had to chuck them in the trash."

Our bodies find each other. *I keep thinking of you, I can't stop. I wonder whose arms are around you now.*

"Babe, you OK?" Carrie reaches for her cigarettes.

"Yeah, uh, need to get ready to see the twins."

Ilse and William smile when I enter their room at the shelter. Tiny hands reach from their crib. I pick them up and place them on the rug. They crawl over me, giggle, grabbing at my medicine bag and red and blue cross around my neck. I settle them down and place blank paper and crayons on the floor. They scribble on the blank paper and mumble to each other in their baby language. They let me in their sweet world. I write their names on their drawings and tuck it in my pocket.

Not so hard to show tenderness, a gentle touch, as a man, a father. What kind of twisted upbringing made my father so hateful? Heat fills my body, and I want to hit something, smash something. Instead, I go for a run to the Cliff House to visit the ocean. I cough, can barely get up the hill. I stop and walk the rest of the way home.

A storm is coming but not a rainstorm or thunderstorm: a desert storm.

"No blood for oil! No blood for oil!" marchers chant while walking down Market Street. Ella and I run to catch up with the crowd. The only reason the U.S. is in Iraq is for the oil. They don't care about civilian life; thousands of innocent people will die, civilians, *children*.

Cops in helmets line the street. Protesters bear signs: "Not My President," "Support Troops Bring Them Home!" Anarchists hide their faces under bandanas. The crowd thickens as pedestrians step off the sidewalk to join in.

"Roots, roots, roots against war!"

Drumsticks smack on plastic buckets, driving the chant. Protestors take the Bay Bridge. Ella and I push along to the ramp. In the distance, a car is ablaze, fiery yellow, orange, and red flames ignite the vehicle. Sirens wail as people start running towards us—will it blow?

"Man, they lit that cop car on fire!" A skinny white man points ahead. In the glow that emanates from the fire, I can make out the silhouette of his face, scruffy beard, and sharp nose. "I'm outta here!"

Sneakers pound the pavement; smoke fills the air. We take off and don't stop till we get to Powell Street.

"They blew it," I mutter to Ella, hunched over, panting.

"The police car up?" She stops in the middle of the street.

"Once it turns violent, we lose our credibility," I sigh.

Waiting at the bus station for the 27 Bryant, glass shattering and store sirens ring in the air. I step on the bus and search my pocket for change.

A guy standing by the bus shouts Ella's name. He scrawls

something on a piece of paper and hands it to her while Ella steps onto the bus.

"Are you coming on or off?" The bus driver is clearly irritated and ready to close the door. She steps up, drops her fare, plops down next to me.

"Who's that, Ella?"

"The train guy. I met him on the train."

Ella

Maps

I spot him in the history section of Modern Times bookstore on Valencia Street. Thick brown hair partially conceals his jaw line.

"Sorry I'm late." I try not to startle him.

He closes his book and places it back on the shelf. We walk up Guerrero Street to Dolores Park. He walks much faster than me. I try and keep up with his pace.

At the top of the hill, clouds roll over the outstretched city. So many possibilities, I open my arms taking it all in.

"Why did you come here?" He sits down on the grass and I join him.

"I didn't want to stay in New York anymore." I yank out a blade of grass.

"What were you doing there?"

"Acting."

"Are you acting right now?"

"No."

"How do I know if you are acting or not?"

"I guess you'll have to get to know me."

"I hope I will."

"What?"

"Get to know you. On the train, you were going through something."

Yes, Ophelia always circling around me trying to take me down the depths. How can I explain that to him? That when I'm up, I try to enjoy it as much as possible before she resurfaces, and I struggle to breathe, to exist—

"Hey, you alright?"

Have I been spacing out that long?

"Yeah, uh, just thinking."

"About what?"

"About how to explain the inexplicable."

"Try me."

"Cassandra. I'm the Cassandra of my family. You know the Greek myth? She takes out her own eyes because she sees the truth and no one else does. And she goes mad." I change the subject. "Why were you in El Salvador?"

"I was writing a piece about cooperative farming. And was detained awhile . . ." His voice trails. His mouth freezes, as if he has no more air around him.

"Mark, what happened?"

"They tried to make me give the names of the farmers organizing, I wouldn't . . . they were my friends, and uh, they did their best to make me speak but I didn't." His mouth tightens into a thin line; his gaze is fixed on something I can't see. This poor guy must have been tortured.

The afternoon sun gives its last blast before retreating behind the San Francisco skyline. My palm covers his fist, his fingers slowly unfurling into mine as the fog rolls over the city.

.   .   .

I relish the quiet in the apartment: no babies crying or feet thundering above. Claude is staying with his girlfriend. Mark comes to mind, our moment in Dolores Park—do I like him?

Before I know it, I dial his number. I throw away old newspapers, pick up clothes off the floor, make my bed. The doorbell rings. I check my face one more time and put on some lipstick.

I take his hand, leading him through the hallway, but he barely lets me close the door before his arms are around me and he's kissing me. His lips taste salty. I study his face.

"What?" He smiles nervously.

We kiss, tumbling onto my futon. His hands slide up my shirt and I lift his off. His chest is cut like an athlete. I want to melt into it.

"Come here," he whispers, and I reach for a condom on my nightstand.

Faint voices from upstairs and heavy footsteps try to interrupt my reverie; they fail.

"You OK?" He asks, tracing his fingers around my face.

"Yes, that was fun. Let's do it again."

"Fun?" His voice has an edge to it. "You know, Ella, I have feelings for you. I'm not playing around."

He sits up on the mattress. "Do you feel anything, for me?"

Whoops. "I . . ."

"What?" His eyes are wild, frantic.

"I'm getting to know you, Mark. It takes time."

He lets out a sigh and opens his arms. I wiggle back under the covers.

They let me go at the Rotunda, since there are barely any customers during the slow season. And Claude is moving out. He found a studio on Bush Street. I get it. Who wants to be roomies with your big sister? And I am kind of a wreck. Don't know when I'll crack and she'll take me. I try and pick up more catering shifts, but catering is slow, too. Claude set me up with an audition for the children's theater company he works for.

The theater is in a small basement in North Beach. The stage is a tiny black platform, dimly lit, with rows of red cushioned chairs surrounding it. Dust mites dance in the spotlight. Here's my chance to do my New York City method-training best.

"Read it like a villain," the director shouts from the front row, with a clipboard in his hand.

I nail it: villains come easy to me.

"Great, how about a confused bird? Like a cartoon."

I squawk around the stage in a high-pitched frenzy. He chuckles.

"Ha, great, now damsel in distress."

My body goes limp, I fall to the stage, my finale. I got the job.

Rent. That four-letter word. Always in the back of my mind. I need a roommate. Mark? It could work out.

He finishes his third beer. This is our last time together before I leave for Minneapolis with Claude. The theater company is flying us there for rehearsals, all expenses paid: hotel and food. Mark turns a bottle cap over and over in his hands.

"So, when are you coming back?"

"It's only a week."

"What is this company?" His tone is sour.

"It's a children's theater . . . Nothing big."

"Any other actors?"

"Sure, it's a theater group."

Why is he asking this?

"Any guy actors?"

Got it. Jealousy. He finishes off his beer.

"Where is this coming from?" I push my plate of chicken tacos to the side. "You know, I was about to ask you to move in with me, but now—"

"Wait, you want me to move in?"

"Yeah."

"You sure?"

I slide over the keys. He reaches over and kisses me across the table.

After Claude and I check into the hotel, we meander around a bit. It is so freezing in Minneapolis that they have hamster tube-type walkways for humans all over downtown. On our first day of rehearsal, we check in with the office manager. Posters of Cher are plastered all over his cubicle.

He resembles Cher, olive skin and jet-black hair.

The director, a plump, friendly, middle-aged man with a toupee that does a bad job of hiding his receding hairline, sits on the stage. His jovial manner puts us at ease. There are two other teams of actors. Tim, a tall man with auburn hair and glasses, stares at me. I look away.

Claude is Captain Hydro, and I am the villain, the water-waster. The show teaches water conservation to kids, so they don't cause a drought by taking long showers or leaving the water running while brushing their teeth. I use puppets and change my voice. We play multiple characters, like kids' cartoons but live. Well. It pays the rent.

After our rehearsal, the director hands Claude a small black bag. He puts his arm around Claude in a fatherly way—what's in the bag? Claude walks towards me smiling.

"What is in it?" I point to the bag.

Claude opens it carefully and there is a wad of cash neatly stacked.

"Woah, what for, Claude?"

"It is our budget for our tour. He trusts me with it, and we need to be careful."

He clasps the bag closed. Of course he would trust Claude, everyone does. I've never seen that much cash. I'd love to spend it on a vacation. Good thing they gave it to Claude.

We all break for lunch. Claude introduces me as his sister who "studied in New York . . ."

Great. Now I have a bunch of potentially envious actors to contend with. I underplay it.

Julie, an actress from Minnesota, the perfect Disney ingenue, chimes in, "Wow! New York City! How long were you there?"

"As long as I could stay before I ran out of money and hope."

Her face is puzzled. Tim raises his glass to me.

"Here's to crushed dreams!"

I laugh, we clink glasses.

"Hey, New York, wanna go out tonight?"

Tim's new nickname for me. I go with it. We end up at a club, strobe lights and blaring bass.

"I'm sorry for dancing like such a nerd."

The actors sit at a table, all except Disney girl; she is staying in to memorize her lines. Claude is talking up Gwen, an older woman with black curly hair.

Tim wipes his glasses on his shirt. Mark's voice booms in my head: "Are there guy actors?" Can't I have a good time? I'm not married. Tim is so easy, no intensity, not walled off. Time to go. We gather our coats and get ready to face subzero temperatures. Thankfully, there is a cab outside the club. We all cram in. Back at the hotel, Claude says he'll be in Gwen's room and breaks into that sheepish smile of his. I laugh and close the door.

So, I have the room all to myself. Maybe I should call Mark? A knock interrupts my thoughts. I open the door; Tim stands awkwardly with a bag of chips.

"Hey, New York, I thought you might want some."

I try to resist him. I try to resist the chips. I watch myself fail.

I turn the key slowly to not wake him. I'm a terrible liar. Once he starts asking questions, I'm doomed. The apartment is darkly lit, empty beer bottles surround him, and the walls are completely covered with maps from all over the world. He rushes to the door.

"What's with all these maps?" I drop my bags.

"Why didn't you call me?"

"I was rehearsing. It was a tight schedule."

"Not one call!" His jawline tenses.

"Why all these maps, Mark?"

Not an inch of wall space is free. He staggers, beer bottles crash into each other like dominos.

"This is home." He gestures to the walls. "This is everywhere I've been—everywhere! Everywhere I survived . . ."

He faces me. "Why didn't you call?"

At this point he is yelling. I hang up my coat and take off my hat. Smooth my hair. He must be drunk.

"I said I was busy."

"Busy! Busy!" He charges after me. "I bet you were busy. Who were you busy with?"

He reeks of beer. I back up, make my way to the kitchen.

"Huh?" He grabs me and pushes me against the wall. "Huh? Ella, answer me!"

"Mark, calm down, calm down."

"What do you want, Ella? You just want sex, huh? Is that it? Is this what you want?"

He presses his body against mine and reaches under my shirt. We freeze like two animals trying to predict the next move.

He is much stronger than me; maybe if I'm still, he will back off.

"Ella . . ."

He starts to weep, hunches over, brusquely wipes his arm across his face and gains his composure. He grabs his jean jacket and exits, slamming the door behind him. I sink against the wall and slide down, down the familiar descent to her clammy, open arms.

I barely sleep. I tear down all the maps, throw them in a pile on the floor. What have I gotten myself into? Click, the key turns in the lock. Mark stumbles in; his eyes are wild like an angry wolf.

"Shhh!" He grabs my shoulders, pushes me aside, and locks the door.

"Ouch, Mark!" His fingers grip my arm.

"They're after me. They know. They know I'm here." His lips form a tense line. Why didn't I bolt the door? "They know what I've seen, where I am."

"Who, Mark?" I try to act nonchalant, like I'm talking to a child in distress.

"Shhh! They can hear us!" He picks up a crumpled map from the floor. "What did you do?"

Uh-oh.

"I was just redecorating." I move towards the bathroom.

"You ruined them all! Damn you!" He charges at me I run into the bathroom and quickly lock the door.

He pounds on the door howling at me, "Let me in, Ella! Ella!"

He finally stops pounding the door. "You want me to leave, Ella? Is that it?"

I don't say a word. I don't breathe. I start shaking, *bony fingers clasp around my neck, Ophelia's white dress balloons around me.*

> *My sweet little babies sold by the devil,*
> *how empty my arms are now.*

Wolves howl. I cover my ears rocking back and forth to her haunting song.

The floor is cold, my head throbs, a baby cries from upstairs. I press my ear to the bathroom door, not a sound. He must have left. I unlock the door and open it slowly. No more maps on the floor. He must have taken them. I bolt the door. Shit. That didn't end well. All I can do is call Claude.

CLAUDE

KNEECAPS

I drop off gifts for Ilse and William before I go on the road with Ella to tour our children's theater show.

"Dada," William says to me.

He thinks I am his father. I hold him closer. Ilse crawls into my lap. Hard to leave them. I kiss the top of their heads and say a prayer for them. *And you, my love. I can save for us, finally enough, and you will be mine, won't you, Vera?* I place my timecard in the slot, punch out, and walk down Fillmore Street to the bus station.

The 22 Fillmore bus is crowded and steamy from all the body heat. I slide open a window, put on my headphones, and listen to Coltrane's *A Love Supreme* all the way home. I slump down on my bed, more tired than usual, and doze off. The doorbell rings.

Carrie stands in the doorway. Her lips are bright red, she offers me a bottle of champagne.

"I'm going to miss you!" She stumbles in, already drunk.

"I'll be back in a month."

She embraces me. "You're the only one for me, the only man."

Her nipples peek out of her T-shirt, teasing me. *If only you would leave my mind, then I could truly be here.* Her body rises and falls on top of me.

"Say you love me, Claude." Sheets wrap around us as we listen to the buzz of cars speeding on the street.

"Yes, I love you, Carrie. Yes, I do." This time I mean it.

Out cold, finally got to sleep; she is peaceful when she sleeps, not haunted by needs and loss. I try not to disturb her, so I can surprise her with coffee before she awakes. The phone? This early? It's Ella, her voice shaky; she's trying to keep her cool.

"I'm leaving now." I hang up the phone.

Carrie stretches, saying, "What's up, babe?"

"Ella. Her boyfriend went crazy—I can't find my keys. Where the heck did I put them?"

Carrie searches with me, finds them in my coat pocket, and tosses them to me. "I'm coming with you."

I don't argue, got to get my sister.

Steam rises on the taqueria's window from hot open grills. Voices drift from nearby tables, chairs squeak on the floor, black plastic bus buckets are full of dirty plates. A mariachi band starts: a violin, accordion, and guitar. Ella appears younger, like a small child. She rests her head against the teal blue seats.

"It's going to be OK, doll," Carrie says.

"He went off the deep end . . ."

"Do you think he's coming back, Ella?"

Her almond eyes are swollen red from crying.

"I don't think so." She takes a sip of water.

"What about filing a restraining order?" I could wring his neck.

"He won't come back; he took all his maps."

"Maps?"

Ella isn't thinking clearly; she must be in shock.

Carrie clasps her hands together, resting them on the table like she's an official at a big meeting.

"I've got connections with the Irish mob. Give me the word, doll, and kneecaps will be blown out," she whispers.

What? Irish mob, kneecaps—Ella looks at me dumbstruck, and we can't help but laugh.

"I'm serious. You just give me the word, doll." Carrie smirks at us and finishes her beer.

Ella dips a chip in salsa. The violinist walks to our table, serenading us. I drop a few bucks in his hat.

"We'll be on the road soon," is all I can manage to say.

"Here's to the road," Ella says, lifting her Coke.

ELLA

Think. Think. Think. I need to think, but all I can do is clean. His clenched jaw and him pinning me down flash into my head as I scrub the kitchen floor, air out the apartment, and sage it three times. I pick up clothes off the floor, gather the towels in the bathroom, and walk to the laundromat across the street.

Women fold clothes, speaking in Spanish. A chihuahua sniffs my feet. I put my first load in; the humming of the dryers and washing machines calm me a bit. Glad to be getting away—leaving tomorrow morning.

"Ella," someone whispers my name.

There he is at the door: a T-shirt, a jean jacket, and a backpack. I can't move. He walks in the laundromat as I lean on a warm dryer, a woman checks him out the way women do when a man enters the room. Vroom vroom, the dryer reassures me.

"I came to see how you were . . ."

I have no voice. He reaches his hand out to touch me. I flinch and gasp. How am I? How am I?

"I'm heading north, probably won't be back for a while."

Am I supposed to feel sad about this? What does he want from me? He traces his finger down my cheek and neck. I swat his hand away, he backs off.

"Ella, I'm sorry."

"Sorry doesn't mean second chances." Am I shaking or is it the dryer?

He glances at me once more before he leaves, looks both ways and turns the corner, loping down the sidewalk like a lone wolf.

This is the part in the movie where the woman runs after her man and insists on joining him, the swelling string music rising as they embrace on the empty street—cut to credits. The dryer stops, I take out the warm clothes, pile them in a basket, and start folding.

Birds chirp faintly, light dims in the apartment. Loneliness seeps into me like brisk air, into my skin, through my bones. Nighttime always wears down my bravado; feelings arise that I can no longer suppress. *Her thin arms grasp for me. Nobody loves you . . .* You are wrong, Ophelia. Claude loves me, he does.

CLAUDE

Toast

Fresno: our third stop. Dusty, hot, dry air makes me cough. We sweat through our first show of the day, two more to go. Ella goes out for a smoke, her back against our bright red rent-a-car that we must be extra careful not to scrape or we'll get charged. She wipes tears from underneath her sunglasses.

"Just two more shows, El."

She exhales smoke rings in front of us and says, "I'll be fine."

She snubs the cigarette out on the pavement. She's on an emotional tightrope, and I'm forever spotting her.

Done with Fresno we drive down Highway 5 to LA: the land of stars. Stars Coffee Shop, Stars Laundromat, Stars Dental Office, Stars Pet Manicure, Stars Enemas, and the stars of Hollywood Boulevard. I will press my hand in the hot cement next to my star, someday—need to do my daily visualizations: *see it, believe it, with you by my side, flashing cameras, red carpet. Inter-*

views on late-night TV. The smooth, golden Oscar in my hand and your adoration—

"Claude, are you listening? Stop at the 7-Eleven. I'm thirsty."

Snapped back to reality. I could use a drink. The air assaults us the second we get out of the car. Feels like we are walking in a hot ashtray. In front of the 7-Eleven, an old woman smokes a pipe next to a shopping cart full of boxes.

She lifts a discarded box from the trash with her wrinkled hand, saying, "This is a good one, something medium, not too important, don't you think, sweetheart?"

"You have a lot of boxes." I point to her collection piled in her cart.

She smiles, wrinkles cover her brown face like a map.

"Can't have enough boxes in this life. This one is good for birthdays, holidays. And this one is good to carry my false teeth in, that is, if I had any." She cackles.

"What do you do with them?" Ella asks intrigued.

"Keep 'em closed, so they don't bother me." She puts her finger to her lips.

"Bother you?" Ella squints.

"The memories. This one here is special," She raises a black and white shoebox. "My wedding. Got to keep collecting new ones."

She carefully places her newfound box in her cart.

"Why?" I ask.

"For the unknown." She raises her hands.

"Like your dreams?" I ask.

"Oh no, you can never box your dreams." She rolls her cart under the shade of a tree. "Dreams tell you where you're going. We're still here, still here. Call us extinct, but like seeds sprouting new trees, we continue . . ."

She must be native to LA; the rest of us are invasive species trying to burrow roots in their land. But who can find any dirt in all this concrete?

Traffic. Stuck. We get off at the Venice Beach exit. Punks on skateboards whiz by. A couple in matching spandex roller skate. A singer on the corner strums a guitar while birds line up above on a telephone wire, facing the horizon.

A few heads bob up and down in the waves. Ella drops her sandals in the sand and runs into the water.

"Come on, Claude! It's warm!"

A wave pummels her from behind, tossing her to the shore like a piece of seaweed. She gets up laughing and runs back into the surf. I throw off my shirt and sneakers and join her. We ride the waves before they take us under or dive into the center of the crest to stay afloat.

As we get out, dripping, flames catch my eye. The box lady is hurling her beloved boxes into the pit of a bonfire. We walk towards the fire, stand close enough to feel the heat on our legs.

"Wait, why are you burning them?" I ask, as she gets ready to toss in another one.

"Got to keep warm somehow."

The box lands in the center of the fire, sending out sparks of golden red.

I run into my former co-star, Duncan, at a café. He invites us to a party at his house in Hollywood. I'm glad to see him sober and upright. He has a nice place, a sweet bungalow tucked inside the hills. Hip hop blasts from the speakers while models or people who should be models pose as they talk and sip drinks. There is not one hair out of place.

"Claude!" Duncan balances his glass as he welcomes us in. He checks out Ella the way all men do. "So, this is the new villain?"

She laughs, that unmistakable loud laugh of hers.

"You're doing well, Duncan, nice place."

It is a palace compared to my one-room studio that has exhaust streaming through the window from the cars on Bush Street.

"Got an agent, a commercial. You should move here." He slaps my back. "Best thing that happened to me was getting fired from that show."

"Great, but you owe me a pair of sneakers."

"Huh?" Wrinkles form on his forehead. He doesn't remember.

"Puking on my sneakers?"

"Oh, yeah! Sorry about that man!" He laughs and starts talking up a cute blond in a silver sequined mini dress.

When will my big break come? Patience, I need patience. I try not to be jealous but instead inspired by his success.

Conversations begin with "How do you know Duncan?" and within thirty seconds, someone name drops: "I got a line in De Niro's latest film, met him on the set," or "Madonna, she is the best to work for. Got a gig on tour as a backup to her back-up dancers."

Ella and I start timing the name dropping; we cruise around the room and come back with results.

"Twenty seconds!"

"Fifteen!"

I won.

"You look like people I should know. You in the biz?" A man interrupts us, obviously taken by Ella. He is white, like most of the guys here, with a few grey hairs.

"We are currently starring in a groundbreaking show—at your local elementary school," I joke, Ella bursts with her signature cackle.

"Seriously, you both have a look, exotic, unique. Here's my card. I run a talent agency in

Mexico."

Sure. Right. Talent agency. Ella takes the card. He grins.

"Let's do lunch. Call me."

I give her my what-do-you-think-you-are-doing look.

"You never know, Claude." She puts the card in her pocket.

My body floats, high-pitched beeping—I can't move . . . a nightmare, it's the alarm. I tickle Ella's feet, poking out of her covers on her bed next to mine.

"No, Claude!" She covers the blanket over her head.

"Come on, time to go!" We have a tug of war with the blanket.

"OK, you win." Ella gets up with her hair all askew.

We get in the car, groggy, drinking bad coffee in Styrofoam cups from the hotel lobby. We drive into San Diego: a richer version of LA. Expensive restaurants and boutiques line the streets for tourists and honeymooners. Business suits, ties— not an artist vibe at all.

We roll our set into the school cafeteria, too tired to talk. A janitor hums while mopping the grey tile floors. Wafts of food smells curl together in my nose: milk, hot dogs, macaroni and cheese, and something sour—like when you open your refrigerator, and something has gone bad—that kind of smell.

Teachers shuffle in with lines of students behind them, every so often turning to keep them quiet. It doesn't work. Children's voices rise to the ceiling, from low mumbles to shrills of laughter. They settle, sitting on the floor while teachers slump back in metal chairs, correct papers, and shush their students, then the magic starts.

Ella misses her cue, and she's behind the backdrop on the floor with her hands over her ears. I end the show early. Ten minutes until the next group arrives. Ella is in a daze, sitting cross-legged on the floor.

"Did I miss my line?" Panic flushes over her face.

"You going to make it through the next shows?"

"Shit! I'm sorry, Claude!"

I don't ask her what happened; we need to get through the next two shows.

She laughs at herself, mutters, "I'm a mess . . ."

The absurdity of it all hits me: standing in tights and a cape, my sister falling apart backstage. We both end up on the floor in hysterics.

Two back-to-back performances with three more schools to go. On the way there, I roll down the car window.

"I can't take this anymore, Claude." Ella lights a cigarette.

"Me neither."

"Five miles to Tijuana." She points to a map.

"Mexico?"

She sucks in her breath. I have a thousand dollars stashed in the bag saved from our budget. Never been to Mexico. I step on the gas.

We end up in Baja and find a nice cottage on a hill overlooking the streets with an ocean view.

And it is cheap. American dollars go a long way here.

Ella contacts the guy we met at Duncan's party. Turns out he really is an agent for Mexican TV. Legit. We land acting jobs, stars of a telenovela, a Mexican soap opera. They don't mind our broken Spanish: they dub over our voices. Our favorite pastime is to watch the shows and laugh at our out-of-synch lips. I am the bad guy; they like to do close-ups to show my scar. I give my toughest looks.

After a month, the telenovela is cancelled, and our funds run low. I miss the twins, Ilse and William. *And you, Vera, my love, I know you will soon to be in my arms . . .*

"Claude, wake up!"

Covers fly off me. Where am I? My limbs feel like wet spaghetti, and I can barely get out of bed. We grab our bags, say goodbye to our little cottage. I slide into the passenger seat and pass out. Ella drives all the way home. It is dawn by the time we get to Bryant and 20th Street in the Mission.

That is the end of my future with this theater company. The director contacted me asking where the money went and why we didn't perform the last shows. I say I got sick, which is partly true, I'm sick now. Ella and I come up with half the money we owe. At least we returned the rent-a-car unscathed. Oh well, the vacation was worth it. I put on my sneakers determined to run this cold out of me. I take my regular jogging route and stop midway, doubled over, hacking. The Saint Luke's emergency room nurse says it is asthma and gives me an inhaler. I use it, but it doesn't help.

My second ER visit, same result: two inhalers. This time, the nurse barely looks up from her clipboard. The third visit, well, she doesn't hide her contempt for me: brown and no insurance. Tells me to keep taking the inhalers. I decide to take a trip home and book a flight.

"Come in, come in. Be sure to close the door now, don't want the heat escaping."

He touches my shoulder. I flinch.

"Sure, Dad."

"Honey!"

Warmth spreads across Mom's face as she embraces me. I try to stifle a cough.

"You are thin. Have you been eating?"

"I'm just tired."

I take my coat off and hang it on a chair. She studies my face. I smile. My beautiful mom—she can see right through me.

"Well, get some rest then."

I climb the stairs to my old bedroom and collapse on the bed.

Classical music swells from the kitchen. They sit at the round wooden table drinking coffee, reading the Sunday paper. Autumn sun fills the room, giving the appearance of warmth, but it is chilly inside.

"Sit down, sit down. Claude, have some eggs." The southern gentleman father pats the chair next to him, gets up, and scrapes eggs from the cast iron pan. "Coffee with cream?"

His tone has a fake jolliness to it, like he is trying hard to be cordial.

"I'll take it black. Thanks."

I sip my coffee in silence while the orchestra rises into a crescendo. They don't talk to each other. My father rustles his newspaper. Mom has a nice set-up upstairs now. Maybe she is down here just for show. Dad folds his newspaper, flops it on a chair, places his dish in the dishwasher.

"Be sure now to put your dishes away," he warns.

She doesn't take the bait, just continues reading. His slippers slap on the floor as he goes upstairs.

Walk. Go for a walk, that will help, Mom says. What a beautiful day, Claude. The trees put on a show this time of year: magenta, golden, orange, and red before winter takes hold, squeezing the day into night.

I cross the street to the playground, passing the brook where we caught crayfish and the field Ella and I walked every day in snow, sleet, rain, trying to make the first bell. We were always late.

I take a deep breath, cough, and walk back to the grey house on the hill. Up the narrow driveway, too small for cars, made for horses and carriages. Gets so slippery and slick with ice in the winter, I was always afraid I would slide right into the street. We used sticks as pretend car keys, riding our bikes around the house.

"Where are you going, Claude?" Ella shouts.

"California, I'm going to California!"

And we raced around and around the house. Funny I ended up there.

On snow days, all four of us jumped off the stone wall, doing flips in the three feet of snow. Adam leapt off the shed. I wanted to be strong and tough like my big brother, Adam. We reamed each other with snowballs packed hard. I pretended it didn't hurt. People skied right down the middle of the street; we waved as they glided by. This land, can I call it home?

I make sure I don't slam the door when I enter the house. That used to really set him off. And the chase would begin. No matter how fast I ran, he caught me.

"Be sure to take off your shoes, so you don't track in mud."

I startle at the sound of his voice, a bit threatening.

"Well, well, have a nice walk?" He switches to the southern gentleman.

He shifts awkwardly to one side; I nod and manage a smile. The light in the mudroom flutters.

"So, Claude, are you employed?"

And the obligatory conversation begins; the subtext is: *"Do I have to give you any money?"*

"Yes, Dad, yes, a couple jobs. Just finished a children's theater tour with Ella."

His face hardens when I mention her name. He does not ask how she is.

"No, Dad, I do not need anything," I lie. I'm broke.

For a moment, we attempt to bridge loss or longing. What do we do when everyone is wounded? He picks up a log and tosses it in the wood stove.

"Going to be bloody cold tonight."

Nothing has changed here. Nothing ever will.

Moonlight shines through the window. *Wish you were here in my arms, keeping me warm.* I can get another job, save money for a house, for Ilse, William, and you. I keep the pictures they drew for me folded in my pocket to remind me love is the strongest power of all. We will be together soon, won't we, my love? The lamp flickers—is that my answer? I turn it off and fall asleep to her sweet scent of rum.

Writhing like a snake on the dirt road, as my Vera stands above me watching, helpless, I grip my side, screaming in agony, like a knife is making its way from the inside of me—poor Henry, what will become of him? He wails and wails. King! My love calls out to me—

I yank the twisted sheets from around me, my side throbbing, sit up on the bed, my pulse is racing. *It was you, my love. When will we be together again?*

I can't sleep. I know each step down the hallway to the main stairway. My hand slides down the smooth banister to the bottom, past the bathroom to the kitchen. I make a piece of toast, sit in the dark at the round kitchen table.

The light flashes on. "Who's there?"

A baseball bat is inches from my head.

"Dad, it's me!" I jump up to the side. Does he recognize me?

"What are you doing?" His knuckles are white, gripping the bat.

"Making toast."

"Creeping around the house." There he is, the other Dad; southern gentleman gone.

"Do you know what time it is?"

"Couldn't sleep," I answer monotone, to not provoke him.

"I thought you were a burglar!"

And I lose it. I start laughing and coughing. If Ella were here, we would be doubled over, on the floor—

"You'll wake Margaret up!"

Does he think I am a thief, a criminal? The thin façade of southern manners, "anything you need," feigning concern, gone. This is the Dad I remember.

"What is going on?" Her voice is loud; she rarely ever raises her voice.

"Margaret, I thought he was a prowler." He sounds like a child in trouble.

"That's ridiculous. It is Claude! Now put the bat down," she commands.

I want to hit him; I want to punch him. He leans the bat against the wall.

"Well, then, I'm going to bed. Be sure and clean up after yourself." He stomps down the hall and up the stairs.

"Mom, I don't know how you put up with this."

"Sit down, Claude. I'll make you something . . ."

"I'm not hungry anymore." I put the plate in the dishwasher and decide I am leaving tomorrow.

The next morning, I enter the kitchen. My parents are sitting at the table reading newspapers and drinking coffee as classical music streams through the air, ensuring everything is in place, correct, like a mathematical solution.

"Good morning, Claude. Coffee?"

Back to the southern gentleman. Not the father that held a bat ready to strike. Crazy is the new normal here.

"I'll get it."

I don't want him anywhere near me. I might lose it and hit him.

"R.J. has something to say to you. Don't you, R.J.?"

She places her cup down like she is playing a game of chess. Oh God, not the apology, as if that is what makes everything better, OK, tidy . . .

"I'm sorry about last night." He won't look directly at me but to the side.

I'm not sure what I'm supposed to say. "Sure Dad, you didn't mean to threaten me with a bat. It's OK, it happens . . .?" I don't say anything, sip my coffee. He folds his paper.

"Well, I've got to make the lecture on time in Cambridge. It's a Buddhist perspective on consciousness. Brilliant author. You're welcome to join." Is he asking me?

"I'm leaving today," is all I can say.

"Well, Claude, certainly nice of you to come visit." He leaves, his feet pounding the floor the way they do.

"Claude, I'm concerned about that cough of yours. Why don't you stay here, and we'll get you a doctor?" She places her palm on my hand.

I want to. I want to rest, to be close to her.

"Mom, I can't stay in this house with him." I slowly try to draw my hand from hers; she won't let go.

"He has his good moments, too. He does care about you."

I hate to see her sad. It is unbearable to me.

"Mom, I'll be OK."

Her warmth travels up my hand, arm, through my body. And I want to believe my words.

I toss and turn all night, can't get comfortable. At my audition for a commercial, the two directors are stunned by my eyes, so open, they exclaim, "they go straight to your soul." They discuss me like I am not there, like I am an apparition in front of them. I don't get the part.

Skinny, you look so skinny, my co-workers say to me. They are concerned, but I try and brush it off. At home, I can barely eat, hot, so hot, I roll in my bed. Call Ella. I think I'm dying.

"It's the flu, Claude. It's the flu. I had it, too. You'll be OK," she says.

I hang up the phone. Maybe I'll feel better tomorrow.

Birthday coming, twenty-nine. *Oh, Vera, my love, will you remember? This is the year, the year we can be together, the year for our love.* I stumble as I steady myself on the bus to meet Ella at our favorite diner on Valencia Street in the Mission. I run out of breath. Stop on the corner. A homeless man asks me for money. I'm dizzy. It starts to drizzle; I open my umbrella.

When did the diner get so trendy? The line this long, even in the rain. Sheets of rain, now. Couples huddle under umbrellas, snuggling in bliss. And here I am, alone again. So tired of being alone. *If you could give me a chance, my love, a chance. Is there a place for our love? For us?*

A man dressed in white, using a walker, plods along the sidewalk. Raindrops trickle down his ebony face, his left leg drags behind him. He moves slowly as he examines the people lined up against the wall.

"I created all of you!" He points to his head: his body wobbles.

"Don't you know who I am?"

He slams his walker on the pavement making a loud drum sound—boom-boom! The line of pale faces ignores him. Some move away, closer to the side of the restaurant. Maybe he is a ghost, a spirit no one can see. The torment on his face is unbearable. I step out of line, hold my umbrella over him.

"Where are you going?" I ask.

He points to a café across the street. He leans to the left as we shuffle across the street, my umbrella barely shields us from the rain.

A bell jingles as I open the café door. It is dark inside. *Afro Blue* by Coltrane plays softly in the background. He sits down carefully, extending his bad leg, resting his elbows on the small square table.

"Your mind is good." He taps his head, points his long finger at me, and nods. "You can see."

He rests back on his chair. This man is mystifying. Coltrane's horn takes a solo, then returns to the hook.

He pauses and whispers, "I am the sky father."

He must be crazy, right? Yet what is sanity? Ignoring the homeless living on the street, waging wars for corporations—what exactly is sane? Time for me to go. As I stand and push my chair in, he nods and points to his temple, saying, "Remember."

OK, I say. How could I ever forget meeting the sky?

"Didn't you hear me?" Ella squeezes my arm.

"Huh?" How did I get here, back in line?

"I've been calling your name."

"Uh, I was helping the man with the walker cross the street?"

"Are you joking? I've been in line right here, trying to get your attention."

I laugh. I must be hallucinating.

"Ella, if anything happens to me, I want you to take my writings and do whatever you want with them. They are in my black trunk, all my writings, do what you want."

She tries to laugh it off, gives me my cue to make a joke, but I don't.

"And if I'm ever attached to a machine, pull the plug."

A hint of fear forms in her face, and she squeezes my hand.

. . .

Palms open wide, take me. Wind, take me. Where can I rest?

"Good evening, this is Claude from Lightning Telecom."

Carrie and I crack jokes in between calls. Not feeling well, I leave early.

Take the new inhalers. Need to lie down. Carrie brings chicken soup and Tylenol for my fever. She has to leave to perform an improv show tonight.

"I'll call you when it's over," she says, kisses my forehead, and leaves.

My love, my love, will I see you soon? A breeze flutters through the blinds as the constant drone of cars speed down Bush Street. I can barely sit up. I pick up the phone.

I limp to a brown minivan. Ella opens the car door for me.

"DonDawn let me borrow his car."

She sings to calm herself down, I know I don't look good. Red circles under my eyes and skinny. She speeds over the curb to the emergency room at Saint Luke's Hospital, where they don't see me. Does anyone see me? I can't walk. Ella runs into the ER entrance and comes back with a nurse and a wheelchair. I manage to get in the chair, they wheel me inside.

Ilse's gurgle, William's laugh. Will my shoulders sprout wings? Nurses mull about me, the same ones that would not look up from their charts, that dismissed me. Ella's at my bedside. She can't stop moving,

"I'm dancing, Claude."

Yes Ella, I see that. I see that. The nurse sneers at her . . . Let her dance! Let her— They put an IV in my vein, they take my blood, they don't prescribe another inhaler. The doctor is furious.

"Who did his intake? How come no one took a blood sample?"

His rage fills the room, nurses scurry. Ella sways side to side. The doctor tells me I have leukemia, and they need to send me to another hospital, UCSF. They wheel me into the ambulance, Ella holds my hand. The sirens shriek.

"I'm scared, Ella."

"I know, Claude. It's going to be OK."

The ambulance twists and turns up and down city streets all the way to the UCSF Medical Center. I breathe in the sting of eucalyptus trees—my first smell of San Francisco, the Sunset District. They hook me up to a dialysis machine to clean my blood. Too many white blood cells.

"I had dreams about this, Ella . . ."

She tries to hide her panic; I feel it underneath her voice. She stays with me, in a chair. I can't get comfortable, wake up coughing.

The nurse says it is best for me to be moved to intensive care, her voice is gentle, careful.

Ella stays close to me, touching my hair, my hand. The nurse pushes my cot through the elevator doors into a room with a large window in the Intensive Care Unit.

"This is the first time I have felt comfortable in months."

IV drips fluid into my arm. The nurse smiles and turns on the TV. Bugs Bunny cartoons, like we watched when we were kids.

"Ella. The road trip, to Mexico. We'll do it again."

"Yes, we will. I love you, Claude." Ella presses my feet.

"I love you, too, Ella."

And she leaves.

Beep! Fingers prod, machine hum, coughing up blood.

"Get him stable!"

Can't move. Stuck. Chest up and down, floating here, floating . . .

Mom. I want my mother. Mom, where are you?

ELLA

PANTHER

The nurse said it was fine to leave, that he was stable, that I could go, come back later. It is morning as I walk out of the building; the sun is cruel to be lighting up the world so bright. I trudge up the hill, down to Market Street, and through the Mission back home. Could this be happening? Is this real?

"He told me he was dying, and I thought it was the flu, Mom." I don't hide my sobs.

"I'll be there soon."

On the phone, her voice is calm and controlled. I strip off my clothes, get in the shower, dress quickly, and take a bus back to the hospital. Up the elevator to the ICU, I have a sinking feeling, and there's Claude attached to a ventilator, his eyes closed, face up.

"He was having difficulty breathing, so we had to put him on the ventilator."

Is that a trace of guilt in her voice? I don't have energy for anger. Claude, Mom is coming. We will get you through this.

His hand is curled into a fist. I massage his slender fingers. Do you feel my hand? Are you still there? I call Carrie on the pay phone in the hallway, voice trembling.

"He's going to get through this, doll."

I grip the phone receiver, hanging onto her words to keep me going.

Carrie strokes his dark curls, whispers to him, "Babe, hang in there, it's me, I love you."

He remains motionless, his oxygen level normal, his heart rate steady. We go downstairs to get lunch.

"I need to tell you something." She leans across the table; she has barely touched her sandwich. "I'm pregnant."

"Is it . . ." I try and keep my cool.

"Yes, it is his." Carrie bites her lip, as if to control her emotions from bursting out. "I would have his baby, I really would. Out of all the men I have met, I would have his, but I haven't been feeling well, and they keep telling me there's nothing they can do. I didn't want to tell you, you have enough to worry about, but I had to tell somebody."

"Oh God, Carrie . . ." I hug her. I wish I knew what to say. "Do you have a doctor?"

"No. The emergency room—don't worry, doll. You take care of yourself; I will be fine."

Her tough-guy persona takes over, and she grabs her cigarettes off the table. "I gotta go to work. Call you later?"

"Yes, Carrie, Take care."

I want to reassure her, but I don't have the energy. Maybe if Claude knows she is pregnant, he will fight more, for the baby. I can only think about Claude.

· · ·

Back in the waiting room, the doors flip-flap open, and a nurse in scrubs hurries to a station. I pick up a magazine to make the time go faster, constantly checking the swinging doors and footsteps. She walks through the doors as calm as a panther. I rush to her, hug her.

"Mom, they had to put him on a breathing machine . . ."

She is silent. I lead her to his room. She moves like she has no weight and sits down next to Claude.

She asks the nurses questions, lets them know she understands the protocols and procedures. She stays with him all night. Reads a book by his side.

"Your father is coming tomorrow," she says.

I have not seen or spoken to him in years. Nothing I can do —I will have to face him.

They administer chemo and platelets, and still, he remains on the breathing machine. I bring him music—Coltrane, Van Morrison. I sing to him, plucking songs from my guitar. I sing to him, so he will rise from the bed, off the machines, and walk beside me, joking. I am sure he will. Carrie's sure, too, that our love for him will buoy him upright on the earth.

Mom continues to talk to nurses, doctors, watching their every move. It is techno medicine, so many people come in and out—who is accountable? There are nurses that care and others that are strictly doing their job: for them, my brother is just another body to lift, to poke, to—

I can't bear it at times, the uncaring ones. Carrie guards Claude like a watchdog, and Mom won't let any procedure go by unquestioned. We take turns by his bedside, making sure we eat, so we can be strong, so we can keep coming back. The nurses that dare to feel, to connect, make all the difference.

"I can tell how special he is through all of you," one says and touches him with gentleness, a sacredness a textbook can't teach.

Carrie doesn't tell Claude about the baby. She says she

doesn't want to worry him. Carrie is paler than usual and skinny. I keep trying to get her to eat more.

DonDawn saunters in the ICU, dressed in white.

He whispers to Claude, "Brother, I know you can do this. I am sending you all my strength."

He places his hands on Claude's side. Carrie and I stand across from him; she strokes Claude's hair; I massage his feet. DonDawn prays quietly. He stays the whole night.

"I'll keep praying, baby, keep praying," he says, before he leaves.

MARGARET

CAPTIVE

I should have made Claude stay and asked R.J. to leave. I could have taken care of Claude, gotten him to a decent doctor. But R.J. wouldn't leave even if I asked him. A simple blood test!

That's all they needed to do! What kind of inept nurses would commit such egregious neglect?

They took an oath to do no harm. Their neglect was harm, and now my boy, my baby boy—

Bronchitis. I thought it was bronchitis, like his father is prone to. I didn't realize, I should have known . . . Oh, Margaret!

Keep reading, keep calm. My heart races; is my blood pressure up? My doctor gave me this book before I left; he was quite concerned about me going alone. He embraced me and kissed my cheek at the end of my last visit before I left. I am starting to have a rush of feelings for him; he told me to call him, and I will tonight. R.J. said he would come later. His son is in the ICU, and he will come later! Incredible! Where is his concern for his son? It's as if he never cared for him, any of them. Nor me. He has left me alone to contend with all these doctors.

Yet, I can't leave R.J.; he needs me. I don't think R.J. could manage without me.

I read the same paragraph over and over, forgetting what I read.

Claude could have stayed up in the attic with me. Away from R.J.'s explosions. I have a breadbox, a toaster oven, and a teapot. I rarely go downstairs. He could have stayed there with me. But he refused, wouldn't stay another day with his father. Oh, Margaret, now look what happened. My poor baby, my poor baby—

Before, I had nowhere to go. Where could I go with four children? Now I have friends; they would take me in, or I could get my own apartment. And now that the doctor has shown affection towards me . . . Is it too late to start over?

R.J. has been a good provider. He can be pleasant, even encouraging at times, and we enjoy our vibrant discussions, films, walks, dinners, and salons addressing the latest science and political issues. His rages, though . . . I never know when they are coming. I am a captive to his rage in that house.

So much like my mother. Yes, I know I married what I knew, what I was familiar with, but it is a bit too late for all that; what is done is done. Where was I? Did I read this page yet? I close my book. I watch Claude's chest rise and fall, like I used to when he was an infant. This is all I can do right now.

R.J

Bloody awful flight. Turbulence makes me nauseous. And the woman next to me keeps snapping her gum. Jesus! I give her a look, but it does not register, and she keeps on snapping like an impudent turtle.

Margaret is already there. Meeting her at the hospital. How much will this cost us? What was he doing walking around without health insurance? What happened? Seemed fine when he was home. I saw nothing wrong. Seemed fine.

Margaret said not to worry about the cost, that Claude is in the ICU, and I should come quickly. I hate hospitals—the smell of ether gets to me, and I can pass right out. I start sweating and memories start coming.

~

I knew my birth was hard. Mama almost died, and I, well, had some injuries. While she about bled to death, the doctor had to get me out with forceps, my body a mangled mess. Pop didn't want children, and when my birth almost killed Mama, he didn't care for me much. There was damage to my spine and the result: one leg—my left leg— grew longer than the other. My right leg was deformed, stunted. I could not walk; surgery was the only option.

My folks drove me to the Shriners Hospital for Crippled Children in Shreveport, Louisiana, a long way from Magnolia, Arkansas. I was two. It was the only place they could afford because it was free.

I didn't know where I was or why I was there, only that my mama left me. Cribs lined up against the wall in the nursery. I grasped the white metal rails trying to get out, crying, shaking the bars—

She never came. I stopped crying. Gave up. Rough hands turned me over to change my diaper.

"If you move, I'll stick yah."

One pin in her mouth, the other in her hand. Scooped me up, to another room, long hallways, strapped me to a gurney, muffled voices, glint of metal.

"There, there, little one," a nurse whispers, putting a damp cloth over my face. Woke to sharp pain, wiggled, tried to get out—

"Administer more ether. We're not done."

Cloth smothered my cries. Bone grafts, many of them, cut into my left knee to slow the growth, and scraped bone from my hip to fill my bent right femur. Don't remember much, just that smell and the nurse's rough hands. Had many surgeries, panicked when they would wheel me down the long dark hallway to the surgery room.

How many? Three? Four?

A tree was right outside the only window in the nursery. I kept watch of birds fluttering on and off branches. The coo of a dove woke me every morning, I waited to see it, to greet it before it flew away.

They covered me in cool plaster, whole body cast. Itched something terrible, cut a hole so I could pee. This was to set my bones, so they would grow straight, and I could walk. I met my dove every morning, waited for the coo.

Was I their experiment? Their little Frankenstein? I am sure I was a scrawny-looking thing when they sawed the plaster off me.

"We'll get this off you, R.J., so you can go home. Won't that be nice?" She smiled.

I was confused. I did not know what home was.

A year later, my folks came to retrieve me. Did not recognize them. They brought me chocolate, and I enjoyed eating it, but I had no idea who these people were.

I was carried into the back seat of a Model A Ford, propped up with pillows, so I wouldn't fall over.

"My baby, my little baby."

She tried to put her arms around me. I jerked away, scooted to the window to search for my dove.

Anytime she came close to me I threw toys and anything I could get my hands on. I crawled away from her pleas. Where was I? Pop wasn't as gentle.

"You mind your mama!" Belt waving in the air.

"I've got him now; I'll take care of him!" Mama picked me up, carried me to my crib.

"Little varmint needs to know his place." Pop slammed the door.

"R.J., it's your mama, it's me, my boy, my sweet boy . . ."

Round and round and round on the red tricycle. Only thing that kept me occupied. Still couldn't walk, but I could ride that trike. Wouldn't let anyone near me, not even Mama. She left food on chairs, easy enough for me to reach, so I wouldn't starve. Sometimes I ate it, other times I threw it. Smash smash, cling clang, splish splosh.

"No, R.J. No!" Mama would holler and take the plate out of my hand before it ended up in pieces on the floor.

Music calmed me; she found a station from New England on the radio that played classical music. I would sit in the living room and rock back and forth. I taught myself to walk, out of my own willfulness. Take a few steps, fall, get up, and repeat. Mama knew not to help me, to stay a distance from me or I'd have a fit.

"Remember who you are, R.J.," she reminded me every day before I left for school. Not sure what she meant by it. Things were routine: after school, help Pop in garage, Bible lessons and church on Sunday and Wednesdays.

Mama was sure Jesus would save me if I would let him in. I suppose I did that day. Unexpectedly, I felt him, the savior, call me, and walked down the aisle, unable to hold back my tears as the pastor held me, hearing shouting from the pulpit: "Amen!" "Yes Jesus!" Mama, crying for joy. I walked as straight as I could, trying to hide my limp.

Dressed in white, submerged in a local pond with the others: the baptism. The pastor glided me under, and I came out in Jesus's name. Birds flying above a few clouds, the rebirth.

Hypocrites, bunch of hypocrites. Talking religion and acting on hatred. I refused to accept the incongruities of Jim Crow and the Scriptures' claim we are all God's children. Didn't add up. Science made sense, and math: neat equations with logical beginnings and endings. Cause and effect.

～

Knew I had to get out of the South, knew I had to leave. And I did, studied physics and met Margaret, and she, well, she changed everything.

Snap, smack, snap. You would think her jaw would ache by now. Thank God, the plane is landing. I wipe my brow, dreading to enter the hospital.

ELLA

TENDERLY

He is shorter than I remember. Why was I ever afraid of him? We don't embrace. I show him to Claude's room.

"Where's Margaret?" he asks.

"Downstairs getting lunch."

He walks in awkwardly. Claude is attached to the ventilator, IVs hang above him, and the constant beep of machines monitor his heart rate and other vital signs.

"Well, well, Claude, oh my . . ."

He drops to the chair next to Claude's bed. Mumbling to himself, he roughly places his hand on Claude's exposed arm and starts wringing it like it was a wet towel.

"Dad, stop you're gonna hurt him!"

He is baffled.

"Is this better?" He slows down but continues to use too much pressure.

"No, Dad, like this." I stroke Claude's arm like it was a kitten.

"Oh, like this?" He mimics my hand and touches his son tenderly.

"Yes, Dad, that's it."

This is the first time I have ever seen Dad touch anyone gently, lovingly—I guess he never knew how.

Dad stays for a week then flies back east for a Buddhist workshop, leaving the three of us to care for Claude.

"I can't believe he left me here, all alone, leaving his son like this. What is wrong with him? Doesn't he care?" Mom doesn't hide her distress; I tell her Carrie and I are here for her: we are here for each other.

The chemo destroys the cancer. Claude lingers on the ventilator. Mom's face grows grim.

We meet in a large conference hall with all the specialists, doctors, and nurses. I sit between Mom and Carrie. Carrie and I are sure Claude will make it: he just needs more time.

"There's nothing more we can do. The cancer is gone, but there is fluid in his lungs. Pneumonia. He's dying." The doctor's tone is compassionate and resigned.

I protest, he can pull through—

"Can't you see what's happening? Don't you see?" Mom's voice is unusually loud and even angry.

Carrie and I are silent. Carrie had a miscarriage; she was unable to visit for a week, recovering from it. And now this? This news?

Claude's voice rings in my head: "If I'm ever attached to a machine, pull the plug."

My big sister, Joan, leaves her horses and flies into San Francisco. Adam, my older brother, joins her. We sit in plastic chairs next to Claude's room, waiting for Dad. He walks towards us in his uneven gait and sits next to my brother, Adam, and every so often puts a handkerchief over his nose. Mom doesn't greet him.

We crowd around Claude.

"All I can say is he is no longer there. That is not Claude in there." Adam's voice trembles.

"At the barn, when a horse is too sick, there's nothing else we can do . . ." Joan cries, and I rarely see her cry.

We say our goodbyes, one at a time. I take out the photo of his poem from my poetry wall in the attic and read it to him:

> *Oh, I love you, my sister,*
> *You are me in too many ways,*
> *And I cry, too, Ella,*
> *And think of our future days.*
> *A special bond is you plus me*
> *And if I fail to respond*
> *I pray that you see*
> *That moods come and go*
> *Like a wave hits the beach*
> *I need you to know*
> *Even if we're out of reach*
> *These waves are not strong enough*
> *To break the love that exists between us*

The time on the lake in Maine flashes in my mind and our promise to each other to not bail—I'm not jumping out of the canoe, Claude. I won't.

Looks like you got to go first. And you better still get my jokes. Our love is stronger than this ending, I know, Claude. I know. I won't ever stop loving you, my brother. His eyes are bulging, facing the ceiling—has he already left?

Adam puts a cassette tape in the boombox and plays Claude's favorite song, John Coltrane's "My Favorite Things."

The melody spirals in and around us, bouncing off the walls, bed, ceiling, and out the window. It riffs off buildings, jams up tree roots, vibrates off leaves, releases to the rolling fog, attaching to droplets, past the pink sunrise.

One by one, spirits walk in with heavy feet, all different shades: a tall man plays a fiddle with a woman in a blue calico dress by his side, holding cowrie beads in her petite hand; a veteran in a blue uniform carries a rifle next to a woman with hair piled high, waving a fan; a skinny one-handed man clasps a fishing pole, a younger man sprinkles tobacco behind him; a Native woman carries a basket arm in arm with a wide-chested man smoking a pipe; a dapper man in a suit uses a golf club as a cane; a man in a porter's uniform embraces a distressed woman clutching a glass vial. Ophelia sings her strange lullaby:

> *My sweet little babies sold by the devil,*
> *buried in the ground, buried in the ground.*
> *My sweet little babies sold by the devil*
> *how empty my arms are now.*

Chills run through my body.

I whisper to Mom, "The ancestors are here; don't you see them?"

My mother's face is blank. We form a circle around Claude. The nurse turns off the machine. Claude's chest rises and falls, the music fades.

Carrie collapses over him, wails, "No!"

Her auburn ringlets spill over Claude's still chest. I place my hand on her back and guide her away from his body. Claude's red and black cross and medicine bag dangle off the corner of the table underneath a picture the twins drew him. I slip them into my pocket.

The nurse begins to wash him.

"No, let me do it." Mom takes the cloth, gently wiping it over Claude's body, her final goodbye.

Claude is no longer there. He disappeared with Coltrane's horn. Dad, Joan, Adam, Carrie, and I walk to the elevator in silence. It is dawn. Words tie up inside my throat. We drive to Claude's favorite spot, the Cliff House.

We walk to the edge of the precipice, streaks of pink and white meet the horizon as the sun rises. Out of nowhere, a hummingbird stops in front of us, hovers a bit then darts away.

"That's Claude telling us he's OK," I whisper.

My dad answers, "Maybe it is, Ella."

I step closer to the edge; waves crash over large rocks. It is time for you to go, Ophelia—go on.

She howls like a wolf, rushes out my guts, limbs, throat, and dives—Ophelia finds her home in the vast ocean. I am free of her, Claude, I am free.

CLAUDE

And as fast as lightning, my life is over. I have no hands, no face, no legs—is this it? Done, dead, gone. She covers me in white cloth silently. She kisses my forehead.

"Mom! Mom! It's OK! I'm here!"

She lifts the blanket over my head. Something so heavy sinks inside her. I flicker the light. She doesn't notice and leaves the room.

Vera, my love! I finally returned to you. There is no fear here—only each pulsing moment, now together forever. And all of you, my loved ones, don't fret. I am watching over you from the in-between sky.

Acknowledgments

I finished this novel many times. Every time I thought it was done, the story asked for more. Many thanks to the following early readers who helped me keep pushing forward: Lisa Terrell, Luz Mena, and James Raggio. Also special thanks to my sister Lisa Terrell for digging into our family history and sharing her findings and much gratitude to Dr. Kate McMahon for sharing her research on Malaga Island. I wouldn't have been able to delve into the horrific history of slavery, eugenics, and racism without my dance/sister community who help keep me afloat: Luz Mena, Melissa Ortega, Lady H, Liz McCarthy, Anna Rodas, Sonya Haggett, Katherine Park, and Elaine Dennis. Special thanks to Gladys Kathman for designing the cover, and editor Ayanna Bennet Meyers.

I was so honored to receive such thoughtful and generous blurbs from Nana Ekua Brew-Hammond, TaRessa Stovall, Luisa Smith, Sharon Coleman, Alix Christie and Sharon Bially.

And thank you Lori Cassels who invited me to read with the Irish American Writers & Artists at Slainte in Oakland, California, and Cathy Dana from the Alameda Poets where I read an excerpt from this novel as well. Thanks to my brother Shawn Terrell, sister Tracy Terrell, the Johnson extended family, my son Luis and Stephen Booth for all your encouragement and support.

Thank you Mike Karpa from Mumblers press and especially you, dear reader for taking this book journey.

It is art that catches us during these challenging times,

Alison Hart

ABOUT THE AUTHOR

National Book award-winning and best-selling author Isabel
Allende introduced Alison and her debut novel *Mostly
White* (Torrey House Press, 2018) at Book Passage in Corte
Madera, CA. Allende praised *Mostly White* as: "So compelling it
gave me goosebumps from the very first lines." Hart's other
works include a poetry collection, *Temp Words* (Cosmo Press,
2015), and selected poems in *Red Indian Road West: Native American
Poetry in California* (Scarlet Tanager, 2016).

Hart's work centers on her Black and Indigenous ancestors
from New England, healing intergenerational/historical
trauma, mixed-race identity, and uncovering the brutal truth of
American history. Hart studied theater at Tisch School of The
Arts, New York University (B.F.A.), and education at Saint
Mary's College (M.A.). She is a mixed-race Passamaquoddy
Native American, Irish, Black, Scottish, and English woman of

color. Hart is an author, musician, music educator and mother living in the San Francisco Bay Area.

Find out more at www.ahartworks.com.

ALSO BY ALISON HART

temp words (Cosmo Press, 2021)

Mostly White (Torrey House Press, 2018)

Selected poems in Red Indian Road West: Native American Poetry
from California (Scarlet Tanager Books, 2016)

A REQUEST

Reviews are the lifeblood of independent publishers and authors. If
you enjoyed the journey of *The In-between Sky*, please leave a review on
one of the many sites that review books. Please also consider signing
up for the Mumblers Press newsletter at https://mumblerspress.com.

Warmest thanks,

Mumblers Press LLC